D0428898

DEBORAH DAVIS

NOT LIKE YOU

CLARION BOOKS
New York

For my sister Susan Gerber

Clarion Books
a Houghton Mifflin Company imprint
215 Park Avenue South, New York, NY 10003
Copyright © 2007 by Deborah Davis

Excerpt from "Love" by May Sarton, copyright © 1980 by May Sarton,
from *Collected Poems 1930–1993*.
Used by permission of W. W. Norton & Company, Inc.

The text was set in 11-point ITC Cheltenham Light.

www.clarionbooks.com

Printed in the U.S.A.

Library of Congress Cataloging-in-Publication Data

Davis, Deborah.
Not like you / Deborah Davis
p. cm.
Summary: When she and her mother move once again in order to make a new start,
fifteen-year-old Kayla is hopeful that her mother will be able to stop drinking and
begin a better life, as she has been promising for years.
ISBN-13: 978-0-618-72093-4
ISBN-10: 0-618-72093-6
[1. Mothers and daughters—Fiction. 2. Alcoholism—Fiction.
3. Single-parent families—Fiction.] I. Title.
PZ7.D28586 No 2007
[Fic]—dc22
2006021867

MP 10 9 8 7 6 5 4 3 2

Acknowledgments

I have many people to thank for supporting and assisting me in the creation of this book. For insightful comments on the manuscript: Peggy Christian, Ann Manheimer, Clare Meeker, Virginia Lore, Kate Willette, Judy Bentley, Terri Miller, Christine Castigliano, Janine Brodine, Susan Starbuck, Lyn Donovan, Emily Hanson, Rosemary Graham, members of the '05 Port Townsend retreat, my Hedgebrook companions, and Betty Lou Davis. For sublime and productive writing retreats: Deb Green, Jerry Blakely, and the two glorious canine companions they entrusted to my care; Kate Miller and Michael DeLongchamp; and the November '03 Hedgebrook staff. And for enthusiasm and support I can always count on, my agent, Faye Bender.

A very special thank-you to my amazing editor, Jennifer Wingertzahn, who asks all the right questions and is patient enough to wait for my answers.

Above all, my love and deep thanks to my husband, Dwight, and my son, Eli, for lovingly accommodating the writer in their midst.

ONE

On a warm May night, Hal and I lay in each other's arms on the mattress that filled the back of his van, waiting for the train. I liked this part—the closeness, the warmth of his skin. It felt promising, and it matched his other promises: we'd sail his aunt's boat on Lake Tawakoni, cruise back roads on his cousin's motorcycle, drive to a bar in Fort Worth with great bands and a bouncer who couldn't calculate ages. "Everyone goes," he'd told me. "You haven't lived till you've been there."

Hal was a senior, two years ahead of me. That was cool—at least, the girls in my sophomore class would have thought so. They didn't know about Hal and me, though. Nobody did. Not yet. That was about to change.

We were parked in the dry riverbed, just yards beneath the train trestle. Thin rays of moonlight shot through the front passenger window. There were no windows in the back, so it was kind of dark, which suited me just fine. I didn't much like being seen, especially with Hal cracking jokes about how we got undressed way too early and would have to time it closer tomorrow night.

Hal was giving a party two days from now to celebrate school being over. I knew because I overheard his friends talking about it. This was our third time under the trestle, and still he hadn't mentioned the party to me. Surely, he'd invite me tonight.

Flicking a condom with his fingers, he checked his watch again and grinned. "Ten thirty-three. One minute to go."

Right on schedule, the train whistle blew, Hal's signal to roll on top of me. The train that crossed the trestle at 10:34 took about two and a half minutes to pass. Hal's challenge was to start and finish within that amount of time.

Overhead, the train thundered past, and Hal squeezed his eyes shut. Closing my own, I tried to block out the grunting boy on top of me by imagining my favorite dog: black and white with a feathery tail. A black muzzle and paws. No purebred—not for me. My dog was one hundred percent, brilliant mongrel. Part Labrador, part terrier, part shepherd, part whatever. A magical mix and the friendliest, best-behaved mutt you'd ever want to share a walk or a swim or a bed with. All of which I did.

He ran next to me, panting. While the van rocked and the train roared, I chased the dog until my heart pounded and my legs burned. We galloped to our house and lay together in the porch hammock and swung and swung and swung. My favorite dog, loyal, gentle, always thrilled to see me.

The last train cars rumbled by, and the dog vanished. Hal groaned, slumped against me, and quickly rolled away. In the dim light his face gleamed. "I made it," he panted. "A perfect night."

I waited for him to say more. The party was only two nights away.

He glanced at his watch again. "If we hustle," he said, "I can even get you home on time."

I pulled on my clothes. He said, "Hey, your T-shirt's on backward," and he smiled at me. I turned the shirt around.

Two nights till the party. He seemed to like me. There was still time.

I opened the door to the apartment and froze. The place had been ransacked. Cabinets and drawers stood open. Clothes, magazines, pots, and dishes were strewn everywhere.

Before I could call out for my mother, a stack of empty boxes and a full bottle of her favorite whiskey caught my eye.

Oh, my God, no. Not again.

There'd been no burglary. Mom was packing.

I heard her in the bedroom. She'd have beer in there. She'd warm up on that and switch to the whiskey. A binge and a move—my mother's answer to debts and dumb boyfriends and a lack of employment. All of which she had.

Mom's footsteps crisscrossed her room, but she wouldn't be on her feet long. Not with a full bottle of Wild Turkey in the apartment and all our stuff to pack. By the end of the night, she'd be on her ass. And in the morning, worse.

Damn, just when I had a chance here. Hal wanted to see me again. He said so right before he dropped me off. He didn't mention the party, but there was still plenty of time. Two more days. Nearly forty-eight hours. This guy was so promising. Not like the others.

When I stepped into her bedroom, she was throwing shirts and dresses from the closet onto the bed. Carefully folded clothes lay neatly in a couple of old suitcases and boxes and in stacks on her bed. "Are we going somewhere?" I asked, scanning the room for beer bottles. I didn't see even one.

She spun around. "You're home early."

Her clear eyes and steady voice startled me. "No," I said, "I'm right on time. As usual."

She noted the clock. "Good. We've got a lot to do. Start in the kitchen, okay?"

I dropped to the floor to grab a belt from under her bed, checking to see if she'd hidden any bottles there. Nothing. Nor did I smell any booze on her when I leaned over to hand her the belt.

I crossed back to her doorway and leaned against it. "We can't leave, Mom."

She scooped pantyhose and lingerie into her arms and dropped them into a suitcase. "Why not?"

"Because . . ." She'd freak if I told her about Hal. I'd said I was going out with some girls. "We're just getting settled." I picked up a magazine and pretended to study the cover.

She looked around the room. One of the two windows was boarded up, had been that way since we moved in a few months earlier. "You want to settle here?"

My mind groped for an answer. "I could probably fix that window."

She folded her arms. "Kayla, I hate this place. So did you, until about a week ago."

My face grew warm. I'd started seeing Hal about a week before. Now I knew for sure Mom wasn't drinking. She was never this rational once she started guzzling. "I've got . . . friends here," I said. Maybe not now, I thought, but two more days and I will.

She squinted at me. "You hardly mention them, you don't bring them around."

My eyes shot back to the boarded-up window. "I could, I guess."

She shook her head. "Too late. We're out of here in the morning."

"To where?"

"I'll explain tomorrow." She emptied a drawer onto her bed. "It's a long story, and we've got way too much to do."

"You won't even tell me where we're going?"

"Tomorrow. We've got a long drive. Start in the kitchen, would you?"

I threw several empty liquor-store cartons into my room and slammed the door. It didn't take long to pack my stuff. I was reading through my poetry notebook when Mom knocked. "Let's finish in the morning," she said. "I'm gonna hit the sack."

I cracked open the door. Trying to keep my voice even, I asked, "Where the hell are we going?"

She smiled. "It's a surprise."

I shut the door in her face. I'd heard that before, and I knew what it meant. It was her way of saying she didn't know.

I should have seen this coming. Our moves were predictable; each one—four in just the past two years—followed a week or two of blowout booze fests. Mom's one-night binges weren't too bad, because she could pick herself up in the morning and muddle on. It was the three-, four-, six-day benders that worried me. I hadn't exactly seen her drinking or puking lately because of my evenings with Hal and my early-morning dog-walking jobs, but she'd stayed out late almost every night for over a week. That and the quart of whiskey on our kitchen table were a sure sign that within twenty-four hours we'd be on the road, searching for a new place to call "home." Mom was dead sober when I went to sleep that night, but I knew her clear-headedness wouldn't last long.

Our apartment was so quiet the next morning, I felt sure she must have put a big dent in that bottle of Wild Turkey. Now she'd be passed out—or glued to her mattress by a hangover.

I dragged myself out of bed, hoping she had changed her mind about leaving or—if she'd finished the bottle—that the whiskey had changed it for her. If getting drunk stopped her, at least I wouldn't have to break my back hauling everything down the three flights of stairs while she lay on the sofa, babying her aching head. How she always convinced me she could drive hundreds of miles but not help load the car first was a mystery.

I padded around in my T-shirt, looking for her. The whiskey sat untouched in the kitchen, and there was no sign of Mom or most of our stuff—just a calendar on the wall, a couple of boxes, and some trash. Her room was completely cleaned out. I almost wondered if she'd conned someone into carrying everything to the car and taken off without me, but then the door flew open. My thin, wiry mother strode in, red-cheeked and smiling. There was no way, from the perky look of her, she could have been drinking last night.

"Good," she said. "You're awake. Get some pants on and help me with the last boxes. My arms must be six inches longer by now."

I stared at her. She'd actually worked up a sweat, and it wasn't from a romp in her bedroom or a night in some dive bar.

"Pants," she said, flicking her fingers toward my bare legs. She snatched a camisole the color of blood and an exercise video—both gifts from the guy she'd been seeing—off the floor, along with blank forms from the Dallas MLK unemployment office, and chucked everything into a large trash bag.

I stepped into my jeans. "What about Rocky?" That was my nickname for her latest bed thug, a wannabe boxer.

"I'm done with him. All he wants to do is have sex."

That was a new reason to break it off. I didn't point out that she had seemed more than enthusiastic about having it with him.

"You and I are off to a whole new start," she said, sounding mighty pleased.

It was a relief to see her sober, but her cheerfulness was grit under my skin. Crossing into the kitchen, I yanked our calendar marked with appointments off the wall. The thumbtack holding it flew across the room and got lost in the scattered garbage. I dropped the calendar into the trash bag.

"Maybe we should keep that," Mom said.

"Why? We're off to a whole new start."

She grinned. "You feel it, too?"

I turned away so she couldn't see me roll my eyes.

Most of what we owned fit into our rusty Escort wagon, the boxes and bags and loose clothes reaching to the roof. She insisted we lug the tattered couch down to the street, where we'd found it. The other crappy furniture was the landlord's, so we left it where it was.

One box of books remained on the sidewalk. Our last books. The collection got smaller each time we moved.

"What about these?" I asked.

"Pitch 'em," Mom said, carrying bags of trash to the Dumpster. "There's no more room." I shuffled through the box and pulled out two books of poetry, three on dog care and training, and a beat-up copy of *Alice's Adventures in Wonderland*. I hesitated over the second half of *The Joy of Cooking,* which I'd found near the Dumpster. Neither of us had ever cracked it open. Still, I crammed it and the other books I'd selected into the car.

When Mom returned, she told me to lock up and leave the keys in the landlord's mailbox.

"What about the rent we owe?"

"Covered," she said, smiling. "The landlord's got our damage deposit and last month's rent." She pulled a wad of bills from her shorts pocket. "Your eighty-six dollars. I didn't need it." I'd earned that money walking three spoiled Chihuahuas, and I'd given it to her for the phone bill. She saw that I was puzzled. "I worked extra hours this week and last," she said. I stared at the money as she climbed into the car. I thought she'd been out with Rocky all those evenings.

"Hurry up," Mom said, already seated behind the wheel. I ran upstairs. From the doorway, I surveyed our trashed apartment. I picked through the rubble, checking inside drawers and under furniture. The Wild Turkey stood unopened on the kitchen table. For two years, I'd lived with a shadow over my head, the possibility that she would drink herself into oblivion again and I'd be sent back into foster care. It was always there, the hushed murmur of wrenching, impending doom, even when my mother was holding it together. Hearing her quick, light footsteps on the stairs, I grabbed the bottle and shoved it under the kitchen sink.

Mom appeared, breathless. "Forgot one thing," she said, then disappeared into the bathroom and returned with a pink bathrobe that had hung behind the door, unnoticed during our packing.

I leaned against the sink, my legs rubbery. When she left, I turned off the lights, locked the apartment, and hurried down the steps after her. One of my boots made a tapping sound. I looked at the heel. The thumbtack from the calendar was stuck in it.

TWO

It was midmorning, as our duct-taped car rattled across West Texas, when my grandmother Esther rose from the dead. Up until then, I thought we were leaving Dallas much the way we'd left Ashland and St. Louis and Wichita—aimlessly and in a hurry, a trail of broken appointments and head-shaking teachers behind us—with one big difference: Mom wasn't nursing a Texas-sized hangover. As she sipped her second cup of truck-stop coffee, I asked as casually as I could, "What's the surprise this time?"

She cleared her throat. "This time," she announced, "we're going *to* something. To some*one*. Esther Hanes. I found her in a nursing home in Rio Blanco, New Mexico."

"Your mother?" I asked. "Isn't she dead?"

She lifted her chin. "Just set aside, let's say. Until the right moment."

I stared at her. I had good reason to think my grandmother was six feet under: Mom had always told me she was "gone." She may have even used the word "deceased." I grabbed a map out of the glove compartment and looked for Rio Blanco. It was a small dot just north of Albuquerque and a long way from where we were now.

"When did you see her last?"

Mom scratched the back of her head. "Thirteen years ago."

"Why haven't you told me about her before?"

Muscles in the side of her face twitched. "She's been as good as dead. I've had nothing to say to her."

"And now you do?"

She hesitated. "I'm a whole new woman now."

Outside the car window, West Texas yawned, hot, brown, and empty, while I digested this news. Tumbleweeds piled up against the fences lining the highway. I had a grandmother. Alive. A new branch on our withered and rootless two-person family tree. The ride had been tedious before, but now that I knew we had a solid purpose and a destination, it felt endless.

I knew better than to try to squeeze too much information out of my mother at one time. I slumped against the door, wishing I could fall asleep and catch up on the hours I'd missed the night before. No such luck. I was too wound up and too uncomfortable. We were baking in the car with the window closed, but opening it turned my eyes and mouth into sticky paper. The air conditioning didn't work, and even if it did, Mom wouldn't have turned it on. We didn't have enough money to pay for the extra gas it would use. She'd said her wallet was so empty, we'd be lucky to make it to Rio Blanco, and she refused to take more money from me.

"Is she glad we're coming?" I asked.

Mom looked at me sideways and readjusted her grip on the wheel. "She doesn't know. We're going to surprise her."

Terrific, I thought. We're going to burst in on a frail old woman in a nursing home. I hoped the shock of seeing us wouldn't kill her. "Why haven't we seen her all these years?" I asked, flicking the loose knob on the end of the window crank.

Her fingers wiggled against the wheel. "It's a long, complicated story," she said.

I swallowed. "Well, we only have about ten more hours of driving."

She pressed her back against the seat. "You want to take a break and check if there's a busted fuse or something in that radio?"

"Did that already. It's not busted. Like I already told you."

"Oh." A semi pulled alongside us and Mom winked at the driver.

"You told me Esther was *gone*."

She sipped her coffee and frowned. "She was pretty far gone, all right," she finally offered, and blew a lock of hair off her forehead. "Jeez, it's hot." I watched her, waiting. "She had a stroke when I was nine," Mom said, pressing one fingernail repeatedly into the cardboard, leaving tiny indentations. "Left her unable to walk. I was expected to do everything—wash, dress, feed her."

I sat up straighter. "What about your dad? Wasn't he helping?"

She scowled. "He turned to faith healers. Mother prayed for her miracle for years." She gunned the engine to pass a slow-moving RV. When we were well ahead of it, she added, "All she got was more strokes." Mom stretched her neck in one direction, then the other. "The sicker she got, the more my father kept me home to care for her and pray."

"Is that why you ran away?"

She flexed her fingers, then gripped the wheel again. "I can still hear her: 'Can't you do anything right?'"

"You never saw her again?"

"Five years later, when you were a baby. She wouldn't even let us in the front door. Said I was the picture of sin." She shook her head. "Tried again when you were two. Same results."

I wiped sweat from my upper lip. "I don't get it. What are you going to do now, grovel at her feet?"

Mom's brow creased. "It's not groveling." She tucked some flyaway hair behind her ear. "I'm going to make amends. When you put booze behind you, you have to apologize for anything hurtful you did. So you can move on with your life."

Maybe she'd been working late for a week or two, but she'd been going out with Rocky for a couple of months, so the booze couldn't be all that far behind her. Besides, though I wasn't sure how long she'd been dry this time, she'd gone days, weeks, even a month or two without drinking before.

"What about what your mother did to you?" I asked.

"That's not supposed to matter."

"How could it not matter?"

"The thing is," Mom said, a tinge of impatience in her voice, "you're just supposed to clean up your past mistakes."

It didn't make sense to me, and I had a feeling she didn't really get it, either. "What did they say when you called the nursing home?" I asked.

"That she's a gentle soul who prays a lot. Very close to God."

I nearly choked. "Wasn't she praying and buddying up to God when she ordered you and me off her porch?"

Mom pursed her lips. "I think she's going to be different now, Kayla. No one ever called her 'gentle' fifteen years ago. Obviously, she's mellowed. People do."

During our talk, the speedometer needle had crept up to eighty-seven, and the front end of the car now started shaking something awful.

"Mom . . ."

She eased off the gas.

Under the intense midday sun, the road ahead shimmered and everything around us gave off a flat, whitish glare. I had to get some air, even if it sucked me dry. Rolling the car window down partway, I gripped the cloth purse that held my dog-walking money. At least this time we weren't running from any angry bill collectors. And we had something else going for us: a place to live. Mom said she knew someone who knew someone in Rio Blanco, and she had it all set up. A miracle.

I shoved the boxes at my feet to one side so I could stretch my legs. It was even more of a miracle that we were going *to* someone. A relative. Not just another sea of completely unrelated strangers. Of all the relations we could have hooked up with, Grandma Esther wouldn't have been my first choice, but I supposed even a cranky, ailing grand-mother was better than nothing. Not that I had much to choose from. Just her and a dad I'd never met named Desmond. He and Mom had split up before I was born, and she always dismissed my questions about him: *Don't even go there, Kayla,* or, *Honey, he's not worth talk-ing about.* I could read between those lines: clearly, the slimeball had abandoned us. We were better off without him. Still, I wouldn't have minded meeting the guy who fathered me, just for a minute. Maybe even exchanging a word or two.

As if she could read my mind, she said, "Nice to have some family and a place of our own to go to, isn't it, Kayla?"

"I guess." I fiddled with the radio, just in case it had magically repaired itself. "Are we going to see Esther today?" I asked.

"That's 'Grandma' to you."

"Whatever." It was hard to think of her as my relative.

Mom shook her head. "It'll be too late. Let's save the fun for tomorrow, okay?"

I shrugged and turned to look out the window.

"Kayla, are you feeling a little shy about meeting her?"

"You haven't exactly made her sound like a joy ride."

"Well, her bark is worse than her bite."

Was she trying to convince herself of something? Maybe I shouldn't have been so surprised that Mom would pull something like this. How many times in the past two years, through all our moves and countless attempts to stop drinking, had she declared she was a "whole new woman"? According to her, everything we did now was a "new leaf" or "new chapter" or "new episode." Apparently, this week's episode would include seeking out and making apologies to the woman who'd treated her like dirt.

By late afternoon, when the sun was broiling us alive, I wished des-perately that I could do some of the driving. Fifteen-year-olds should be able to drive—at least the smart ones. I was ready to do almost anything to distract myself from the heat and the 694 miles that Mom was hell-bent on covering in one day. I'd tired of reading poetry and dog-training books, and a girl can distract herself with recipes for only so long—in my case, about six minutes. Too bad we were so broke and Mom was in such a rush. Some of our best times happened when we had extra money and could check into a motel with a pool.

I considered digging out my notebook and taking a stab at a new poem—something inspired by shimmering asphalt and oil rigs—but I didn't like writing in front of anyone.

It was too hot to eat much, but we stopped anyway at a diner. My clothes were sticking to me, but Mom hopped out of the car looking cool and comfortable. Of course, she wasn't wearing a T-shirt and heavy jeans like I was. She had on a tank top and cut-offs, and more of her was uncovered than covered. Her leg muscles were firm and smooth, her arm muscles had definition, and her thighs didn't rub against each other like mine. I envied her wiry body. And her small boobs, which she complained about. I'd have traded my big jobbers for my mother's petite ones in a minute. My papayas for her half lemons, as she put it.

Inside the diner, I rolled up my sleeves. Mom glanced over at me. "Kind of warm, huh?"

"I'm okay." Outside, dazed travelers stepped stiffly from their cars and pickups.

"Want to dig out something cooler to wear?"

"I'm fine."

"I don't know why you hide yourself in all that."

I ignored her.

"Maybe you're saving it," she said, taking out a compact and lipstick and sliding the lipstick across her lips. "That's okay. Nothing wrong with saving it. Just a bit warm, is all."

Saving it? If only she knew. If only I could tell her about Two-and-a-

Half-Minute Hal. "Hiding it" was more accurate, but my body was another subject I avoided with my mother. She wouldn't let me use the word "fat" when talking about myself. "You're a full-figured girl," she'd say. I'd studied the doctors' charts for the past two years, ever since I began to sprout in every direction. Height, above average. Weight, above average. All that horizontal sprouting. A regular vegetable garden. Next to my mother, I felt huge and awkward. At least, I felt that way when I caught a glimpse of us reflected in the diner's big plate-glass windows. When we stood at the register to pay for our greasy food, the truckers gave me a once-over but studied my mom as she dug into her back pocket for her thin wallet.

Out past the parking lot, a herd of dark brown cattle stood facing the fence by the highway as if waiting to cross to the other side. We got back into the car. Maybe we were truly off to a fresh start. Come to think of it, I hadn't actually seen Mom take a drink or heard her complain about a headache in more than a week. It wasn't like me not to notice. Hal must have been taking up an awful lot of space in my brain.

Maybe she'd keep a good job this time and I wouldn't have to cook or grocery shop or piece together enough dog walking to hold off bill collectors. Maybe we could get that house I dreamed about, with a hammock I'd write poems in and a frisky dog I could take roaming. We could have Grandma over for Sunday dinners, get her out of that nursing home. We'd set the table with a bright blue cloth and yellow candles. Mom would roast a turkey, and I'd learn how to make apple crisp. When no one was looking, I'd sneak scraps to the dog.

THREE

She had to be kidding.

Thirteen hours after we'd left Dallas, with the sun low in the sky, Mom steered our car up to a pile of junk in front of a trailer on the outskirts of Rio Blanco, a nothing town north of Albuquerque. The trailer was the color of old cooked oatmeal, with mustard yellow trim, and seemed to tilt slightly to the left. I'd been picturing a doublewide. This one was smaller than a single.

"Mom, this is *it?*"

She sucked in her breath, nodding slowly. "Well." She flashed a smile at me. "It's you and me and my lonely desert in this little trailer for now."

I bit the inside of my cheek. Her "lonely desert" had nothing to do with the dry lands of New Mexico. When she had a man in her life, the lonely desert transformed into the happy jungle.

I picked my way across the wasteland between the trailer and us, dodging a cracked sink, sections of plastic pipe, and broken fan belts (you drive around this country as much as we have, you get to know fan belts). Even at dusk, heat jumped off the packed earth.

"You call this a yard, Mom?"

She sat in the car still, looking a little deflated. She called out, "Sure. Redbone did."

"Who the hell—"

She shot me a look. We'd agreed on the long drive not to swear so much.

"Who the *heck* is Redbone?"

She rummaged in the fringed black leather backpack she used as a purse, pulled out a slip of paper, and read aloud, "Key on nail under right side of porch."

I found the key, climbed the cement-block steps onto the tiny wooden porch, and unlocked the door. The knob turned, but the door wouldn't budge. I pulled hard and it flew open. Mom marched inside. A wave of stale heat wafted out of the trailer while I stood rooted to the little porch. She'd told me the place was "private, with a yard, next to acres of wilderness." I could have hit our neighbors' trailers by throwing a stone with my left arm, and I had half a mind to. The so-called wilderness behind the trailers looked as inviting as the moon and just as barren.

Mom stuck her head out a window. "Cute curtains," she chirped. I wanted us to get back in the car and drive off. But she'd already paid the landlord—I was guessing that was who Redbone was—the first two weeks' rent, and she had such high hopes for reconnecting with her mother. I grabbed a box from the car and went inside.

Setting the box on a small table, I glanced around. This old trailer was about four times the length of our Escort and maybe two and a half times as wide. Faded beige curtains printed with lassos and red cowboy boots fluttered on all the windows. Maybe having curtains on the windows was what she meant by "private." That would be new for us. In our St. Louis apartment, the shades had rolled up with a snap when we pulled them down, or they'd hung limply when we tried to raise them. In Wichita, we'd had metal blinds that were bent and broken and angled every which way. Dallas had been the worst—half the apartment windows were boarded up, the rest with no curtains or shades.

Mom pointed to the real wood paneling. "Classy," she gloated. "None of that vinyl and plastic shit"—now I glared at her—"I mean, *stuff* that newer trailers are made of." She ran her hand over the edge of the kitchen counter. "Real stainless. This is all right."

She didn't seem to notice the grit in the cracks of the linoleum. While she pointed out the trailer's other fine points, I tried to get the warped front door to latch. The *only* door. Probably violated some fire code not to have a second escape, but she wouldn't think to check on that. What finally worked was slamming it hard.

I went on inspecting. The living room and kitchen were all one small, narrow room, the kitchen part separated from the rest by a counter. A dingy turquoise two-seater sofa and a tiny table and three chairs with metal legs took up a lot of the space. A narrow hall led past a minuscule bedroom and a bathroom with a toilet, sink, and stained shower. Everything was tiny. I felt like Alice in the rabbit's house after she'd taken a swig of the stuff that made her grow. I half expected my head to hit the ceiling any minute now.

The hall ended at a small bedroom filled with a double bed, which Mom had already claimed by dropping her backpack on it. My bedroom—the minuscule one—had a twin bed pressed against the wall and a set of built-in drawers at the foot of the bed. It was so narrow I could almost touch both walls by stretching my arms out. I tried to look at the bright side: it would be easy to keep this place clean once we'd wiped off the dust coating everything. And we were still together. That was something.

But when a truck roared into the yard and a stocky man wearing a Bullwinkle cap hopped out carrying two six-packs of Coors, I felt a chill start in my chest and shoot outward to all my limbs. Normally, we were in a new place at least a couple of weeks before Mom got reacquainted with alcohol. Mom sidled onto the porch and walked down the steps. "You must be Redbone," she said. I stayed in the doorway.

"Housewarming gift." Bullwinkle man held out a six-pack of sweating beer cans to her like the two of them were old friends. "This one's straight from the cooler."

I held my breath, and my heart began to thrash around inside my rib cage. She glanced back at me, then turned to him, shaking her head but smiling. "You didn't have to."

"C'mon. Is your refrigerator too full of these already?"

Sweat trickled down my sides.

"No, as a matter of fact, we don't have any. It's just . . ." She wrinkled her nose.

He stepped past her, but I stood firm in the doorway.

"Carly?"

"Kayla."

"Redbone, here. How do you do? I'll just set these inside."

"She doesn't want them."

He laughed, a gruff, snorting laugh. "After a long, hot day on the road?" He looked back at her, confused. She smiled and shrugged.

I asked, "Are you the landlord?"

"That depends," he drawled.

Now I was confused, and he saw it and laughed. "Not if something needs fixing."

My mom laughed, too. I didn't see what was so darn funny.

"What is it, darlin'?" he said to me.

"This door's hard to open. Even harder to latch." And I'm not your *darlin'*.

He looked at me as if I were a car that wouldn't start, set the six-packs on the step, and climbed onto the porch. I didn't like being close to him, so I stepped down.

"You've got to give it some muscle." He shoved one hip into the door. The latch clicked. I looked at him. "I'll get it fixed, girl. Don't worry." He came down the steps and hesitated by the Coors. "It'd be a shame not to enjoy these cold ones, Marilyn."

My insides rolled into a tight ball. All she had to say was *No, thanks. I don't drink.*

Instead, she rubbed her thin, bare arms up and down as if she were cold, even though it was still at least eighty degrees. "It's tempting," she said.

"Nothing like a cold beer on a hot day," he replied.

Despite the heat, I shivered.

"You go ahead," she told him.

Laughing, he broke two cans out of the carrier and tossed one to her. "*You* go ahead."

She caught it. Turned it around in both hands. Looked at me.

I shook my head very slowly.

For a moment, eyes closed, she touched the sweating can to her cheek. Then she swooped past Redbone, handed him her beer, and scooped up the six-pack that wasn't cold.

"Another time, Redbone," she said, her voice breezy. She yanked open the door. "One sixer is enough for us. That was sweet of you. You take the other home."

I turned hot then as a drop of sweat ran into my eye and burned, and I waited for Redbone to go. I feared that if I turned my back, he'd follow me in.

He shrugged, picked up the other six-pack, and ambled to his truck. "Later," he said.

"Much later," I muttered.

"Why'd you take that?" I pointed to the beer she had set on the kitchen table.

"It's rude not to accept a gift, Kayla. Anyway, it'll come in handy for visitors."

"Remind me who else we know here besides your sick mother and the illustrious Mr. Redbone?"

Mom put the beer in the refrigerator. "Kayla. We'll get to know lots of people."

The Coors was the only thing on the empty refrigerator shelves, and we'd never gotten to know many people before. Panic rose in me like a geyser. There was eighty-six dollars in my pocket, a lot less in hers, and an unsuspecting and potentially rabid grandmother awaited our arrival. Mom's getting plastered seemed like the worst possibility in the world. Remembering how she hated warm beer, I suggested, "Why don't we keep it in a cupboard until we have a visitor who drinks?"

She stood before the open refrigerator for a long time, her shoulder blades like small, twitching wings. Slowly, she took the beer out and put it in the cupboard.

I went outside and stood on the steps, sucking air from the massive sky before I got more stuff from the car.

FOUR

A chainlink fence around the turquoise trailer next to ours corralled two German shepherds. Across the road, rolling land dotted with cactus, juniper, and sandstone outcroppings stretched downhill to a sprawling adobe house with huge windows. I'd heard barking from down near the house but hadn't seen any dogs yet.

My mom sat next to me on the cement-block steps.

"Did Redbone say we could have a dog?"

"I forgot to ask."

I sucked on my lip. That was the only thing I'd asked her to find out. What the heck had all those long phone conversations been about? The sun slipped behind low, thin clouds. The sky turned wonderful shades of purple, gold, and pink, but her almost taking a drink sat between us like an unwelcome third person, ruining the view.

"There's a phone here already," Mom said, as if that should console me. "We just have to put it in our names."

"Good," I said grudgingly.

"Are you hungry?" she asked.

"Sort of. Mostly tired. I'll fix us corn flakes."

"No milk."

I sighed. "Right."

The sun dipped behind the mountains. The whole world was in shadow. A relief.

"Let's get milk." She took my hand, jumped up, and hauled me with her.

The inside of the Escort felt huge without all our stuff. Mom hummed, and her good mood encouraged me. If she was a new woman, I could at least ask a few more questions.

"Did Grandma know Desmond?"

She looked at me like I was nuts. "That would have been a pretty picture." She steered from our dirt road onto the main drag.

"You've never told me his last name."

"I haven't?" Two reddish splotches appeared on her cheeks.

"Nope," I said, studying her face. I'd never seen her blush when talking about a man. "What was it?"

She pursed her lips. "I don't know."

I cleared my throat. "But you lived with him, right?"

"Half a year."

"That's long enough to learn a person's last name."

She shrugged. "What can I tell you, Kayla? That was more than fifteen years ago."

"Where does he live now?"

"I have no idea. He moved." The color faded from her cheeks.

I asked, "Why didn't you go with him?"

"I've *told* you," she said. "There was nothing between us."

Other than me. We came into town, passing a couple of auto repair shops, a Circle K, a Mexican café, and a hardware store. I shifted my focus back to our newly-raised-from-the-dead relative. "All these years, you and Grandma never talked or wrote even once?"

Mom turned into a busy parking lot. "Remember when we lived in Colorado?"

"Of course." When I was ten, we moved to a town surrounded by mountains. Each fall, the aspens turned bright golden yellow. Mom worked steadily and took a night class, leaving me with the woman who lived in the other half of our duplex.

"Our second year there, I got word that my dad had died. Mom wanted me to come home, but I had a kid to take care of," she explained, as if I weren't that same kid. "I wasn't going back to be her slave again." She made it sound like staying with me was the lesser of two evils.

We left the car and I followed her through the lot, remembering more: the woman next door had a baby who cried all the time. When I turned twelve, Mom stayed in bed too much, and her room stank of old sweat and whiskey. I made us hundreds of peanut butter and jelly sandwiches that year. She hardly ate any of hers. The day I couldn't wake her, I ran next door. The neighbor woman called 911 while the baby screamed in her arms.

Later that day, a social worker took me to see my mom in the hospital. I sat in the hall while they talked in her room. I couldn't hear everything they said, but I caught Mom's last words to the social worker: *"Take her."*

The social worker led me to Mom's side, made me tell her good-bye. From there, she took me to a foster family I'd never met before. She told me on the way that their last name was Patella, which means kneecap, and she laughed. "Isn't that funny?" As she was leaving me, she said it would be two months until my mom could take care of me again.

Before my mother managed to come for me, two months turned into an entire year.

Mom led me past a liquor store, her eyes flickering over the banners declaring RUM SPECIAL! $3.99! Once inside Bailey's Grocery, I turned toward the dairy cases, but she tugged me in another direction.

"I thought we came for milk."

"Let's have a real dinner."

I followed her past aisle after aisle toward the wall lined with vegetables and fruits. Meat was at the back of the store. She darted into the frozen-food aisle. I stopped, just yards from the fresh stuff. Mom held a freezer case door open. "Fish sticks or chicken potpie?"

My stomach curdled. "I dunno. Cereal sounds better."

"Nah." She selected two potpies and handed them to me along with a ten-dollar bill. Keeping a five, she told me, "Meet me back at the car."

I started to say, "If we were going to have a real dinner . . . ," but she had already slipped through the crowded aisles, out of earshot. And with the five bucks. Rum was only $3.99. I hurried to the endlessly long checkout lines and stepped up to a big-bellied man with a heaping cart and asked if he minded my cutting. He nodded curtly and let me step into line.

In front of me was a woman buying a real dinner: lots of vegetables, boneless chicken breasts, fresh parsley, and milk. That was when I remembered that we had forgotten to get milk, but there was no way I would have gotten out of line now.

I knew how my mother shopped for booze: she took her time, cruising the aisles, selecting expensive bottles of wine and brandy and examining the labels, finally choosing the item she knew all along she was going to get, the four-dollar gallon of wine or whatever whiskey was on sale. She would turn to the cashier with a smile and say, "Just this today," as if she'd be back in a day or two for a case of the expensive stuff.

When it was finally my turn and the cashier asked me for $4.28, I handed her the ten, which I had crumpled into a damp ball. She moved in slow motion, counting five ones into my hand and calling to the next checker, "Give me a roll of quarters, would you, Jeannie?" I was tempted to leave without my change, but we were too broke. Finally, I got the coins and ran to the liquor store, where I searched every aisle.

She wasn't in the store. Outside, she walked toward me carrying a large box. I hoped she hadn't seen me leave the liquor store. On the box, I read *Oscillating Fan.*

"It's for you," she told me. "Your room has no cross draft."

Her thoughtfulness caught me off guard. "How'd you pay for it?"

She shifted from one foot to the other. "If you have to know, magic plastic."

"I thought you destroyed that."

"After we're settled," she said. "And by then, maybe we won't have to."

I followed her to the car, calculating how long it might take to pay off the credit card debt if we could pay a hundred dollars a month. I'd be done with high school, maybe college, even—if you can go to college with no money and big debt. I pushed the thoughts away. I'd barely finished tenth grade. College was years away—and might as well be on the moon. It was just an idea. She hadn't gone. But she had bought me a fan for my hot, stuffy room. I should think about that.

On the way home, she asked, "What were you doing in the liquor store?"

I stared out the window. It was an unfair question. She knew what I was doing in there. I didn't want to be the one to say it.

The breeze coming in was warm, and a small truck with huge tires blared Latino music. Our rusty Escort looked out of place in this land of shiny cars.

"You've got to have more trust in me."

I turned to look at her, but she was concentrating on the road. Her knuckles looked pale against the dark gold steering wheel.

"We have beer at home. If I wanted to, I could drink that."

I was quiet, ashamed that I didn't trust her and angry that I couldn't.

"Kayla, I'm not going to drink."

"What about with Redbone?" I asked, my voice embarrassingly high.

She tapped one hand on the steering wheel. "What about it?"

"Why didn't you just tell him?"

"Tell him what?"

"That you don't drink."

"When you say that, people think you have a problem."

Now the car felt fuller than it had packed with all our stuff. I wanted to get out and walk, but there was no sidewalk, and in the dark I wasn't sure I could find the way to our trailer.

"It's been three whole weeks, Kayla."

"Three weeks."

I sounded like an idiot, repeating her words, while in my head a battle raged: there *is* a problem, there *isn't* a problem. By the time she shut off the engine and the headlights beside our very own garden of junk, I was numb with exhaustion and desperate to go to sleep.

FIVE

I woke in the middle of the night disoriented, jolted from a dream of a dog just out of reach. A weird cry came from behind our house: half human, half animal. I shot upright, terrified that something had happened to my mother.

Moonlight filtered in through the one tiny window over my head, and I remembered where I was. A second, more doglike cry joined the first, coming from a different direction, a piercing, lonely howl that dissolved into yipping. The neighbor's dogs joined in, and I lay back down, comforted by their more familiar barking. The other howls, I figured, must be coyotes. Their cries gave me chills.

It was quiet when I woke again in the morning, though the coyotes' forlorn wails still echoed uncomfortably in my head. Even though Mom planned to leave my money alone, I knew it wouldn't hurt to round up some more. I wasn't sure what else I'd do all summer in this puny town. Mom had insisted on cruising up and down all the streets in the business district last night. That drive lasted about as long as it took me to yawn.

"You're going out like that?" Mom asked when I came into the kitchen. She sat at the tiny table, drinking coffee from a big mug. I held up the flyer I had just made.

"I'm a dog walker, Mom, not a fashion model."

"Still. You could tuck in your shirt. Or I'll lend you one of mine. How about the red tank? It's cute with jeans."

I didn't say anything. "Cute" had nothing to do with me.

"Your hair, then."

"It won't lie flat. It's too short. Besides, I like it spiked."

"Bandannas are in." She rummaged in a suitcase and pulled out a bright yellow bandanna.

In? I thought. Wasn't that a couple of decades ago?

"Put it on. You don't want to scare away your customers."

What did it matter to her? She'd said she was done taking money from me. My new and improved mother planned to be fully on top of our finances. I swiped the bandanna from her hand.

"If you can wait a couple of hours," Mom said, "I'll drive you into town. We'll go see your grandmother. You can do your errand after that."

I couldn't wait. I'd discovered that if I flung myself onto my bed, the trailer shook. I needed to get outside and feel my feet on solid ground. "That's okay." I took a dollar from her purse. "For copies," I explained when she raised her eyebrows.

"What about your money?"

"I'm saving for college," I said.

That shut her up for a minute, but as I was leaving, she said, "Kay, I don't want to take more money from you, but I could use a little loan for more groceries." Reluctantly, I handed her half of my eighty-six dollars.

When I stepped outside, my ribs widened at the sight of the sky expanding in every direction. I went down the road, past the German shepherds, who lunged to the ends of their chains, snarling and barking. Safely beyond them and around the curve, I blew my nose in Mom's yellow bandanna and stuffed it into my pocket.

At the bottom of the hill, I came to a long dirt driveway leading to the sprawling adobe with the big windows. A silver BMW sat in the driveway, and a golden retriever trotted out from behind the house, wagged its tail, and barked at me. He was chained and frustrated. The front door didn't look too used, so I walked around to the back. The retriever barked and jumped up on me, tail still wagging, and tried to lick my face. Gently but firmly, I brought my knee up. He got the message and dropped down.

Before I got to it, the back door opened and an older guy rushed out wearing crisply ironed cream-colored khakis and a deep purple shirt that looked like silk, the way it caught the light. He seemed startled by the sight of me and said, "Whatever you're selling, we're not buying today."

Without thinking, I grabbed hold of the dog's chain close to his collar and yanked it toward the ground, commanding, "Sit!" The surprised dog obeyed me.

Halfway into his car, the man straightened up. "What do you think you're doing?"

Embarrassed, I shrugged. "Just . . . showing him what to do. I have a business, walking dogs. And I train them. This one"—I leaned over and scratched the dog behind one ear—"must be a pest, the way he is."

The man shook his head. "I don't recall hiring you."

I laughed nervously. "Maybe you should. What's this dog like to live with?"

He looked at his chunky gold watch. "I don't have time to discuss this."

I gave the dog another quick scratch and hurried over to the car, surprised by my own boldness. "Can you give me a lift into town? I could tell you more on the way."

He hesitated, looking at his watch again. His silver hair was perfectly combed back. I'd never seen such elegant hair on a man. "Get in."

He started the car before I could get around to the passenger side, but he didn't drive away until I'd buckled my seat belt. The inside of the car smelled of leather. I felt the seat with my hands, hoping he wouldn't notice.

"Where do you live?"

I pointed up the hill. "Just moved into the oatmeal-mustard trailer."
I held the flyer out for him to see. "I'm going to make copies. For my business."

He took it from me, scanning it as he drove. "What do you do when someone hires you?"

"Walk their dog. Feed it and play with it, too, if the owner is out of town. Train the dog if it needs training, and teach you how to give commands so the dog listens to you."

He nodded and glanced at me.

"My prices are fair, too. Ten dollars an hour. Most people charge at least twice that."

"I wasn't looking for help with the dog."

I swallowed. "But you sure could use it. Look how he jumps and barks. How many times has he gotten your nice clothes dirty? I've lived here less than twenty-four hours and I've heard him barking a lot. Haven't any of the neighbors complained? He's a bother, and he's lonely. I can take care of both of those problems."

The guy laughed. "You're quite a saleswoman. Ten dollars an hour? What can you do in one hour?"

By the time he pulled up in front of a store called Kopy Kats, we'd almost agreed to six hours a week of walking and training. We exchanged names—his was Sam Coltan—and then he offered his hand. It was warm and smooth and probably had never held a leash or thrown a stick. "I'll think on it," he said. "I run Moonstar Gallery." He hesitated, maybe waiting for me to recognize the name. "We've got a string of important shows coming up. But my son should be coming home soon. It's his dog. Then I won't need any help."

"When's that?"

He placed both hands on his leather-wrapped steering wheel. "I don't know exactly," he said softly. "It should be soon."

I had questions, but he looked at his watch again, so I climbed out. "Leave the dog's leash by the back door tomorrow," I said. "I won't charge you. I'll just take him for a walk. We'll check each other out."

He nodded. "Okay."

After talking the Kopy Kats woman into giving me the five-cent rate, I walked around town finding bulletin boards to pin my flyers on. It wasn't a bad flyer. It read:

DOG IN, DOG OUT
Reliable, experienced pet care while you work or travel.
Ask about our foolproof pet-training services.
Reasonable rates. References available.

Below the words, I'd pasted a black-and-white magazine drawing of a posh-looking woman walking a groomed poodle. At the bottom of the flyer, I'd put *Call Kayla at . . .* and written our telephone number vertically fourteen times, then snipped between each number to make little tabs that people could tear off.

I'd hesitated about saying I had references. I didn't. I couldn't exactly ask any of my previous pet-care clients for them. We always moved so suddenly, I'd left most of them in the lurch. If anyone actually asked for a reference, I'd get Mom to write a fake one. How could she refuse, after all I'd done for her?

I found bulletin boards in a supermarket, a health-food co-op, a senior center, and a coffee shop. Two hair salons, a bookstore, a shoe repair shop, and a car repair place let me tape them to the windows. The last place I stopped was Shirley and Sherrie's Big-Time Bargains, a used women's clothing store, where headless mannequins holding swords and ostrich feathers posed in the front windows.

Shirley and Sherrie turned out to be big-time women themselves, one being tall and thin and the other about my height but wider than our trailer's front door. They each wore large rhinestone pins that spelled out their names and sparkled against their polyester exercise outfits.

"What have you got there?" the tall one labeled Shirley asked me, reaching for my flyer. "Sherrie, c'mere. This girl is a businesswoman like us. Got herself a dog-walking business."

Sherrie, who was hanging clothes on racks, peered around Shirley and down through bifocals perched practically on the end of her nose. She glanced quickly at the flyer and studied me as if she was trying to decide if I was truly in the same league. I resisted an urge to smooth down my spiked hair.

"How many of these have you put up?" asked Shirley.

"This is my tenth."

Shirley lit up and slapped Sherrie on the back. "You hear that? She's a hard-working, diligent businesswoman. Whaddya think?"

It seemed like a lot of fuss over hanging a flyer.

Sherrie nodded. "Looks promising." I didn't know if she meant the flyer or me. She rested her elbows on the counter, fingering her name pin. "How old are you, honey?"

"Almost sixteen."

Sherrie sighed. "I thought you were older. Shirl, wasn't the last one fifteen? The boy that tried to get Cocoa to smoke a Pall Mall? Set off his asthma. Nearly killed the poor thing."

"*Him?*" the tall woman said. "I thought *he* was a *girl.*"

"Can't hardly tell these days. Well, whatever. He had promise, too. Just didn't know where to put it."

"I know where he can put his promise," muttered Shirley. "Pall Mall. *Hmmph.*"

Sherrie made a clicking noise with her tongue. "Cost us a bundle, too."

"Excuse me."

They looked at me, a little startled.

"I just want to hang this flyer."

Sherrie smiled at me. "Sure, honey. Go right ahead, but come back here tomorrow to meet Cocoa. If it works out, we can pay you, or we can trade for merchandise." Her arm swept toward the many racks of clothing.

I cleared my throat. "Who—or what—is Cocoa? I do pet care. I don't baby-sit."

Sherrie clapped her hands together. "I'm sorry, hon. We should have explained. He's our dog. He could use a midday walk when we're tied up with the store, and a little extra training."

"Extra?" Shirley leaned toward me. "I don't think dressing him in a tutu and getting him to jump for truffles should count as basic training, do you?"

Sherrie scowled at Shirley. "Never mind that." She looked at the flyer again. "Kayla. Can you come by tomorrow? Or later today, after I pick him up from the salon? He's getting a shave and a 'poo."

"A what?"

Shirley rolled her eyes. "That's short for shampoo. Sherrie, you ought to take along some salve for Beryl's scratches."

"Nah. I'll bet Cocoa loved it this time."

"He hates it," Shirley declared to me.

"I can come back," I said. "Probably tomorrow." I didn't need clothes as much as I needed money, but their offer intrigued me. Mom couldn't borrow from me if I got paid in clothes. Or would that be disloyal? I pushed the thought aside. "Do you have T-shirts?"

"Scads of 'em," said Shirley.

"Second round rack on the right," added Sherrie.

I wandered over to look. There were more T-shirts than I could wear in a lifetime. Solid and striped. Printed with dogs, horses, feathers, camels, and cupids. On my way out, the women called, "You come back now!" at the same time. Sherrie slapped Shirley on the arm and they both shrieked, "Jinx!" and cracked up laughing.

The mile-and-a-half walk home felt long. I found Mom unpacking, and she had set my two boxes of clothes on my bed. It didn't take long to put my things away. I had a few pairs of jeans; a bunch of T-shirts, flannel shirts, and sweatshirts; and a couple of jackets. Underwear, socks. One pair of sneakers, flip-flops, and the boots I was wearing. At the bottom of one box was my poetry notebook, which I shoved between the mattress and box spring of my bed.

"Time to go meet your grandmother, Kayla," Mom drawled, now curled on the faded turquoise sofa in the living room, one forearm draped over her eyes.

I sat down on the arm of the couch. "Tell me again about the last time you saw Esther."

"*Grandma* to you, remember? You were two years old. I took you to see her. She threw us out. End of story."

"Why?"

Mom rubbed her face. "I guess she was still mad that I'd left her. And partly it was a religious thing. She thought your father and I should be together. But he was gone, and I didn't know where to find him. If I even wanted to."

I wondered for the millionth time why he left, but I didn't ask. I hated hearing *Men do things like that* or *Some people always think the grass is greener.* Honestly, I wasn't sure I wanted to know the reason, even if she could give it to me. I picked dirt out of my thumbnail. "I need a shower before we go."

"Ditto."

"Couldn't you just make your apologies and then we go someplace else?"

She rolled onto her side to face me. "Kayla, we're in a brand-new phase."

"Right." I headed for the shower. "Anybody told *her* that we're in a new phase?"

She rolled onto her back again. "All it takes is for one person in a family to change. Then everything changes."

I almost asked aloud which person that would be, but I bit my tongue. Mom was trying so hard. Still, that line about change must have come from one of the many counselors and caseworkers we'd been through, or from the self-help books we'd left behind several moves before.

The showerhead sputtered and spit as much air as liquid. Fortunately, the heat in our trailer made up for the lack of it in the water, but I wondered what showering would be like in winter.

My mom dressed in purple fringed boots, a black tank dress, and a long, lacy crocheted sweater. She piled her hair into a mass of frizzy curls, wisps hanging every which way, a style that looked annoyingly cute on her. I put on a clean T-shirt, my jeans, and my boots.

It was late afternoon by the time we left the house. The nursing home squatted just off the main road, between a drugstore and a bowling alley. After killing the engine, Mom stayed in the driver's seat.

"Aren't we going in?"

"Yeah. Just a minute." She pawed through the contents of her black leather backpack. "Where the hell is it?"

"Heck," I prompted.

"What?"

"You swore. I thought we made a deal."

She ignored me and kept digging until she held up a lipstick. Looking in the rearview mirror, she traced her lips with it. Her hand shook. "Damn."

"Don't you mean darn?"

"Dammit, Kayla, just lay off me, would you?"

I pressed my back against the vinyl seat, staring out at the parking lot.

My mother frowned at herself in the mirror. "Kayla, do you have a tissue?"

Slowly, I pulled the crumpled yellow bandanna from my front pocket and handed it to her. She hesitated before taking it and wiping misapplied lipstick from her upper lip.

"Damn, damn, damn," she muttered. She handed the open lipstick to me. "Do it for me, would you, honey?"

Sherrie had called me "honey" that morning, and I hadn't minded, but coming from Mom, the same word irritated me. Mom parted her lips and pursed them slightly. As I drew the lipstick smoothly over her mouth, I could feel heat coming off her face. It didn't exactly burn, but I had to concentrate not to jerk my hand away. Her skin was pale except for two red blotches on her cheeks and bluish gray smudges under her eyes, like smoke. I had the impression that my flesh-and-blood mother might at any moment dissolve and evaporate into the air.

A few strokes and she was repaired. I handed her the lipstick.

She made a face in the mirror and tossed the lipstick into her pack. "Let's go."

SIX

The inside of the nursing home smelled like fish sticks. At the front desk, my mother asked where we could find Esther Hanes, adding, "I'm her daughter, and this"—she gestured to me—"is her granddaughter." No one had ever called me a granddaughter. The title pleased me, even though I felt like an imposter. Maybe the woman behind the front desk thought I was one, too, because she exchanged glances with another woman filing papers nearby. "Do you have identification with you?" she asked Mom.

"Of course," Mom replied, taking her driver's license out and handing it to the woman, who reached for a thick file folder on her desk and checked Mom's ID against something inside it. She frowned, returned the license, and said, "Excuse me a minute."

The woman knocked on the door of a back office and went into it. Through the glass pane separating the office from the front desk, we saw her speak to a man with a bushy mustache. The man came out, smiling, and extended his hand to Mom. "Ms. Hanes?"

Not smiling, Mom hesitantly shook his hand. "Where is my mother?"

"I'm Ben Stokes, director of operations here. Please join me in my office."

"Where is she?" Mom asked, more insistently.

He stepped toward the back room. "Please. Let's go where we can talk in private."

Mom started to protest, but I grabbed her arm and drew her toward Mr. Stokes's white-walled office. "Mom! Let's go," I hissed.

She let me lead her there, and Mr. Stokes followed, carrying the file folder the front-desk woman handed him.

"Sit, please," he said, and he closed the blinds on the window between the two offices. When we were all seated, Ben Stokes folded his hands on top of the folder on his desk. "Our Mrs. Hanes may not be the person you are seeking," he said.

"What do you mean?" Mom asked.

"I'm sorry to say, but our files indicate that Mrs. Hanes has no living relatives."

Mom's eyes narrowed. "What the hell?"

I touched her shoulder. "Mom, let's go."

She ignored me. "I called every damn nursing home in this state. I was told she's here."

Mr. Stokes stroked his mustache. "I'm sorry. Whoever you spoke to must not have checked the files—or understood our policies about releasing information to callers."

"Stop being so damn sorry about everything." Mom leaned toward him. "My mother and I have been out of touch for years. She doesn't even know if I'm still alive." She stood up. "Just take us to her now. She'll tell you who I am."

Mr. Stokes sighed and tapped his fingertips against each other. "I'm afraid she can't do that. Our Mrs. Hanes died two days ago." He paused, pulling on one side of his mustache. "Her remains are at a nearby funeral home."

My mom's face turned as chalky white as the walls, and she lowered herself back into the chair. In a rasping voice she said, "You'd damn well better let me see her now, because if she isn't my mother, then I'm going to have to keep searching, aren't I?"

Mr. Stokes looked like he'd just swallowed a frog. I didn't understand what the big deal was. The woman was dead. She wouldn't care if the wrong folks looked in on her. Why couldn't we just take a peek and give him a yes or a no?

Telling us he'd be back in a minute, Mr. Stokes left the room. Mom locked the door behind him.

"What are you doing?" I thought she'd gone nuts.

"This is insane," she said. She grabbed the file folder on his desk and started flipping through the many pages inside. "Esther Hanes, widowed . . ." Some pages she read silently; others she turned with barely a glance.

"Mom, he's going to come back!"

She ignored me, continuing to read, frantically leafing through the thick file.

I peered through the blinds to the outer office just as Mr. Stokes approached the door.

"He's coming!" I hissed.

"Not once," she muttered. "She didn't mention me once."

The doorknob turned, and then the whole door shook as Mr. Stokes tried to open it.

"Mom!" I pleaded quietly. "Let's get out of here. It probably isn't even her."

Closing the file, she looked up. "Turn the doorknob," she whispered. "Don't open it. Just shake it! Like you're trying to open it." She leaned her forehead on one hand. "How could she?"

Mr. Stokes banged on the door. "Ms. Hanes? Can you open the door?"

"Mom, what should I do?" I whispered.

"We're trying!" she called out. To me she whispered, "Keep rattling." She grimaced at a few last papers. "What the hell was I expecting?" Then she came around the desk and nudged me aside. "Gosh!" she exclaimed, fiddling with the doorknob. "What's wrong with this?" She unlocked the door and opened it. Mr. Stokes stood flustered in the doorway. "Does it do that often?" she demanded.

The man looked around wildly at the doorknob, at the folder on the desk, and at us. "That was strange," he said uneasily. "It's never stuck before."

Mom dropped into a chair and held her head in both hands. "I can't believe this."

"I'm sorry to have kept you waiting," Mr. Stokes said. "I had to clear it first. Now I can take you to see our Mrs. Hanes. If you don't mind, though, just one question first."

Parting her hands, Mom peered at him.

He glanced inside the folder. "Ms. Hanes, did your mother have any birthmarks or other identifying physical characteristics?"

Mom pondered what should have been an easy question for her, then shook her head. "Her skin was flawless," she said. "Absolutely beautiful."

Mr. Stokes appeared disappointed but seemed to recover. "I have a feeling you *will* get to continue looking for your mother, Ms. Hanes. This woman has a large red birthmark on her left forearm."

"Oh," Mom said, and then she smiled, though her smile didn't reach her eyes.

Mr. Stokes wrote down the address of the funeral home where Mrs. Hanes had been taken and offered to lead us there in his car.

Subdued, my mother rose stiffly to follow him. "Thank you," she said.

The woman who wasn't my grandmother lay under a sheet in a chilly room that reminded me of a walk-in refrigerator and that smelled, oddly, of antiseptic and popcorn.

"Are you ready?" Mr. Stokes asked. Mom nodded. I felt a little queasy and decided I didn't need to see this. I turned to leave the room, but Mom grabbed my hand and gripped it tightly, startling me. I couldn't remember the last time she'd taken my hand. An employee from the funeral home lifted the sheet. My mother gasped and covered her mouth. It was a creepy sight: a bluish waxy-looking face; stringy gray-black hair; a body so still that I found myself breathing hard into my own ribs, as if her lifelessness might be contagious. A blotchy, red-brown birthmark encircled her forearm.

"Ms. Hanes, is this—"

"No!" She blinked rapidly and held the back of her hand across her mouth. "No," she repeated. She grabbed me by the shoulders and hugged me hard. Too hard. "It's *not*," she gasped, pulling me by my hand out of the room. "Oh, God. *Thank* God."

"Are you sure, Ms. Hanes? You'll want to be absolutely sure. You seem—"

"I've never seen a—a dead person." She smiled apologetically. "That's all." She stopped in the doorway, gripping my hand so tightly that my eyes filled with tears. I looked down at my feet, trying not to yelp or pull away.

"Mister . . . ," Mom started in a strange voice. Her eyes were bright and her lipstick was smeared and the weird grin on her face sent a chill down my spine. "Thank you so much. I am so sure. You have . . . This has made my day."

It's a wonder that we didn't get a speeding ticket.

"Mom?" I asked as she barreled out of town.

"Shh."

"But I don't understand."

"Later, Kayla."

We rode in silence, my mother hunched forward as if she couldn't get away from the funeral home fast enough. At the trailer, she shut off the engine.

"Mom, where do you think she is, then?"

She stared through the windshield. "Back there."

"Where?"

"In that funeral home."

"It *was* her?"

"A bitch right to the end."

The car engine ticked. "I thought what she did wasn't important."

She closed her eyes.

"Why didn't you tell him?"

She shook her head. "Are you kidding? She had a huge bill. What if they came after me for it?"

I felt shaky. "Are you sure it was her?"

She rolled her eyes at me. "Wouldn't you recognize your own mother?"

I didn't know what to say to that. "What about her funeral?"

My mother leaned her head against the headrest. "Do you know what funerals cost?"

The German shepherds next door sat on their haunches, watching us. "Why did we come here?" My voice sounded high.

She dropped her forehead against the steering wheel and moaned. "I don't know. I thought she'd be different."

That part certainly came true, I thought. Esther was different, all right. Not to mention closer to God, like they'd said. Probably his right-hand woman by now.

"People do change, you know?" she mumbled. "Shit." She sat up suddenly, pulling a folded piece of paper and a lighter from her backpack.

"What's that?" I asked. "What are you doing?"

She held the paper out the window and clicked the lighter. I expected her to set the paper on fire, but she kept the paper and flame apart.

"What is that?" I repeated.

"A list," she said dully. "My amends to her."

Good, I thought. Burn the damn thing. Be done with it.

She shut the lighter, crumpled the paper, and jammed both back into her pack. "At least there might have been an inheritance. Social

Security," she said. "*Something.*" She held her head and shook it back and forth. "God. Nothing left, and still she cuts me out. What did I expect?"

She wasn't making sense. "So, now what?" I asked quietly.

She rolled her head to look at me. Her eyes were red-rimmed but dry. "How the hell do I know?" she said, and turned away. "Get out of the car, Kayla."

"What?"

"Just get out."

I had to force my limbs to move. She started the engine.

"Where are you going?"

"I need some time to myself."

"Don't . . ." *Don't drink,* I wanted to say. But I stopped, because I didn't want to give her any ideas. Maybe she wasn't thinking about drinking.

Yeah, like kids don't think about candy. Like boys don't think about getting into girls' pants.

She backed the car onto the road. "Don't worry about me, Kayla," she yelled out the window as she gunned the engine, leaving me coughing in a cloud of dust.

SEVEN

My mother's snores announced her presence when I woke the next morning. I was surprised that I hadn't heard or felt her come in—the whole trailer shook when we slammed the door to get it to close. I took a long time making and eating a piece of toast, then puttering around the trailer, waiting for her to wake up. Finally, I admitted to myself that she must be hung over. Not wanting to see her puffy face or hear about her killer headache, I took off for Sam's house. Halfway there, I realized I hadn't left Mom a note. Sometimes she got upset when I didn't let her know where I'd gone, but just as often she didn't say anything. I kept on going.

Sam wasn't home. A webbed nylon leash and silver choke collar with a ten-dollar bill stuck in it hung off the back doorknob. When I knocked, the dog barked, and his long nails clicked frantically on a hard floor. I tried the door and it wasn't locked, but I didn't open it.

"Calm down, dog."

He barked louder and hurled himself against the door.

"Easy does it," I crooned. It took about ten minutes of talking gently to him through the closed door before he quieted down. Finally, I heard him drop onto the floor with a sigh.

I opened the door and the dog leaped, but I was ready. We'd lived in Dallas long enough for me to take two of the three Chihuahuas that I walked there to dog obedience school, where I'd watched how to handle big dogs. Quickly, I slipped the choke collar over his head. He started to jump again, but this time I blocked his jump with my knee and yanked on his choke collar.

"Down!" I commanded, and he didn't dare rise from the semi-crouched position I'd forced him into. I checked the brass bone-shaped tag on his collar for his name: Rebel.

We left the house just as my mom drove past, heading to town. I called to her and waved, but she didn't see me. A trickle of guilt worked through me, and I turned my attention to the dog.

For the next half-hour, Rebel and I were all business. We practiced "Sit," "Stay," and "Heel," up and down the long driveway. I thought golden retrievers had lost most of their brains through overbreeding, but he learned fast—especially when he realized I had a pocket full of treats. After the lesson was over, we walked around the huge property and I gave him more lead, letting him sniff out rabbit holes and pee on dozens of spiny plants.

When our hour was up—plus a little more—I put the dog inside and wrote a note to Sam thanking him for the money and telling him the training went well. I hung the leash on a hook inside the door and stepped through a tiled hall to a bright kitchen with exposed wood beams and floor-to-ceiling windows. Lined up neatly on the counter were a few bills, an art magazine, and a shopping list you'd never see in our trailer: *game hen, brie, crackers, chablis, arugula*. Posted on the refrigerator with a magnet was an eight-by-ten photo of a cute guy, a younger version of Sam. Off the kitchen was a large living room, probably ten times the size of our trailer, where a plush couch and chairs made a roomy half circle around a massive sandstone fireplace.

The photo on the fridge drew me back to the kitchen. I'm not one to run around declaring to my friends which guys are hot—a lack of friends being one obstacle—but this guy was scorching. He had long dark hair pulled into a ponytail, green eyes framed by thick eyebrows, and tanned or maybe naturally light brown skin. His head was tilted slightly and he wore an "I know you know I'm gorgeous" smile. His arms loosely embraced a guitar. It was hard to say how old he was—at least twenty, I guessed. It was the kind of photo you'd see posted outside a bar with *Saturday at 8:00!* scrawled underneath in thick black handwriting. I used to study those photos while waiting in the car for Mom, faces with hard edges that the smiles didn't soften.

Except this guy's expression did have some softness. I felt a flash of envy for the guitar in his arms. I was so mesmerized by the look on his face—a mix of arrogance and tenderness—that I hardly noticed Rebel jumping and pawing at my ribs.

I pushed him away. "Later, Rebel." Then it hit me how disobedient he was being and how distracted I was. I tore myself away from the photo. I was acting like those big-haired Dallas girls in my last school who swooned over the latest country singer to hit the top of the charts or the bare-chested actors on magazine covers. "Bad dog. Lie down."

Rebel panted at me, wearing a big dog grin, until I grabbed his choke collar and snapped it toward the floor. He dropped. "Stay!" I commanded. He whimpered but didn't move while I continued exploring. On the coffee table in the living room lay a large book with paintings by someone named Georgia O'Keeffe. I lifted the cover and glanced at a few pages: bold, tantalizing flowers stretched across each one. I sat on the floor with the book and after a while ripped a sheet of paper off the large pad on the counter and kneeled next to the coffee table. The only teacher I liked in Dallas had shown us paintings to inspire us to write poems. I thought for a moment before writing:

Love isn't always what you want
or where you want it.
It's burnt sienna when you wanted magenta.
A high, dry desert when you longed for a meadow.
A marching brass band when you needed one wooden flute,
one simple melody.

Not bad, I thought. Suddenly, Rebel ran barking toward the back door, which opened. I slipped my poem into the book, slammed it shut, and jumped up. A guy with a low, smooth voice bent over the dog, murmuring, "Hey, Rebel. Down, boy. How's it going?"

I called out, "Is that you, Sam?" though I knew it was someone else.

When the guy from the picture on the refrigerator walked into the living room, I felt as if half the air in my lungs got sucked out of me. He was not as perfect as in the picture, but in the flesh, he was even more striking. His eyebrows were darker, his cheekbones stronger. What surprised me first was that he was suddenly real; second, that he was just a little taller than I was, so his startling green eyes were almost even with mine; third, that he seemed as overly confident as I was suddenly unnerved.

I blurted, "I was walking the dog."

He looked amused. "In here?"

"No." I felt myself blush. "I was done. This book, this one, caught my eye. I'm sorry. I can go now." I pulled the ten out of my pocket. "Your dad already paid me." My cheeks burned and I doubted that I was making sense, but my mouth had a mind of its own. "Or, aren't you his son? Sam? Sam's son?" I couldn't get enough air into my lungs.

He smiled at me, his head tipped back slightly, his neck smooth and graceful, his shoulders square. He wore a T-shirt and baggy green army fatigues, and on a thin brass chain around his neck hung a small old-fashioned brass key. He swung around and picked up a guitar case. He moved like a cat. "I am. I am Sam's son. Son of Sam." He laughed, showing straight, white teeth. I couldn't help laughing, too. He sat on the couch, unpacked his guitar, and expertly picked a melody. Frowning, he tuned the strings. "I'm Remy. And you?"

"Kayla."

"Daughter of . . . ?"

I said the first thing that came into my mind. "Dracula."

He raised his eyebrows and picked a fast succession of notes.

"Make that Draculetta."

He nodded and broke into a blues melody. He sang, *"Draculetta, let me be, can't you see I'm so lonely. But I don't like your pointy smile. I'm bound for lovin' that ain't so vile. . . ."*

I couldn't help grinning. When he'd finished, I said, "I really should go."

He drew his hand slowly across the guitar strings. "How often do you walk Rebel?" He nodded toward the dog, which had settled heavily at his feet.

"This was my first day. Sam said you'd take over when you got home."

He studied me, his face serious for the first time. "Did he?"

"Well, he thought you might."

He laughed again and I joined in, louder than I'd intended, someone else's laughter in me. All of a sudden, I couldn't wait to get away. "I gotta go." I made myself walk calmly toward the door. The dog clicked after me.

"You better come back tomorrow," Remy sang after me, strumming his guitar.

I wasn't sure if he was singing to me or just to himself. I wanted to get away so badly, it was hard to stop. "Me?"

His fingers worked the guitar. "I won't have time to walk the dog."

"Okay." Rebel eyed me adoringly, dying to go out again. "Sorry, pup," I whispered, and slipped out. In the spot where Sam had parked sat an old Volkswagen bus, bright orange with a white top and trim. Under the searing blue sky, I felt myself relax, until I remembered that I'd left my poem inside.

EIGHT

Mom wasn't hung over when I got home. She whirled about our tiny kitchen, unpacking Cheerios and bran bread and a gallon of non-fat milk, dusting off shelves.

"Where'd you go last night?"

"Heck if I know." She laughed. "I shot out of here like a cannon-ball, didn't I?"

I nodded and tried to laugh with her.

"Took some dark highway somewhere, out past a state park and a casino. Drove till I thought, Where the heck am I going? So I turned around, wound up at a place Redbone told me about. New Horizons. It's for women starting over. They were having some kind of support group thing. I just sat in." She put one stick of butter in the refrigerator and three others in the freezer.

I'd stayed up worrying, dozing and jumping every time a car drove past or the neighbors' dogs barked. "You could have called," I said.

Mom took a package of sponges out of a grocery bag and dropped them on the table. "How? I didn't have the number."

I scribbled our new phone number on a scrap of paper and slid it across the table to her. She studied it as if I'd written in Greek. "Thanks," she said, tossing it into her leather backpack.

"I guess we're staying, then," I said, sitting on one of the small kitchen chairs.

Mom pulled two cans of refried beans from the bag. "Why wouldn't we?"

I picked up the sponges and tossed them into the air. "With your mother gone, I thought maybe there'd be no reason to stay here."

"On the contrary," Mom said, setting the beans on a shelf. "There's still a whole new world for us here. Might even be better this way."

I opened cupboards to see what else she had bought: canned soups, chocolate chips, microwave popcorn, peanut butter, jelly. I didn't know much about families or death, but it seemed strange to me that a family member we'd come all this way to see had just died, yet my mom was cheerfully shelving jars of mayonnaise and cans of beans.

"You don't even want to sneak into her funeral?"

Mom scrunched up her face. "What for?"

I hesitated. "It seems kind of sad that she won't have any family there, and we're right here."

My mother continued putting groceries away. "She did it to herself."

Though I hadn't known my grandmother, I wanted to defend her. Taking a deep breath, I said, "I thought we came here for something. Maybe you could still make those amends."

She gave me a withering look. "Amends? To a dead person? What's the point of that?"

My chest felt hollow. "I thought it was something you had to do. That it didn't matter what the other person said. Or did." My mouth had gone dry. "Maybe she can still hear it."

Mom rolled her eyes. "Sure, hon. We can have a séance, too, and ask her if she wants us to walk on hot coals or howl at the full moon." She took a carton of eggs out of a grocery bag. "Do you want them to find out we're related?" She waved the carton at me. "Go ahead. Then you can figure out how to pay the bills they saddle us with." She spun around to open the refrigerator and the egg carton slipped from her hand and crashed to the floor. "Dammit, Kayla!" she cried. We watched as yolks and whites mixed with cracked shells oozed across the linoleum.

"What did *I* do?"

She started to speak, then stopped and sat down heavily at the little table. "Can we just not talk about your grandmother anymore? It's over." She sighed. "What a mess."

I wasn't sure if she meant the eggs or the situation with her mother, neither of which felt over to me. When she didn't move, I began mopping up the broken eggs with sponges and paper towels. I resented that she wasn't helping, but it bothered me more that we'd come all this way to see Esther and now we were pretending she didn't exist. We could have gone anywhere, but we were here. The least we could do was go to the funeral and give the old lady some respect, and give ourselves—what? I wasn't sure, but it seemed important to go. Maybe someone who liked her, a friend or a nurse, would talk about her, and I'd at least learn a little about who she was, beyond what my mother had told me.

I glanced up at Mom, but she was looking away, biting her lip, and then I felt sorry for her. What had I lost? I didn't know her mother.

It took forever to clean up the eggs, the whites spreading around and sticking to the floor and soaking dozens of paper towels before I cleaned up the last bit. Still, no matter how many times I wiped the floor with a damp sponge, it remained sticky.

"Enough, girl!" Mom finally said, her mood shifting again, adding to the strangeness of that day. "At least we're in fat city here. Redbone's letting me pay by the week, and we've got nearly a month's worth of food, I'll bet."

I sat next to her. "Looks like you spent more than the forty-three dollars I gave you."

"Courtesy of New Horizons. They advanced me money for groceries."

"Just like that?"

"You should see the list of jobs they're recommending me for."

"How much did they give you?"

"One hundred."

"Dollars?"

She reached for the plastic grocery bags and stuffed them all into one. "No. Clamshells."

"Just gave it to you?"

She hesitated. "I had to sign some forms." From her backpack, she took several magnets that said *Create your own reality* and stuck them to the refrigerator. "A gift from New Horizons." She grabbed my hands and tried to spin me around, but I resisted. She released me and spun around by herself. "I am on a *roll,* girlfriend!" She shook the plastic bags at me. "We're even going to *recycle*. Imagine that, Kayla." She pitched the bags as if she were shooting a basketball, and they landed in a cardboard box next to the counter. Then she snapped around to face me. "Hey. Where were you earlier? Why didn't you leave me a note? I was worried."

I didn't answer right away. Was she really worried, or had it just occurred to her that she should have been worried? I decided to give her the benefit of the doubt, and let some satisfaction creep in over the thought that she was concerned about me. "Sorry, Mom. I was just down the road. It looks like I've got a job."

For a moment, she looked startled, or maybe it was disappointment that crossed her face. I suspected she wanted to be the first to find work.

"It's just walking one dog," I explained, not sure whether to feel apologetic or proud. "And training him. He's a total dork. Jumps on everybody, doesn't know simple commands."

"Where is it?"

I pointed out the window. "That big place down the hill."

She looked and nodded. "Good for you," she said slowly, and then, with more enthusiasm, "You go, girl! You're my rock," which made me flinch. She looked out at Sam's house again. "How much are they paying you?"

"It's just one man." That slipped out before I could factor in Remy.

But it was his dad who was paying me, and I didn't even know if Remy lived there. "Ten an hour. I'm walking and training the dog an hour a day, six days a week."

She whistled. "Not bad, Kayla."

"And I've got flyers up around town," I added, though by now I felt rattled. I could just about see the dollar signs, hear the *ka-ching!* in her head.

"Oh, yeah." She darted around the trailer, picking up magazines and boxes and looking under stuff. "Where did I write that message? Somebody called about a pet turtle that needs walking or something. She sounded a little crazy. It's probably just as well that the number's missing. I don't think you should follow up on that one. Said Shirley and Charlotte or somebody raved about you, like we'd know who the heck they are. Hey, I've got the 'heck' thing down pretty good, don't I?"

"Hell, yeah."

Laughing, she pretended to swat me. "C'mon, we can't be foul-mouthed forever."

Encouraged by her playfulness, I pushed aside my concerns and volunteered more: "It's Shirley and *Sherrie,* and they own the big thrift store we passed on the way to the market, Mom. I hung a flyer there. They have a dog that needs walking and training, and they can pay me in clothes if I want."

Mom appeared way too interested. "Another job, huh?" she said. "Well, the trade might come in handy. My work wardrobe needs some sprucing up."

I knew I'd said too much. At least I hadn't spilled anything about Remy. Besides, what was there to tell? A lot of breathlessness and blushing on my part was all.

I spent a couple of hours helping her put the trailer in order and then she gave me a ride back into town so I could meet Cocoa. After dropping me at Shirley and Sherrie's, Mom cruised off to get her hair done for free by a New Horizons grad who liked helping the newbies.

At the thrift store, not only were the two women glad to see me, their smiles flashing like their rhinestone pins, but Sherrie—the short one—immediately snatched a V-neck T-shirt off a rack behind the counter and handed it to me. "Had to fight off three customers to save it for you." Shirley, who'd been writing in a spiral notebook, put down her pen.

On the dusty rose–colored shirt, cartoon dogs posed wearing big hats, drinking bubbly drinks out of fancy glasses, and dancing with feather boas wrapped around their necks. I didn't believe she'd fought off anyone to keep it for me, but I felt flattered that she was making a big deal of it. Plus, I liked the shirt, goofy as it was.

"Perfect color for her, don't you agree, Shirl?"

"Made for her. It's that garment-dyed kind. Those go for more than twenty, new."

"At least," Sherrie agreed. "Go try it on."

I set it back on the counter. "I don't have money for clothes right now."

Sherrie pushed it back to me. "It's our welcome-to-town gift. You just take it. Nothing owed." She grinned at me. "Try it."

Their kindness put a lump in my throat. I took the shirt without looking either woman in the eye. In the dressing room, I noticed that my own shirt had a large gray-black streak across it. The T-shirt fit and looked good on me.

"I guess I'll keep it. Thanks," I said to the women after they stopped crowing about how great I looked. "So, what about Cocoa?"

Sherrie blinked a few times and smiled at me. "Let me tell you a few things about him, Kayla. You look like a smart girl who can be firm with a dog, but—"

"Quit stalling, Sher, and quit trying to butter her up," Shirley grumbled. She stalked down a back hallway and opened a door. A fat brown and white dog with ridiculously short legs waddled forward two steps and sank to the floor. Sherrie hurried over to pick him up.

The dog leaned out of her grasp to lick Shirley's face. "Ugh. He reeks," Shirley said, stepping away.

Cocoa panted in Sherrie's arms, staring bright-eyed at me. He was the oddest-looking dog I'd ever seen, with a long body, those short legs, long floppy ears, and a cropped tail, all covered with short, curly hair. He had the square snout of a terrier, and his head looked too large for his body. Sherrie beamed at him.

"He's . . . unusual," I said. "What is he?"

"An abomination," muttered Shirley.

Sherrie shot her a disapproving look. "His father was a dachshund and his mother was mostly Airedale, maybe with some basset hound. Can you imagine?" She laughed, and my face grew warm. She shook her head. "Now, if the *mother* was the dachshund, it would be easier—"

Shirley interrupted. "We get the idea, Sher." To me she said, "We need you to walk him once a day, except on Mondays, when we're closed, and also teach him all the basics—to come when called, sit, stay—all that. He's completely untrained."

"But you should know," added Sherrie, "the poor thing has a hard time walking."

"Stop feeling sorry for the little monster," Shirley growled. "If you didn't pick him up all the time, he'd walk just fine."

"He had a rough start in life," said Sherrie. "Have you worked with dogs that have some history?"

I wasn't sure what she meant. "I don't know. Probably."

"Hmm," said Sherrie uncertainly. "Look, why don't you come by in a day or two, after Shirl and I have had a chance to talk?"

Shirley folded her arms across her chest. "What's to talk about?" she snapped. "Kayla, you have yourself a job."

NINE

As I walked from the thrift store to the salon where my mom was getting her hair cut, I worked up a pretty good feeling about myself. Two dog-care jobs, and we'd been here just three days. I found the Escort unlocked in front of the salon and got in. Whatever was keeping my mother inside for so long, I didn't want any part of it. I hated hearing how cute I'd look if only I'd grow my hair out like my mom's. I'd wait outside.

It didn't take long for me to grow restless. Waiting for my mother always took me back to other times: a social worker's waiting room, a girl with small round scars on her arm, her nosy questions. *Is this the first time you're here?* Twelve years old, under the Patellas' sun porch, the smells of bacon and fresh biscuits taunting me from the kitchen above, the oldest Patella girl telling me I'd die if I went any farther back because that was where Ollie croaked. Who the hell was Ollie? A man? A boy? A chicken? Waiting in Ollie's death place until that awful girl with her poking stick got bored and left me alone. Waiting for Mom to come. Waiting. A whole year.

I left Mom a note and started walking. The sun was high overhead, and halfway home, my nostrils felt like they were cracking from the dry air. I needed a drink of water. My jeans stuck to my skin and my feet were sweating inside my dark boots. Cars whizzed by and the air filled with a fine, irritating dust. I found Redbone in our yard tossing junk into the bed of his truck: the broken pipes, the cracked sink, the fan belts.

"Where's your mother?" he asked, throwing a tangled mess of wire into the truck.

I hesitated. What if I said she was getting her hair done, and he wanted to come in? I didn't like the idea of being alone in the trailer with him. It wasn't that I didn't trust him; I just didn't want to play hostess to the guy. If I said she'd be home any minute, he might hang around waiting, and I didn't have a clue when she'd arrive. I took so long to answer, he stopped working to look at me. "In town," I finally said. "Finishing up errands."

I sat on the porch and out of the corner of my eye watched him work. He was deeply tanned, but sometimes his T-shirt sleeves rode up, exposing lighter skin. His creased, leathery neck looked like reddish brown turtle skin. He was clean-shaven, though, and not bad-looking when he wasn't sneering. "There isn't really hot water in the trailer," I told him. I meant to say it in a matter-of-fact way, but it came out more like an accusation.

"Yeah. That water heater will need replacing." He kept on chucking things into the truck.

"Should we tell you again when it stops making piss-warm water and we're taking purely cold showers?"

He walked over to me and stood with one hand in his pants pocket. "Carly, your mother pays just four hundred dollars a month for the two of you to live here. Do you know what a steal that is? I could get two, three times that."

At that moment, so many things ticked me off about Redbone, I couldn't have listed them all. That he never got my name right was just the first.

He said, "I own fourteen properties, and I take care of every one of 'em by myself."

Whoopee. Aren't you the big man.

"When I heard you were coming without beds or nothing, I furnished this place for you."

What did he want, me to kiss his feet?

"I'll get to that water heater just as soon as I can," he said, getting in his truck. He rested his elbow on the door. "I hope you're being some kind of help to your mother."

As he drove off, my insides churned. Who the hell did he think he was? He should only know what kind of help she'd been getting from me. For *years.*

I turned and kicked the dirt. I'd forgotten to ask him about getting a dog.

Now the yard looked less cluttered but more forsaken. The bits of wire, plastic, and glass left behind made it even less hospitable than when it was a mini-junkyard. A dog kept here would cut its paws on the sharp edges of glass and metal. I searched behind the trailer for some kind of rake but found only weeds and a few cinder blocks. I checked inside the trailer, too, although I knew there was nothing that even resembled a rake in there. My hunger, which had slunk off at the sight of Redbone, returned now with a vengeance, so I made myself a cheese sandwich. While I ate it, I couldn't help checking to see if all six beers were still in the six-pack in the cupboard. I counted only four, and they'd been shoved to the back, behind two jars of applesauce. I wondered if Redbone had drunk them. Maybe some-one else had stopped by. Maybe she'd poured two out. I checked the box of recycling, but there were no cans in there. Good, I thought. Probably she gave two of the beers away.

I stared out the window past the cowboy curtains. When Sam's car turned into his driveway, I took myself down there.

Rebel careened into the kitchen and pushed past Sam to greet me, but he didn't jump up.

"Kayla," Sam said. "How'd it go this morning?"

"Like water over a waterfall. He's a good dog. Want to see what he learned?"

Sam checked his watch. "I've got to run. Just keep on doing what you're doing. How do you want to get paid? Weekly? Every other week?"

"You still want me to walk him?"

"Sure. Why not?"

"I thought with Remy here . . ."

He looked puzzled. "Do you know Remy?"

I pointed to the photo on the refrigerator. "That's your son, Remy, isn't it?"

He nodded.

"You don't know he was here this morning?"

"No."

I pointed to the couch. "He sat there and played a guitar. Made up songs on the spot." A little anxious, I asked, "Does that sound like him?"

Sam sighed. "To a tee."

"Maybe you won't need my help now." I didn't mention that Remy said he wouldn't have time to walk the dog. I figured that was between him and his dad.

For a moment, arms folded, Sam stared at the floor. "Look," he said finally, "let's keep our arrangement until I talk to Remy."

"Okay." I started for the door. "Uh, Sam? Have you got a rake I could borrow?"

While he showed me the garden shed, he asked me again how I wanted to be paid—"assuming that Remy doesn't take over"—and we agreed on every two weeks. Then he showed me a small hollow under an outdoor sculpture, where he kept a house key hidden.

The first message on our answering machine when I got home was from a woman who lived outside of town and needed her old Saint Bernard driven to the vet twice weekly for kidney dialysis while she was at work. The other was from my mother, saying that she'd stopped by New Horizons to check the job list and they'd recommended that she stay for their "Circle of Support." Whatever that was. I called the woman with the dog and explained that I didn't have a car.

I spent the rest of the afternoon lying on my bed, with the rake leaning against the wall and the fan turned on high. I imagined what it would take to clean up the yard really well, build a fence and a doghouse, get some thornless plants in. I'd given up on the idea of growing grass. Mom was already grumbling at me about the water bill if I showered for more than five minutes.

She came home after four with an ugly gray-green plant resembling a hairless tarantula, which she fondly called a Christmas cactus. "A gift from New Horizons. They say it blooms when you least expect it." She set it on the windowsill over the kitchen sink. "That place is amazing!" she exclaimed. "They know what I need before I do."

I jerked my thumb toward the cactus. "You needed a pathetic little plant?"

Laughing, she poured water from an unwashed coffee cup onto the cactus. It drained through the soil in the cheap plastic pot, spilling onto the sill and the counter, carrying with it a stream of dirt. She wiped up the water but missed the dirt. She didn't seem to notice, turning instead to pull papers out of a canvas bag with the New Horizons logo: beams of sunlight shooting upward between silhouettes of women holding hands in front of a rising sun.

I said, "What is this, some New Age voodoo brainwashing cult?"

Mom laughed. "That's Bell's influence. She acts a little out there, but she's as down to earth a woman as you'll find anywhere. They all are."

"Who's Bell?"

"Didn't I tell you? She's my co-coordinator at New Horizons. Sort of a counselor or case manager, except they call it a co-coordinator. We're kind of a team, figuring out my future."

That sounded suspiciously like a social worker to me.

"Check this out." She spread lists and workshop schedules on the kitchen table. Using the New Horizons magnets, she stuck them to the refrigerator. She taped a rainbow-colored poster that said *With My Circle of Support I Can Fly* to a cupboard. On it, a woman sprouting feathers flew toward the clouds; below her, a circle of women gazed upward, except they didn't seem to be watching the woman in flight.

"You should see this place, Kayla!" She was flushed. "In Circle, women in all stages of the program share stories—how they got office-manager training or school scholarships or mortgage loans. New gals like me talk about bills they can't pay or how they can't find childcare. More experienced women tell how they dealt with similar problems. One woman spent twelve years in prison, and now she's applying to medical school." She grinned at me.

It sounded like Losers Anonymous to me, but it sure made her happy. She bopped around the kitchen, putting away dry dishes, folding dishtowels, wiping crumbs off the counter. Then she took the four Coors cans out of the cupboard and put them in the refrigerator.

She turned and saw me staring at her. "Bell is coming by," she announced.

I felt my stomach roll over. I'd know right away if Bell was a social worker. They clutch clipboards to their suited chests, smiling as they pry into our lives. The one who had checked up on us after my year at the Patellas' snooped in the kitchen cabinets and wrote indecipherable notes on her clipboard. "Maybe you should just offer her a cup of coffee or tea."

"I could offer that, too." She paused. "You're right. Forget the beer." She yanked the Coors out of the fridge, returned the cans to the cupboard, and kept bustling about as she talked. "I was so ticked off after getting turned down for three jobs today that I had to do something. I stopped by New Horizons, and Bell could see I was out of sorts, so she made me stay for Circle. I really dumped there. One place thinks I don't type fast enough. Another wants a three-year

62

signed commitment." She scowled. "The last one wanted me to work double shifts three times a week and be on call the other days."

"Did you tell them about your mother?"

Mom picked at a price tag on the bottom of a coffee mug covered with red hearts and the words *Love is all around you*. Then she sat back and crossed her arms over her stomach. "No, I did not. This is a small town. No one needs to know."

I wiped up the dirt that had drained from the ugly cactus. Mom sat holding herself, as if loosening her grip would result in pieces of her flying around the room. I felt tense and ready to start catching and reassembling.

"Why is Bell coming?"

Mom must have noticed the edge in my voice. "It's nothing, Kay. Social as much as anything. She can't help me visualize a new life unless she can see the one I've got."

"Visualize a new life?"

She shrugged. "I guess you have to picture it before it can happen." She swooped over to the couch and began tidying up. "C'mon. Help me with this mess."

Not counting Redbone—which I didn't—Bell would be our first visitor. Ms. Create Your Own Reality. As I folded newspapers and threw away used tissues and a half-full can of Diet Coke, I couldn't help seeing the place as Bell would: a claustrophobia-inducing hovel.

Wrong again. Bell turned out to be a big-boned woman wearing a bright orange blouse, a long yellow peasant skirt, and flat sandals who, as far as I could tell, never found fault with anything. She greeted me as if she was thrilled: "The fabulous Kayla! I've heard great things about you from your mom." She followed Mom around the trailer, commenting, "Cute . . . Not bad . . . Has potential . . . Needs a lamp or two. A tight fit, but it could be worse." Settling onto the couch, she asked, "The landlord furnished this place for you? Left his phone? Who is this guy?"

My mother blushed, and Bell raised an eyebrow. "Name's Red-bone," my mom said. "Real name's Richard Bonebrake or Bone-bright or something like that."

"Bonehead," I muttered.

Both women turned to look at me. Bell broke up laughing.

Mom looked annoyed. "He's been good to us. Gave us a deal on this place."

Bell looked around. "I hope you're not paying more than eight hundred dollars."

"Just half that, and he's letting me pay a week at a time," Mom said. "And no deposits."

Bell whistled. "You've got nothing to complain about, girl." She looked at me kindly. "What about you? Have you met any kids your age yet?"

I shrugged. "I'm doing okay. I've got two jobs—one at Big-Time Bargains."

Bell smiled. "Those characters. A couple of gems, but they're not teenagers. I'll see what I can do."

I bristled. "I don't need anyone to make friends for me."

"Kayla, don't be rude. She's just trying to help."

"It's okay, Marilyn." Bell sat back, eyeing me. "You're independent."

I didn't say anything.

"No, that's good. I should have asked. My own girls are grown, gone off to Albuquerque and Boston. But I know some girls your age. You want to meet them?"

I did and I didn't. I pictured girls who'd grown up in this town, who didn't work two jobs, who had time to hang out and paint their toenails and walk around in small, tight groups.

I shrugged again. "I guess. When I'm not working."

"Okay, then." She turned back to Mom and, to my relief, changed the subject. "Tell me more about those job interviews."

TEN

A few days later, while Mom attended a class at New Horizons on how to impress job interviewers, I tried to rake up the fragments of glass and metal in the yard. Most of them slid right through the tines, so I threw down the rake and picked up the sharp bits by hand. Right away, I cut my finger on a glass shard. Cursing, I washed the cut, squeezing my finger to stop the bleeding. I was certain we didn't have any Band-Aids, but I looked anyway. Pressing a piece of wadded tissue to the cut, I searched the bathroom, the kitchen, and my mother's room. In a box under her bed, I found two empty Coors cans. I took one out to the sink and tilted it. Not one drop fell out. She drank them a few days ago, I told myself, trying to quiet the shivery feeling in my gut. She didn't overdo it. She's taking classes, interviewing. Visualizing her future. Two beers is nothing to get worked up about.

While the sun grew hotter, I picked over the yard, this time with toilet paper and duct tape wrapped around my cut. When I was finished, I returned the rake to Sam's—no one was home—walked Rebel, and thought about fences. I wanted to build a wood fence for my own dog, but chainlink was cheaper. I wondered what bamboo would cost. Once, I saw a pretty bamboo fence around a cute garden with a grape arbor and a border of purple irises and orange lilies— though I doubted it was in a place as dusty and dry as this.

Later, when Mom came home, she yelled for me to help her. She was grinning madly and clutching two bags. One held something like birdseed. "Get the cage out of the back, would you?" She marched into the house, leaving me to haul a large cage from the back seat of the car. It had two levels inside connected by a wire ramp, and a small plastic dome nestled in the fresh wood shavings that covered the bottom.

When I lifted the cage out of the car, a tiny black-and-white whiskered face appeared in the doorway of the plastic dome. It looked like a rat. I balanced the cage on one knee and slammed the car door. Rat-Face disappeared.

Mom held the trailer door for me, still grinning, though not quite so enthusiastically. She watched for my reaction. "Come on, bring him in."

A he-rat. I carried the cage into the trailer, turning it sideways to fit through the door. "Where do you want it?"

She stopped peering at me as if she was waiting for me to pop and surveyed the room. "Good question." She cleared the table and patted it with both hands. "Right here, for now, Kayla." I set the cage down. The rat poked his head out again, sniffing the air, his whiskers twitching. Mom looked hopeful. "Isn't he cute? They're supposed to be very personable."

"Sure, Mom." I crossed my arms. "Why on earth did you get a rat?"

She smoothed some loose hairs back. "He's for you, honey. A pet."

"I wanted a dog."

"I know that. I know you wanted a dog." She slung her leather backpack onto a chair and took a small plastic bag of grayish brown cylindrical pellets—rat food, I guessed—out of a bag. "You can't have a dog here, Kayla. I talked to Redbone. He doesn't allow it. Most landlords don't, you know. But he was okay with a caged pet."

"So I get a rat."

Mom was quiet for a moment. "Kayla, I asked at the pet store for the best kind of caged pet. They recommended a rat."

"Great. So it's a conspiracy."

She handed me a bottle with a U-shaped wire bracket and a curved tube coming out of its cap. "Here's his water bottle." Brushing her hands like she had finished a dirty job, she went into her room. I stood with the bottle in my hands, staring at the rat as he sprinted around the perimeter of the cage. The sight of his hairless tail made me cringe.

I yelled to her, "Mom, there's no room here for this cage!"

"Yes, there is." Her voice drifted out to me, singsongy. "The space at the foot of your bed is perfect."

She was right. Between my bed and the wall of drawers was just enough room to fit the cage. It annoyed me, that perfect spot, and I'd have to move the cage to open the bottom drawer. I careened out of my room, nearly colliding with Mom. "What's Redbone's problem with dogs?"

Sighing, she held up her hands. "I don't know. Probably that they scratch the doors and dig holes and leave their business all over the place."

"Will you ask him again?"

She shook her head. "We're lucky to have this place. I don't want to push it. Fill that water bottle and hang it on his cage, will you? Rats need to drink constantly. Apparently, they die without water." She noticed my finger wrapped in toilet paper and duct tape. "What happened?"

I slid the makeshift bandage off my finger and crammed it into my pocket. "Nothing," I mumbled. "What if I don't want it?"

She put a finger under my chin and lifted my face so she could look me in the eye. "Give the rat a chance, Kayla. It's the best I can do."

To hide my disappointment, I turned away and got busy filling the water bottle and a small food bowl. She had also brought home a book marked down from $8.95 to $2.95—*Your Pet Rat*—a bargain book to go with my bargain pet. The cover showed a smiling, chubby girl with long braids. A tawny rat perched on her shoulder. The table of contents listed *History of Rats, Care and Feeding, Signs and Symptoms of Sickness, Training Your Rat,* and *Showing Your Rat.* When I took the cage into my room, I wanted to kick it into the space at the foot of my bed.

Mom came in and sat down, her hands in her lap. She had changed into worn jeans and a short-sleeved flowered blouse, and she looked soft and even a little nervous. I stifled an urge to yell *Take it back to the store!* What if this *was* the best she could do?

We both watched the rat, now clutching the cage wires like a prisoner behind bars. I wanted to hate the little rodent, but I couldn't.

"You can take him out," Mom said. "He's used to being held. The woman at the store showed me." She stood up. "I'll leave you two to get acquainted."

I wasn't having any of that. Not yet. I followed Mom into the kitchen and made myself a bologna sandwich. When she mentioned that the yard looked nice, the bread caught in my throat.

That night I had trouble getting to sleep. I sat up, hugging my pillow to my chest, the cut on my finger a stinging reminder of the cans I'd seen in her room. A faint scent of wood shavings blended with the musty smell of my tiny room. Twice I got out of bed. A light shone under Mom's closed door. *I know you meant well,* I wanted to tell her, *but I really don't want a rat. I can wait until we have money and space for a dog. And by the way, what were those two beer cans doing under your bed?*

I kept chickening out and lying back down. The questions faded, leaving me with one torturous desire: to get into bed with her, just for the comfort of being close. But you can't do that when you're fifteen.

I rolled over and tried to settle down. I knew what would happen if I crawled into my mother's bed: *What the hell are you doing here?*

How do you expect me to sleep with you breathing all over me? I actually considered seeing whether the rat would cuddle with me, but I was scared that I'd roll onto him and crush him.

So pathetic. Who ever heard of sleeping with a rat?

ELEVEN

Our water heater quit that night, so my shower in the morning consisted of repeated short blasts of icy spray. The sun warmed me on my walk to Big-Time Bargains, where Sherrie led me down the back hallway. "Welcome to the Dog Palace!" she announced, opening the door to reveal a cozy room that looked like a cross between a kennel and the private quarters for a harem. A daybed covered with a camel-printed bedspread and colorful pillows hugged the left wall. Opposite that stood a pretty roll-top desk. Gauzy reddish curtains gave the room a muted light, and the walls were painted various shades of deep gold. Cocoa lay in a sheepskin-lined dog bed on the floor, and scattered across every surface were half-chewed rawhide bones and tattered, fleecy stuffed animals.

"It's beautiful," I managed to say. "Is this all for Cocoa?"

"Mostly," Sherrie said, smiling. "It's had different uses over the years. Shirley likes to write back here when business is slow, and I've been known to take a nap or two. It's our little getaway." She nodded toward Cocoa. "Do you want any help from me?"

I shook my head. "The sooner I start training him, the better." I pulled a handful of dog treats out of my pocket. "I have these. He'll start learning in no time."

Glancing skeptically at my handful of treats, she blew a kiss to Cocoa and left us alone.

"Come!" I called to the dog from across the room. He lifted his head, but that was all, and soon he lowered it again between his paws. On the wall by the door, a row of pegs held leashes, all brightly colored or studded with rhinestones. I chose a gaudy red leather one, snapped it onto his collar, walked a few paces away, and commanded again: "Come!" This time he didn't even raise his head. Gently but firmly, I drew him toward me with the leash. "Come, Cocoa," I repeated. He stood up, stepped out of his bed, and sat down. I ended up dragging him toward me on his haunches. I offered him a dog treat from my pocket. "See, Cocoa? You come, you get a treat." He sniffed at it and turned his head away, slumping to the floor with a sigh.

The door to the store opened, and Sherrie stuck her head in. "How's it going?" she sang out. Cocoa sat up and wagged his stumpy tail.

"Have you tried to teach him to come?" I asked.

"Oh, sure, he comes." Sherrie glanced over her shoulder and then stepped into the Palace. She drew a chocolate kiss from her pocket and unwrapped it, and Cocoa sat up, quivering. "Come, sweetie," she called to him, and he dashed over to her as fast as his little legs would carry him, snatched the chocolate from her outstretched palm, and swallowed it.

"You're giving him chocolate? It's poisonous to dogs!"

She wrinkled her brow. "Is it really that bad?"

"You could kill him. Doesn't he get sick?"

She pursed her lips, thinking. "He does have some . . . well, digestive problems. I don't give him much, though. And he loves it so." She backed out of the room. "Just let me know if I can help with anything."

The dog lay down. "C'mon," I told him. "Let's go out." I stepped into the hallway. Only his eyes followed me. I tugged gently on the leash. "Let's go, Cocoa. Come!"

"Are you taking him outside?" Sherrie called from the store.

"I'm trying."

"Leave him a minute." She waved me over. "Cocoa was a stray with a badly broken leg," she explained. "Now he's used to being carried."

Reluctantly, I returned to the Palace and picked up Cocoa. He was small, but he was no lightweight.

"Have fun," Sherrie called out. "Just set him down a few times so he can do his stuff."

Did she think I was going to carry the lazy beast for an entire half-hour?

Away from the store, I set him on the sidewalk, but a bag of wet cement on a leash would have been more cooperative. If I pulled on the leash, Cocoa planted all four paws and leaned back. I managed to drag him forward, mostly on his haunches, but he choked and gagged until I was sure he was going to throw up. When I eased up on the leash, he plunked himself down on the sidewalk. We struggled like this until finally, I carried him a couple of arm-breaking blocks and set him down on the sidewalk near a vacant lot.

"There you go, Cocoa. Walk just a few feet and you can pee to your heart's content."

Cocoa sat on his haunches, looking over at the dirt lot, wagging his tail, and whining.

"It's yours for the taking." I folded my arms, trying to be patient.

He lay down, nose pointing toward the dirt. Several times he sat up, whimpered at me, and gave his body a little wriggle, but he refused to take a step.

"Your leg is not broken anymore," I told him.

The sun beat down on us. I'd just wait him out. He'd walk to the dirt when his bladder was good and full. Passersby shot curious looks at us. Finally, Cocoa stood up. He looked at me eagerly. "You can do it, fella," I reassured him. He took one step, lowered his rear end slightly, and dropped a pile right in the middle of the sidewalk, just as an orange and white VW bus pulled up to the curb. I checked my pockets and groaned. I'd forgotten a plastic bag to clean up after him.

"Hey," Remy called to me. Cocoa sat conveniently in front of his mess. I stepped between the dog and Remy.

"What are you up to?" Remy asked.

"Just working."

He held out a small white piece of paper. "Is this yours?"

I wasn't close enough to take it. I took a few steps toward the bus, hoping Cocoa would stay parked in front of his stuff, but he chose that moment to walk with me. I took the paper from Remy. It was the poem I'd started at his house, and I felt my cheeks grow hot, embarrassed that he'd seen it. I crumpled it up and stuffed it into my pocket.

"It's good. You should finish it," he said, his gaze drilling into mine, and then he glanced over my shoulder. He snatched a plastic bag from the floor of his bus and handed it to me. "Need this?" Tongue-tied, I took it and watched him drive away, wondering if he would forever think of me as the Dog Shit Girl, if he bothered to think of me at all.

I lugged the dog back to the store, dropping the foul-smelling bag in a trash can along the way. Shirley sat behind the counter writing in a spiral notebook. Sherrie held her arms out for Cocoa. "Back so soon?" She took a chocolate from her pocket, saw me watching her, and popped it into her own mouth.

"How'd it go, Kayla?" Shirley asked, setting her pen down.

"Not bad," I lied. "Only I may not have time for him in my schedule."

"Oh," said Sherrie. "Hear that, Cocoa? Kayla's gonna be too busy for you."

Shirley came over to the counter and leaned her elbows on it. "We'll pay you fifteen an hour, Kayla, but only if you think you can train the little monster."

I looked down at my feet. "I'm not sure I can."

"He was so traumatized," Sherrie said. "His poor little legs."

"He might have been traumatized," I said, "but I think he's just spoiled now. And uncomfortable, with all that extra weight." I looked down again, wondering if Sherrie would be offended. She, too, carried considerable extra weight.

Sherrie frowned, but Shirley said, "Kayla, give it a few more tries, will you? No hard feelings if it doesn't work out. But you have to give it your best." She looked at me steadily.

I glanced at Sherrie, but she wouldn't meet my gaze. "I'm not sure about this," I said, "but I don't think I'll get anywhere if you keep feeding him chocolate. Plus, it'll kill him."

Shirley gave Sherrie a stern look. "You promised."

Sherrie carried the dog to the Palace, protesting, "He's so unhappy without it."

"*He* is?" Shirley's voice was not sympathetic.

"Okay, no more chocolate."

"And the stash goes," Shirley said dryly.

"The stash?" Sherrie said in a high voice.

Shirley jerked her head toward the Palace, indicating that I should follow her. "Hold the dog, Sherrie." The taller woman lifted the camel-printed bedspread, revealing large drawers underneath the daybed. She rummaged among canned foods, gallon water jugs, flashlights, batteries, and toilet paper. It looked as if they were prepared to weather a catastrophe. She lifted out a shoebox and handed it to me.

"Shirl, what are you doing with it?" asked Sherrie, clearly worried.

Shirley ignored her. "Have a party, Kayla."

I opened the box. It was filled with chocolate kisses. Cocoa, smelling the candy, whined and wriggled in Sherrie's arms. Shirley gave me fifteen dollars and shooed me out the door. "See you tomorrow!" I left with the box of chocolate under my arm, the women arguing behind me.

TWELVE

For two days, I lugged Cocoa in my arms on our so-called walks. Taking Rebel out was a whole lot more fun. It helped that Shirley and Sherrie paid me time and a half.

After my third time hauling that spoiled little dog, I walked to New Horizons, where I'd arranged to meet Mom. While I waited in the car for her, I searched my dog-training books for ways to get Cocoa to walk. Mom emerged from the New Horizons building with Bell right behind her.

"Think about it, Marilyn," Bell called to her, stopping near the doorway. My mother kept walking toward our car, not responding. "I can picture you doing it," Bell added, smiling at my mother's back. "Kayla, help your mom imagine working at the Heirloom, okay? She has such a sense of style. She's perfect for the job."

Mom rolled her eyes and hissed at me, "Let's get the hell out of here."

The speedometer read forty-five as we passed a thirty-five-mile-an-hour speed-zone sign on our way home. Wisps of hair blew into my mom's face, and she brushed them away.

"What's the Heirloom?"

"Antiques. Expensive gifts. Potpourri in ugly china."

"Does Bell want you to apply there?"

"She's out of her mind."

"What's the big deal?"

"A job like that, you're just a sitting duck for any rich bitch with too much time on her hands." She spoke in a high-pitched voice. "Dear, do you have any Louis the Fourteenth? How about wild rose potpourri? Is this teapot from the Civil War or just pre–World War One?"

"It sounds to me like you might be good in that job."

"Are you kidding? One slip and you're out."

"Slip?"

She rolled her head. Maybe her neck hurt. Maybe I was the pain in her neck. "In a store like that, Kayla, if a customer or another employee complains about you, you're history. How long do you think I'd last dealing with all those fussy women?"

You'd be the fussiest. "I don't know," I said, "I think I can picture you there."

She was quiet.

"Mom, I don't think this is a good time to be picky, do you?"

"Did you get the job with those two women's dog?" she asked, changing the subject so abruptly that I knew she didn't want to discuss her work situation—or lack of it—anymore.

"Uh-huh."

She nodded, two fingers flicking the air nervously. "Ten an hour?"

"Fifteen. Or clothes credit."

Her eyebrows went up. "Take the money. We need to hire someone to look at that water heater."

"We do? Isn't that Redbone's job?"

Mom braked for a red light. "He's very busy, Kayla."

I wasn't sure which annoyed me more: my mother's assumption that I would cover our bills or Redbone's neglect. "Why are you defending him?" I asked. "The trailer is a piece of junk. He could at least fix what's broken."

"I don't want to hassle him, that's all." She took a cigarette out of her purse, lit it, inhaled, and blew the smoke out the window. Some drifted toward me, reminding me of the pack-a-day habit she'd dropped years earlier. I scowled and fanned the smoke away from my face.

"Don't bug me about this, too," she said, shaking the cigarette at me. The light turned green. She took another drag and steered the car through the intersection. "Cut me a little slack, would you?"

I stared out the window. "Sometimes," she said, "you just ride me. You worry about everything. Things take time, but they work out, okay? I know when to lean on a landlord to fix things, and I know when to back off, just like I know a rat isn't a dog. And I'll know when the right job comes along." Mom stubbed out the cigarette in the ashtray. "If you don't understand something I'm doing, just ask me, okay?"

Right then, there was no way in hell I'd have asked her anything else, yet by the time we got to our road, a question jabbed at me like a hot fire poker. I took a deep breath. "Why do you have two empty beer cans in a box under your bed?"

She looked away quickly, her fingers drumming on the wheel. "Those are from the night we learned your grandmother died, Kayla. Just those two." She gave me a pathetic smile. "I haven't had a drop since."

Neither of us spoke the rest of the way. It felt as if we were driving on quicksand, and if we didn't keep moving fast, we might get sucked straight down.

At the trailer, Mom tossed the two beer cans into the recycling bin. "Kayla, you never did say why you looked under my bed."

"I needed a Band-Aid," I said, feeling sheepish.

"Do we ever keep Band-Aids there?"

I shrugged. "We just moved. I don't know where everything is."

"Find any?"

"Nope."

She wrote *bandaids* on a scrap of paper and stuck it on the refrigerator with a New Horizons magnet. "Kayla, how about we agree not to snoop in each other's rooms?"

"I guess. Sure."

After a strained silence, we were surprised to hear footsteps and a knock on the door. I opened it to find Remy filling our doorway. *It's just Remy,* I thought as my heart tried to run right out of my chest. I must have been quiet for an unnaturally long stretch because my mother was suddenly next to me, looking at us, and finally she said, "Can I help you?"

Remy nodded toward me. "I'm just looking for her phone number." My mom's eyebrows went up, and I could see from his fraction of a smile that Remy was enjoying himself. "My dad and I are taking Rebel up to Taos with us tomorrow, Kayla, so we don't need you to walk him. Dad wants to be able to call you next time we go away." Nodding, I turned to get some paper and a pencil and tripped over a suitcase, catching myself before I sprawled across the floor. I couldn't find paper or a pencil, and I was having trouble talking, as my brain and my tongue had gone for a ride with my galloping heart. I looked at my mother, who was watching me with a mixture of confusion and amusement. "Pencil? Anywhere?" With those words, hot blood rushed up to my face, as if my heart had quit trying to bound off and decided to erupt instead.

Remy watched me, too, but he was also taking in the whole scene: cowboy curtains, shoddy furniture, smirking mother. When I handed him a piece of paper with my phone number, he took his time folding it and slipping it into a back pocket.

Mom asked, "You live right down the road?"

"That's my dad's house. Sam Coltan. I'm just visiting."

"Where do you call home?" she asked. She talked so easily with Remy.

He looked down at his feet, kicking gently at something I could not see. "I'm actually between homes right now," he said, looking straight at Mom. "In transition."

Mom folded her arms across her chest and leaned against the counter. "Sure."

He asked her, "Did I see you coming out of the pet store with a big cage a few days ago? I was across the street at Dan's Music."

"Probably."

"What did you have in that cage?"

Mom looked at me. "You want to show him?"

I spun around and headed to my room so they wouldn't see my face go up in flames again. I didn't expect him to follow me. Did Mom send him back to my room after me? Did he just saunter in? Whatever happened, there he was, making my tiny bedroom six times too small. I pointed to the cage. "There." I sat on the bed, then stood again. I didn't know what to do with myself. I certainly didn't want to bring up the incident with Cocoa.

Remy unlatched the cage door and held his hand out to the rat. "Male or female?"

"Male, I guess."

The rat ran up his arm and onto his shoulder. He gave it his other hand to sniff, and it checked out his neck, his cheek, his ear. He chuckled when the rat's whiskers tickled him. Scooping it into one hand and holding it in front of his face, he said softly, "Aren't you cute." He looked at me. "Does he have a name?"

I shrugged. "Not yet. My mom just got it. I didn't want a rat."

He looked at the rat. "She didn't want you? She'll change her mind. She doesn't know how great rats are."

I couldn't help smiling. "I wanted a dog."

"Nah." Remy shook his head. "Everybody and his uncle has a dog. This is unique." He held the rat out to me, and I took the small creature from him, my clumsy hands brushing his warm and steady ones. Music-making hands. The rat was full of energy, running up one arm, across my shoulders, down the other arm, making me giggle. Remy peered at me intently. "You finish that poem yet?"

I took a step backward. "No. Why?" I tried to smile, my insides jittery.

"It hooked me. I keep thinking about it. You're good with words."

Mom appeared. "Would you like some coffee? Or a beer?"

"That's okay," Remy said. "I should go."

A little giddy from Remy's praise, I put the rat back in its cage. Remy was already on the porch when I came out. "You can walk Rebel again the day after tomorrow," he said.

"I will." I tried to keep my smile from taking over my face.

He left as quickly as he had appeared. Mom watched me, and I felt big and awkward.

"Why do you suppose Sam didn't come himself?" Mom asked.

I sat and reached for a basket of laundry, started folding each item neatly. "Beats me, Mom. He runs a gallery, and he seems pretty darn busy—"

She looked amused. "I thought you said Sam lived alone."

"I said he hired me—and he's the only one who takes care of the dog. As far as I know, he usually does live alone." I pulled a black sock from the pile of clothes.

"When did you meet Remy?"

"The other day, when I went to walk the dog." Keeping my face turned away, I dug through the basket for the matching sock.

"He's a looker."

"Oh, yeah."

"And he's looking."

"What?"

"At you, precious. And he's too old for you."

"Don't worry. I'm not interested." I held up the other sock and rolled the two together. "Why'd you send him back to my room, anyway?"

"I didn't. He waltzed back there like he owns this place."

I snatched a wrinkled T-shirt and shook it out hard. "You should have stopped him."

I didn't mean that. That close encounter was terrific—once I got over the worst of my terror. Remy seemed like shiny bait on a sharp hook, and I was a bottom-grubbing catfish looking for a ride up to the sun. Better she should think I was happily swimming down in the dark.

"Mom, don't let strangers follow me to my bedroom! That was embarrassing."

She sat down and folded her hands on the table, looking mildly contrite. "I'll try." She stayed quiet for a moment, and I could see that she was trying not to grin.

"What?" I demanded, and grabbed a pair of jeans from the pile.

"That laundry?" She chuckled.

"What about it?"

"You don't need to fold it. It hasn't been washed yet."

I lay on my bed with my head near the rat's cage. When he stood on his hind legs, his body took on a pear shape, reminding me of a documentary I'd seen on Elvis Presley and how he got all bloated at the end of his life. The rat was happy to see me so close; he poked his nose out to sniff my fingers and ran around in lively spurts. "You are Elvis," I whispered. I recalled the gentleness of Remy's hands as he approached the rat and lifted him out of the cage, and thought about how his energy filled any room he entered. I decided I had a choice; to either sink or swim in that energy. Just so I didn't keep flailing around, like I had been, as if I were about to drown.

THIRTEEN

That night I dreamed about Redbone digging a pit with a backhoe under the end of the trailer. Shirley and Sherrie lay on beach chairs in big floppy hats and skimpy bathing suits, sipping cool drinks, completely unselfconscious about their aging bodies. Elvis scurried into the freshly dug pit, and Mom went after him. I waited anxiously for them to climb out. Mom emerged halfway, holding the rat, which turned into a baby. Suddenly, I realized there was nothing holding up one end of the trailer. I tried to scream to Redbone, but my voice was barely a whisper. The trailer tilted and began to slide.

I woke and stared into the darkness. Elvis rustled in his cage. Tiptoeing into the kitchen for a glass of water, I stepped on something sharp. Startled, I dropped my glass, and it shattered. A moment later, my mother padded unevenly from her room.

"Be careful, Mom! I broke a glass."

She shuffled back to her room and returned wearing boots. Cowboy boots, with her above-the-knee silky nightgown.

"Nice outfit," I said.

She turned on the hall light and squinted. "What the hell were you up to?"

"Sorry. I stepped on something sharp. My glass slipped."

She rubbed one eye. "Jesus, Kayla, clean it up and get to bed."

What did she think I was going to do? "I need shoes," I pointed out.

She sighed and went back to her room, her boot heels striking the floor, and returned with another pair. Her boots, two sizes too small for me.

"Mom, your shoes don't fit me."

She stared at the boots, her gaze unfocused. "Since when?"

I shivered. "Just toss them to me."

She did, badly, and they landed in the broken glass. Mumbling "Sorry," she shut off the hall light and went back to her room, leaving me in darkness. I picked up the boots and tugged them over my feet. They hurt, but I could stand it for the few minutes it would take to clean up. I yanked the chain on the small fluorescent light over the sink. Among the glass shards on the floor was the thing I had stepped on: a bottle cap. I didn't have to examine it to know it was from a bottle of beer. I yanked open the cupboard. We still had four cans of Coors. She must have bought herself this bottled stuff.

While I swept up the mess, I heard Mom muttering "Oh, Cheez-Its" from her room, and then I realized she was saying "Oh, Jesus." By the time I went to bed, the muttering had stopped. I tossed for a while, eventually falling asleep.

She was drinking. It was a red-lettered banner across my brain when I woke late the next morning. I stalked into the kitchen with every intention of confronting her about the night before, but I couldn't connect the beaming woman in a frenzy of list making with the cranky, muddled person I'd encountered a few hours earlier.

Mom wore a green cardigan, a white blouse, and a straight black skirt that fell just below her knees. She'd even put on stockings and low-heeled pumps, and her hair was pulled back loosely into a bun at the nape of her neck. I'd never seen those clothes or that hairdo on her. She could have been anybody's mother. Anybody's but mine. The only sign that she might have been drinking was some puffiness around her eyes—but she had that at other times, too.

"That shower of ours is certainly invigorating," she said, flashing a smile at me.

The night before seemed to be nothing more than a bad dream, and I felt bewildered. "Mom, where are you going?"

"Where am I *not* going is a better question." She dumped everything out of her backpack and began rifling through the clutter, rapidly selecting lipstick, wallet, keys, tissues, breath mints, deodorant, barrettes, and a hairbrush and dropping them into a black leather purse that nearly matched her shoes. I watched her hands to see if they shook, but she moved too fast to tell. She scooped up the remaining items—a bottle of vitamins, a Swiss Army knife, a wadded ball of pantyhose, and a tiny book titled *Life Isn't Meant to Be a Struggle*—and shoved it all into the backpack. Hesitating, she took the book back out, added it to the purse, and removed the deodorant. "Get me a glass of water, would you?" I did, and she opened the vitamins—B-Complex High-Stress Formula—and swallowed three.

"When will you get back?" I asked.

She gulped down the rest of the water. "That's next," she said, taking a wall calendar from under her new purse. "Here's my schedule this week."

Each square on the calendar had a vertical line drawn down the middle. *Heirloom interview, Resume update wkshop, Circle,* and *Re-Imagine Your Life* were some of the things she'd written, all to the left of the vertical lines.

"This side," she said, tapping the right half of a day's square, "is for you. I need you to write your work schedule and anything else you leave the house for." She smiled. "I don't want you to worry about me or me about you. With both of us coming and going so much, this will help us keep track." She slung her purse to her shoulder. "I have to run."

I wanted to bring up the night before, but now it seemed impossibly long ago.

She hurried over to me and planted a hasty kiss on my cheek, making the morning even more unreal. The clatter of her pumps on the steps echoed inside the trailer.

Less than twenty-four hours earlier, she couldn't be bothered with a job that catered to fussy women. Now she was going to interview for it. I should have been pleased.

I sat outside on the steps and breathed the pungent morning air, wondering about the night before and whether I was just imagining things.

Before I went into town to walk Cocoa, I melted a little of Shirley and Sherrie's chocolate in a small pan, added carob chips I'd found at the health-food store, and dipped two handfuls of small, round dog treats in it. While the coating cooled and hardened, I took a teeth-grittingly cold shower.

At Big-Time Bargains, Cocoa refused to come to me until I waved a chocolate-covered treat under his nose. Then he couldn't get out of his cushy bed fast enough. He trotted over to me, took the treat I offered, crunched it twice, and dropped it on the floor. He looked surprised. He tried to lick the chocolate off the treat, but it was too small for him to hold down with a paw while he licked. Finally, he ate the whole thing.

"Probably the healthiest thing you've had in weeks, Cocoa." He wagged his tail and headed for his bed, but I clipped a leash on him. Opening the door, I walked into the hallway a leash length away from him. "Cocoa, come!"

He hesitated. I waved a treat at him. He whimpered, but he came to me. It took three more treat bribes to get him to the front door. Sherrie wasn't around, but Shirley witnessed all this, shaking her head and making disapproving noises.

"I thought we took chocolate off the menu," she said.

"These are regular dog treats dipped in a chocolate-carob mix," I explained. "Next week, they'll be half dipped, then a quarter."

"You're weaning him." It was a statement, not a question.

"I guess you could call it that."

She looked thoughtful, then gave me a sly smile. "Give me a few of those, would you?"

When I brought Cocoa back this time, both women were working behind the counter, their backs to each other. Shirley tried to stifle a smirk when she saw me. Sherrie's eyes got big when she noticed Cocoa walking.

"The poor thing," she murmured.

"He's okay, but you probably shouldn't feed him tonight," I cautioned, handing Sherrie the leash. "To get him to walk, I bribed him with a lot of treats."

Shirley did her best not to laugh, but she was ready to explode. She poked Sherrie with an elbow. "Those chocolates were pretty filling, huh? Should we skip dinner, too?"

Sherrie glared at Shirley. "You're disgusting."

I had to bite the inside of my cheek not to laugh.

Shirley bent over, cackling. "She's brushed her teeth three times to get rid of the taste!"

Sherrie lifted a stack of T-shirts and carried them stiffly to a shelf. "It wasn't funny."

Shirley composed her face, looking down at the floor, but only for a moment before deep laughter erupted from her. She gasped, "I didn't mean for you to *eat* them!" I couldn't help laughing, too. Sherrie stood with her back to us, shaking her head, but when she turned around she was trying not to smile.

"Kayla," Shirley said, "I hate to change the subject, but your mom came here yesterday."

"She did?"

"She got some clothes she said she needed for work."

So that explained her new outfit. "Okay."

"She said you wouldn't mind if she charged the clothes against your credit with us."

I stared at her.

Shirley shook her head. "I'm sorry. I had a feeling I should have checked with you first."

I shouldn't have been surprised, but I was, and the warmth I'd felt from laughing with the two women faded. Mom trusts me, I told myself. She counts on me. That's a good thing.

"I'm sorry," Shirley repeated. Sherrie, hanging clothes across the room, watched us.

"It's okay, I guess," I mumbled, and now I had a sinking feeling— disappointment, maybe, or anger. I wasn't sure which. "Don't worry about it."

"Are you certain?" Shirley asked.

"Yeah. I'm sure." My insides were quivering like Jell-O. I turned to go.

"Kayla?" It was Sherrie now. "What about next time? Because she'll want to do it again."

I took a couple of breaths. They could see that about her. Just from meeting her once. I scratched my head, thinking of what to say.

Sherrie said softly, "You're probably a big help to her."

"But it's your money. Your hard work," Shirley added.

"Let me think about it," I told them, and I fled.

When I got back to the trailer, my mother was actually wearing an apron over the same clothes she'd worn to New Horizons and her job interview. I didn't even know we owned an apron. Some hair had escaped from her bun, and she repeatedly pushed it out of her face with her forearm as she stirred something on the stove. I put Elvis on my shoulder and peered into the pot.

Mom stepped back abruptly. "Don't bring him so close!"

"We're curious."

"Kayla, a rat does not belong in the kitchen."

"Well, leave, then."

She peered at me. "What's that supposed to mean?"

"Just joking." I offered Elvis to her, but she flinched, so I set the rat on her shoulder and took the long wooden spoon from her. She shrieked and cupped the rat with her hands. Elvis poked his nose out from between her fingers.

"I don't want him to climb down my shirt!"

I buttoned the top button of her blouse. "You made sauce from scratch?"

She blushed—or maybe she was hot from cooking. "I figured it's time I learned to cook."

"Hmm." I didn't want to look too pleased. "How did the interview go?"

Her shoulders sagged. "They said they'd call me."

"What's wrong with that?"

"That means they won't."

I decided not to bring up the clothes credit right now.

Through the window, I saw Redbone's truck pull into the yard. We heard the engine cut, the truck door open and slam.

"Put Elvis away, would you?" she asked, shoving the rat at me. "Before he walks in."

Holding the rat, I unlatched the trailer door, kicked it open, and had the pleasure of seeing Redbone jump. He carried a bottle of wine in his hand.

My mother snapped, "Kayla!"

"Didn't mean to startle you, Redbone," I said. "The door's sticking worse than ever." I put Elvis on my shoulder.

He scowled at the rat. "Where'd you get that?"

"Mom got him for me. I guess I have you to thank, in part. Want to hold him?"

"Sure. Let me just grab one of my traps from the truck first."

"Funny."

"You know they carry plague?"

I shrugged. "He only bites when he senses a person doesn't like him."

Redbone took a step toward the doorway, but I shifted sideways to block him. "May I?" he said.

I wanted my apron-wearing, job-interviewing mother to myself. "We're about to eat."

"C'mon in, Red," Mom sang out, and then she cleared her throat and said to me, "Redbone is staying for supper."

I looked from one to the other and escaped to my room, leaving the door cracked open.

He asked Mom, "You wanted me to meet a rat?"

My mother laughed. "No. Come on in."

"Smells good in here," he said. "Thank you for inviting me."

The man was a walking testament to good manners. He must have been saving them up for special occasions. I shut my door and set Elvis on the bed. He ran about, stopping and sniffing at tiny bits of lint. The room felt stuffy, so I turned on the fan, but I was afraid Elvis might stick his face into it and get hurt, so I shut it off.

Mom knocked on the door.

"Wait." I put Elvis back in his cage. "Okay."

She slid the door open. "Supper's ready."

"I'm not hungry," I lied.

She stepped inside and slid the door shut. "What have you got against him?"

"This is how you're going to tell him that the hot-water heater died?"

She tapped her fingernails against the doorframe. "It's better than him hearing about our troubles over the phone."

"He doesn't have to eat dinner with us to be informed of his responsibilities."

She crossed her arms over her stomach. "Look. He usually rents this place to single people. It took a lot of work to convince him to let the two of us stay here. And the way things are going, I may need a break on the rent. It won't hurt to let him eat with us. And . . . he's been good to us, all he's done. You've got to look at the bright side."

Elvis picked up bits of food and furtively carried them into his little dome house. I suddenly saw myself as an extra appendage of my mother—an arm sprouting from the middle of her back or a leg shooting out of the side of her hip. I wished I could make myself very small—Elvis-sized—get rid of most of my belongings, take up less space. Breathe at half my usual rate.

I leaned back against the wall. "I stepped on a bottle cap last night."

She looked puzzled. "What are you talking about?"

"Last night, remember? There was a bottle cap on the floor. It hurt, and I dropped a glass and it broke. A beer-bottle cap."

She looked down at her feet. I braced myself for her confession.

"Kayla," she said, looking up. "I don't know what you're talking about. I need you to come to the table. Now." Wheeling, she turned away, leaving my bedroom door open.

My thoughts tumbled into each other. I shook my head, as if that would sort everything out into separate but compatible truths: She was drinking. She wasn't. She must have blacked out. She's lying. I know what she's like when she's drinking. It was only a bottle cap. It could have fallen out of an old grocery bag. She's getting too friendly with Redbone.

Reluctantly, I joined them. Redbone looked disgustingly at home, seated at our little table. Mom stuck two candles into empty vitamin jars, lit them, and served the spaghetti.

Redbone opened the bottle of wine with his pocketknife. "Wine for you, Marilyn?"

He really annoyed me. She was filling the sink with soapy water and didn't seem to hear.

"Wine, Marilyn?" he repeated.

She set the colander and two pots in the soapy water and smiled at him. "Sure."

She looked at me only a few times during that loathsome meal, but never when she raised her glass to her lips. My heart dropped each time she drank. The arm's length between us might as well have been a hundred miles. I wanted to knock the glass out of her hand, but everything was going eerily well: the polite conversation, Redbone laughing at Mom's jokes and helping with the meal, my mother looking relaxed, happy, and pretty in the candlelight.

The spaghetti was overcooked and tasted like paste. A layer of red-tinted water separated from the sauce and covered our plates, soaking into our salads. Redbone told my mother the dinner was delicious. As soon as I was done eating, I moved to the couch to watch TV. I wanted to go to bed, but I had this idea that if I left them alone, he'd end up in her room. I didn't think I could stand that.

Redbone and my mother cleared the table. He picked up her wineglass. It was about a third full. "Are you done with this?"

"I'm done," she said.

Done? I'd never known her to leave a drink in her glass unless she'd passed out. She took the glass from him and submerged it in the foamy suds. As if it was nothing. As if she dumped half-full glasses of booze every day.

"Redbone, about the rent . . . ." Mom began. She smoothed the apron across her belly. "I'm interviewing, but I'm not hired yet."

He held up his hands. "It's okay. We'll work something out."

"It's not okay," I said. They both looked at me. "I can pay it."

Redbone's eyebrows rose. He looked at Mom, who explained, "She makes a small fortune with her pet-care business. More than a hundred a week."

He looked me over. "I thought you were pretty smart soon as I met you."

I ignored that. I didn't want his compliments.

He rubbed his knuckles. "Kayla, till your mom's employed, why don't you pay me fifty dollars a week? I don't want to take all your money. You need it for other things."

He looked from Mom to me, awfully pleased. I glared at the two of them. If he was going to kiss her goodnight, I was going to witness it. Ruin it for them, too, if looks could kill. He offered his hand to me, but I pretended I didn't notice.

He kept his extended. "I always shake on a deal."

Reluctantly, I took his hand. He held mine firmly, for too long. He wasn't hurting me, and I could have taken it back, but it would have been so noticeable, my pulling away. Mom watched us. His hand was warm and callused. He put his other hand over mine, holding it in both of his. The one time my mom took me to a church—for a free dinner—a preacher had done the same thing. Embarrassed, I started to draw away, and he held on just a second more before releasing me.

Between the money I had left over from walking the Dallas Chihuahuas and what I'd collected so far from Sam, minus a little I'd spent on myself, I had about a hundred dollars. I gave Redbone fifty of that. The remaining bills felt thin in my pocket.

He put on his Bullwinkle cap and tipped it to my mother. "Good night, ladies."

FOURTEEN

Bell knocked on our door one Saturday afternoon with a lanky girl whose straight dark hair fell to her waist. I'd just come back from walking Rebel and was heating up a can of chili.

Mom let them in. "Welcome to our castle."

Bell introduced the girl as a New Horizons member as if it were a club, adding, "I thought you and Luz could hang out while I help your mom with her resumé."

You thought wrong, I wanted to say. The girl examined her nails, unsmiling, and shot Bell a look that said *I knew this was a bad idea.*

"C'mon back," I said to Luz. "I'll show you my pet rat."

Bell grinned, the happy matchmaker. Luz shrugged, gave Bell another look—sour or uncertain, I wasn't sure—and Mom folded her hands, looking satisfied, *Kayla has a friend* written all over her face. I fled to my room, and Luz followed.

At first, Luz didn't want to hold Elvis. She tentatively held her hand out so her fingertips rested on my arm, and Elvis ran down from my shoulder and up her arm.

Big-eyed, Luz watched him. "Why'd you get a rat?"

"I didn't. My mother did. I wanted a dog."

"Whoa. Not even close."

"I'll say."

"I used to want a dog, until I got Celie."

"What's Celie?"

"Not a what." Luz smiled, the first time since she'd come over. "She's my daughter."

"How *old* are you?" I blurted. Her smile vanished. She handed Elvis back to me, as if she'd decided that being a mother and playing with a rat were incompatible.

"I'm seventeen. Celie's twenty-two months." Luz raised her chin.

"That's cool," I said, groping for words. "Where is she now?"

"With my mom. Her dad's going to pick her up later." She stretched her arms wide and yawned. "I've got the whole day to myself. Doesn't happen much."

"Does Celie's dad live with you?"

She made a sound like a soft snort. "We split up when Celie was nine months old."

I put Elvis in his cage, and we watched him run around.

"I just never knew anyone—I mean, anyone close to my age, you know—who had a kid. There were a couple of girls in my last school—"

"Sure." She lay back on my bed, closing her eyes. "I'm one of *those* girls."

We were quiet. Then she opened one eye.

"I don't recommend it. But I wouldn't trade her for the world."

I got two Diet Pepsis from the kitchen. Mom and Bell barely noticed me.

"I've never been an administrator," Mom complained to Bell.

"We can pull your administrating experience out of these jobs and stick it at the top."

I carried the two glasses back to my room. "Is Diet Pepsi okay?"

Luz made a face but reached for a glass. "Why do you drink this? You don't need to diet." She took a sip. "Bleah."

"I feel like a house."

Luz looked puzzled, then burst out laughing. "Round, like a hogan?"

"What's a hogan?"

"A round Navajo house. Traditional kind. My grandmother owns

94

one on the reservation. She's always asking me, how come you girls want to look like you're starving? You look good, Kayla. Some girls pay surgeons a lot of money to look like you." She put down her soda. "This stuff's nasty. You shouldn't drink it."

"Easy for you to say."

She looked down at herself and shrugged. "You get what you get."

"Yeah. And you don't throw a fit," I added.

Luz flopped back, laughing. "That's good. That'll come in handy with Celie."

"Are you in school, Luz?"

"Community college. Eventually, I'm gonna go to law school. Another eight years and I should be finished." She chuckled, piled her hair on top of her head, and let it fall. "Make that twelve years and I'll have a piece of parchment to hang on my wall."

We watched the rat, who was running in and out of his house.

"Have you always lived here?" I asked.

"Always. Except for a few months." She sat up. "I used to want to get out of this town, so I stuck out my thumb on the highway. Got a ride from a trucker whose cab was full of postcards. One said *Thanks for the ride, Bill. With your help, I never looked back, and it has made all the difference.* I thought I had it made."

"What did the others say?"

"I don't know. It got too dark to read the rest."

"Why'd you come back?"

She smirked at me and with her hand made a big loop in front of her belly. "My parents help us out a lot, and Celie's other grandmother is pretty cool. Leaving now depends on where I get into school and who offers the best financial aid." She stood up. "I've got a car. Let's get out of here."

"And go where?"

"Anywhere. Celie's a doll, but I like to roam when I don't have her. C'mon. Let's tell them we're going."

"We don't have to tell them. I have another way," I said.

She followed me out to the kitchen, where I wrote on the calendar, *Into town with Luz.* My mom looked up at me and I winked at her.

Outside, Luz said, "Let's take Elvis. Will he stay on us?"

"Probably. I don't know. I've never tried it. He's scared of running in open places."

"Let's get him," Luz said. "I think we can have some fun."

Our first stop was the bank where I had opened a savings account. I had to have Mom's name on the account, but I kept the ATM card that went with the account. Sam paid me on Fridays, and I wanted to deposit a hundred of the nearly hundred and fifty I'd saved. I asked Luz to hold Elvis while I went inside. "Just put him in your shirt pocket," she urged. When Elvis poked his face out, the bank teller grabbed a thick pamphlet and blocked the opening in the barrier between us.

"Is that a rat?"

"It sure is," Luz answered before I could say anything.

"Will it run in here?"

"No," I answered.

"Unless you're wearing lipstick," said Luz. "He loves lipstick."

The teller jumped up and snapped at the teller next to her. "You'd better finish this one."

I handed the rat to Luz. "You should probably take him outside." Luz was laughing so hard, she could barely hold on to Elvis.

The tellers stared at me, wide-eyed. "Sorry," I said. "I just want to make a deposit."

Next, we took Elvis to Shirley and Sherrie's. They shrieked over him, but they laughed, too. "Don't let Cocoa see him," Sherrie warned.

"Don't worry," Shirley said. "Long as you don't dip the rat in chocolate."

Shirley wouldn't touch Elvis, but Sherrie set the rat on her shoulder when a customer called to her for help. "Be right there!" she sang out, and trucked over to the unsuspecting woman with Elvis perched next to her face, his tail curled around the back of her neck. We heard the woman gasp, and I thought Sherrie was going to die laughing.

Luz was impressed. "Does she *know* that woman?" she asked Shirley.

"Been a customer for years."

"Might be the end of that," Luz remarked.

The customer reached out to pet Elvis, so Luz and I decided to do some browsing of our own. We tried on hats and gowns and anything that looked tight and sexy, and I slipped into some black leather pants.

"Jesus, Mary, and Joseph!" Luz declared. "Give this girl a Harley, or an electric guitar, or maybe one of those big groomed black French poodles with the little red bows, and I think we'll have a whole outfit here. You've got to ditch that T-shirt, though." She found a gold-sequined tank top and got me to put it on, then took a lipstick from her purse and quickly traced my lips with it. Shirley and Sherrie and the customer all came over to look at me.

They were quiet. Elvis sniffed Sherrie's ear. Finally, Sherrie said, "Girl, you are a sight. Fifteen going on thirty-five. You want me to put that outfit on hold for a few years?"

After I was home again, when Bell and Luz had gone and Elvis was back in his cage, my mother sat at the little table with six drafts of her resumé spread out and her eyes closed.

"What are you doing, Mom?"

"Wait." She held up one hand. "I've almost got it."

I helped myself to a glass of milk and leaned against the counter.

She opened her eyes. "Darn it. I almost had it. Don't talk when I'm visualizing."

"How was I supposed to know? What are you trying to *get*, anyway?"

"An image of me in my perfect occupation. Bell says the resumé will flow from that."

I lay on my bed and wished I could have hung out with Luz all evening. It was going to be a long night.

FIFTEEN

A few days later, Mom was scheduled for a full day at New Horizons. I wrote on the calendar before she woke that I was taking Rebel out from eight to noon. I wanted to explore the mesa above us. I took water and one of her energy bars, since there wasn't much else in the house, unhooked Rebel from his chain at Sam's, and headed out.

It was scorching hot, so after just two hours I'd had enough. Arriving back at the trailer around ten, I found Redbone's truck in our yard but no sign of him outside. I hoped he was inside working on the hot-water heater. When I got close enough to the trailer that I could almost feel the heat shimmering off it, I heard a woman's high-pitched laugh, a man's low voice like water sliding over rocks, and then the woman giving out repeated, punctuated gasps. It sounded like two people having sex. My feet froze to the ground. My mother was out. Why was Redbone hooking up with a strange woman in our trailer? *My mother isn't here* droned in my mind. No car, no mother, no car, no mother, until the woman declared, "Right there!" in a voice eerily like Mom's. But Mom's car isn't here, I thought.

When the woman exclaimed, "Redbone!" and burst into laughter, the wall between this mysterious person and my mother crumbled. Her low moan sent me hurrying down the road, fearful that they'd look out the window and see me. Against my will, I pictured them entwined on her bed.

My limbs seemed disjointed as I fled what felt like the scene of a crime. If I hadn't been so angry, I'd have stormed in there, grabbed the calendar off the refrigerator, and flung it at them. That calendar was nothing but a way to keep track of me so she'd know when she could sneak Redbone into the trailer.

By the time I reached Sam's driveway, my palms hurt from digging my nails into them. If the calendar was a sham—which it had to be—then everything my mother did was in question.

Chained outside, Rebel hurled himself at me, an explosion of excitement and adoration. I kneeled in the dirt and hugged him tightly, letting him lick my face and ears. He bounded away only to race back to me for a second goodhearted assault. "Good dog," I was telling him when the back door opened and Remy stood there. He leaned against the doorframe in a wrinkled T-shirt, jeans, and bare feet, smiling at me.

He pushed his hair out of his eyes. "Thought you'd already come and gone."

"I had to run home for a minute. But we didn't finish our walk," I lied.

"Mind if I join you two?"

I shook my head.

He put on sneakers and took the leash off its hook.

"I don't think we'll need the leash. He stays close now, even heels on command." I hesitated, not sure of anything. "You could bring it, just in case."

Remy stuffed the leash into his pocket, and the three of us set off. Rebel bounded ahead and Remy strode easily beside me. I felt stiff in comparison.

Remy chatted about his band, but I could barely pay attention. I kept thinking about my mother and Redbone.

"Kayla?" he asked.

"What?"

"I asked you a question."

"Sorry. What was it again?"

He repeated it, something about whether I thought male or female vocalists had more impact emotionally, and I couldn't even make sense of the question. "I'm—I'm . . . not sure," I stammered.

"Is something wrong?" he asked.

I felt myself blush, and I looked away.

"I don't mean to pry," he said.

"It's okay."

He took hold of my shoulder and turned me toward him. "Are you all right?"

God, he was sweet. I couldn't help smiling. "I'm fine."

We followed the curve of the land down to the arroyo, where Remy took the lead. I followed him up the dry riverbed. I didn't mind that he was leading; it was his dog, after all. But as the arroyo curved toward my trailer, I had to say something.

"I'd rather not go near my place."

He glanced at me, then up at Redbone's truck, still parked in the yard. I hoped he wouldn't ask questions.

He whistled to Rebel, who had gone ahead. "This way," he said to me, and headed off to the east on a deer trail. Grateful, I followed him.

Not speaking, we skirted the trailer in a wide arc, Rebel crisscrossing our path and sniffing deer tracks. The trail was narrow but clear and began to climb the hills, angling back toward the arroyo, which was narrower up here than it was below but just as dry, an empty creek bed. The absence of water made me imagine it splashing over the rocks, swirling in small eddies on slabs of sandstone, sticks and leaves piled up in tiny dams.

Remy's voice startled me. "Who's at your place?"

I tried to keep my voice steady. "Landlord."

"Something broken?"

You could say that, I thought. "Yeah."

"You don't like him." It was a statement more than a question.

"He's not my type." I wished immediately I could take back those words.

Remy smiled. "What type is he?"

I shrugged, afraid of digging a deeper hole. "Just a landlord. I don't know. I don't really know him." A rock turned under my foot and I stumbled forward. Remy grabbed my arm and steadied me. Pleased and embarrassed, I mumbled "Thanks" and kept walking. Only now I was leading on the trail, and I was sure his eyes were on me. I felt as though my arms and legs were shooting out in odd directions and thought my butt probably looked huge. The more graceful I tried to be, the clumsier I felt. Finally, I glanced back at Remy to see if he really was watching me, but he was gazing off to the east, where Rebel was galloping around cactus plants and shrubs with small yellow flowers.

He turned and gestured toward a stand of junipers ahead. "Almost there."

I should have realized he had a destination in mind. The trail climbed more steeply. Sweat trickled down my sides, and I wiped some off my upper lip.

Remy passed me, rounding several trees and disappearing behind a huge boulder. I came to a small, flat clearing bordered on three sides by boulders and an overhang and open to the arroyo. Remy sat beneath the overhang, patting the ground beside him. I wasn't sure if he was beckoning to me or to the dog, but Rebel didn't hesitate. He leaped up there and tried to lick Remy's face. "Down, boy," Remy commanded, and the dog settled beside him. Remy patted the ground again. "It's cool in here, and there's room for you, too." He moved over, leaving a space between him and Rebel. The dog groaned as I nudged him over so that I could sit without pressing against Remy.

"Do you come up here a lot?"

"Used to," he said. "When I lived here."

"How long have you been gone?"

"Gone?" He laughed. "Hard to say. I keep coming back."

"But did you first leave after high school?" I was trying to figure out how old he was. The way he looked at me, I wondered if he knew why I was asking.

"During high school, the first time," he answered. "Middle of senior year, the second time. Can't keep track after that." I was no closer to knowing his age than when I started asking questions. Unwanted thoughts of my mother and Redbone crept in. What did it matter how old Remy was? The shade cooled me, and I raked the fur on Rebel's belly with my fingers. Remy lay back with his hands behind his head and closed his eyes. Sweat dried on his forehead. His lashes were long and dark against his skin, and his lips curved into a faint smile. The air smelled of dry earth and sage, and occasionally, when a breeze skipped into our hideaway, I got a sweet, musky blend off Remy. Hal had smelled like sweat, too, but his was a sour odor that made me want to pinch my nose shut.

I lay down, too. Remy shifted beside me, and I felt him brush against my shoulder. Opening my eyes, I saw that he had rolled onto his side and was facing me, his eyes still shut, a half smile still on his lips. His face was just inches away from mine. I wanted to bolt upright but held myself still. He opened his eyes. I sat up quickly. He covered my hand, which was pressed into the dirt, with his own. "Do you write a lot of poetry?" he asked.

"Some," I replied. "When I feel inspired."

Part of me wanted to yank my hand away and part of me wanted to turn it over and lay my palm flat against his, entwining our fingers. That made me think again of my mother entangled with Redbone. An unwelcome intrusion.

"What inspires you?"

"I don't know," I said, but that sounded stupid. "Colors. Paintings." I laughed. "Dogs."

"Oh, yeah? Show me more, when you write some." He closed his eyes again.

I drew my knees up and took long, slow, and what I hoped were silent breaths to calm the racing in my chest. Slowly, I slid my hand out from under Remy's and examined my palm, wondering what a palm reader might say about me—about life and love and the pursuit of happiness. Remy waved his fingers and, with his eyes still closed, found my hand and traced a route from my fingertips to my palm, where he rested his fingers. Pleasurable and disturbing pinpricks shot down into my pelvis and farther, to my toes. The world was holding its breath. I forgot to breathe until a puff of breeze on my warm cheeks reminded me to take in some air.

I could have curled my fingers around his; instead, I withdrew my hand and wrapped both of my arms around my knees, hugging them to my chest. He pushed himself up, spinning around and sitting cross-legged next to me, barely an inch of thick, charged air between us.

"How old are you, Remy?" The question surged out of some part of me that just wouldn't play along with the glory of this moment. I sounded like my mother. *I don't want to know,* whispered the rest of me. *Don't tell me.*

"Twenty-four," he murmured. Still looking out across the arroyo, he asked, "And you?" as if his question were a minor thing, a bit of information he didn't really need.

Nine years between us seemed like too much. "Seventeen," I told him.

He looked at me. His eyes slid down to my chin, up to my hair. I was grateful that he didn't stare at my breasts. "Seventeen," he whispered, as if he were saying a prayer. The truth flapped inside me like a landed fish, but I held it in. I *felt* seventeen—sort of. Surely I could add months or years based on everything I'd seen and heard and been through. Not to mention my woman-sized self. All that should count for something.

Still, I could not hold his gaze.

Closing my eyes, I waited for him to laugh in my face and tell me I wasn't fooling anybody. I hoped I looked calm, and I pretended I was enjoying everything: the dry, fragrant air; his company; the sleeping, twitching dog by my side. I could sense Remy leaning close before his lips pressed against my cheek, sending an electric current through me. I kept my eyes closed and didn't move, waiting to see what he would do next.

"Is that okay?" he asked.

He peered at me from under his eyebrows and seemed genuinely interested in my answer. I nodded.

"You're really sweet." His voice was low, and he shook his head, like maybe I wasn't supposed to be so sweet. Standing, he brushed dirt off his butt and offered his hand to me. "Come on." I let him pull me up. He whistled to Rebel and let out a whoop, and we all ran down the slope, back toward the road and my trailer. He turned onto the same deer tracks that took us in a wide semicircle around the trailer, and I noticed that Redbone's truck was gone. At the road, we slowed to catch our breath. I wanted him to take my hand and I thought of reaching for his, but we didn't touch all the way back to his house.

He stood in the driveway coiling and uncoiling Rebel's leash. "My band plays tomorrow night at Billy's. I'd like you to come."

"Where does Billy live?"

He laughed. "Billy's is a bar. It's on Avenida Real."

"Remy, I don't think they're going to let me in."

"Go to the side door. It's marked *Authorized Personnel*. You see anyone, tell them you're with me."

I nodded.

"Or I could pick you up."

"No. I'll be in town already. I'll get there on my own."

He leaned forward and kissed me quickly on the cheek.

I didn't have a clue how I'd get to town at night or what I'd tell my mother—certainly not that I was going out to a bar to hear a twenty-four-year-old guy and his band. Walking home, I played the two kisses over and over, wondering about them. Hal had wanted to be my boyfriend. No, Hal had wanted to score—I could admit that now. Remy's approach was altogether different—sweet, respectful, kind. I decided, as I turned into my yard, that Remy's touch was more like that of a brother or a good friend. That was all he wanted. Something my mother would approve of. Maybe I could even tell her about going to hear the band. And she could explain about Redbone.

When she came in an hour later, however, with a bag of groceries and a sack of lies about her terrific long day at New Horizons, I didn't mention a word about Remy. It didn't seem right to trust her with my secrets if she wasn't going to tell me hers.

SIXTEEN

Shirley and Sherrie were glad to see me the next day. They introduced me to a girl named Lisa, who worked for them occasionally and had stopped by to pick up her paycheck.

"You're early for walking Cocoa," said Shirley, after Lisa had left.

"I'm ready to cash in on my work time, too," I said.

"You know where the T-shirts are," Shirley told me, turning back to the pink Looney Tunes spiral notebook in which she'd been writing. Sherrie was singing "Somewhere Over the Rainbow" while she hung clothes in the kids' and maternity sections.

"I've got enough T-shirts already."

Shirley put down her pen and sat up straight. "What do you need, then? We'll help you find whatever it is."

"That's okay. I'll just look around."

Shirley adjusted her bifocals. "Kayla, everyone can benefit from a second opinion when it comes to clothes."

Irritated, I moved off to the racks. I picked out a few silky blouses and one scoop-neck sweater and carried them to the dressing room. The sweater was tight fitting and low cut. It made my boobs stand out, and I wouldn't be comfortable with that. When you wear loose shirts all the time, switching to a tight fit is like announcing, *Hey, check out my big papayas!* It was fun to try on, but no way would I wear it outside the dressing room. The blouses were okay, and I decided on a silver-gray one. I figured I could unbutton an extra button if I was feeling daring. The fabric had some shine to it, so it seemed dressy. It would do.

I took everything but the silver-gray blouse back to the racks and laid the blouse on the counter. Shirley was writing intently in the notebook. Sherrie pushed her invoices to one side. "Let's see what you've got."

Frowning, she held the blouse up to me. "Shirl, what do you think about this?" She looked back. "Oh, sorry. I forgot you're working on the book."

Shirley set down the notebook and pen. "I'm at a good stopping place. Victor just buried the knife in the herb garden."

Sherrie winced. "He's burying it? Not slipping it into Camille's carryon bag?"

I cleared my throat.

"Shirley, we'll settle the knife problem later. Don't you think this blouse is too matronly for her?" She held it up again. "Makes you look old before your time. This is something a middle-aged woman would wear to go out for drinks with the gals after work, wouldn't you say, Shirl?"

"I think you're right. Kayla, are you trying to look like your grand-mother?"

I nearly choked. "You wouldn't say that if you'd known her."

"Well, what's the occasion? Are you going someplace special?"

Now I felt really annoyed—but at the same time, I was having sec-ond thoughts about the blouse, especially when Sherrie added, "Honestly, it makes you look dowdy. Color's all wrong, besides."

"I'm going to hear a friend's band."

Sherrie marched over to the rack where I'd gotten the blouse and whipped through a dozen or so items. She held up a black camisole top with a lace neckline. "Nothing slinky here, Kay. It's wholesome cotton, but the lace dresses it up."

I frowned at her. "It's nice, but it's too . . . underwear-ish."

Sherrie looked at the top, considering. "That it is. So we'll add . . ." She found a gauzy white cotton blouse. She put the camisole under it so I could see the effect. "Modest but sexy. Youthful—*and* machine washable. It's you, girl." She handed it to me.

It worked. I felt great in it, and not too exposed. I came out of the dressing room grinning, until I saw Sherrie holding out the pair of black leather pants I'd tried on with Luz.

"I don't think so, Sherrie."

Both women howled. "Just messing with you, Kayla. The jeans you've got on are fine. You gotta be yourself." She held the leather pants against her round belly. "What do you think, Shirley? Is it me?"

"Next life, sister."

Mom had an evening class at New Horizons from seven-thirty to nine-thirty. I told her I was going to see a girl named Lisa who worked at Shirley and Sherrie's and lived near New Horizons. I tried to convince myself it wasn't a complete lie, since I had met Lisa earlier that day.

I took a long time getting ready so we'd have to go straight to New Horizons. Nestled in with my new clothes was a pair of dangly silver earrings that one of the women must have sneaked into the bag when I wasn't looking. They were wrapped in tissue paper and sealed with a pink heart sticker with *Have fun!* in Sherrie's handwriting. I slipped them in my pocket to put on later, and I added a flannel shirt over the sheer white blouse so my mother wouldn't ask questions.

"You've made me late," Mom complained as we drove away from the trailer.

"I don't mind walking over to Lisa's."

"I don't like you walking at night."

"The streets are lit there."

"What's the address? I'll pick you up when I'm done."

"I know which house it is, but not the number. I'll meet you back at New Horizons. Please. Stop worrying!"

It was nearly eight o'clock when I found Billy's. I stashed my flannel shirt in some bushes, put on the earrings, and added some lip-stick—an old one of my mother's that I was pretty certain she didn't wear anymore. The side door was locked, and no one answered when I knocked. Around front, the windows had neon Dos Equis and Miller signs, and another that read POOL, and a poster for Terra Luna—Remy's band. I approached the bouncer, who was seated on a tall stool by the front door. He was broad, bald, and tattooed, with bushy eyebrows that almost met in the middle.

"ID?"

"I'm with Remy. He's in the—"

"Then especially you need your ID."

I fiddled with one of my earrings. "I didn't come to drink. I'm just here for the music."

"I can't let you in."

I drew myself up tall. "Believe me, I'm old enough. I know I should have brought my ID, but I was kind of rushed. I'm sorry."

"No deal."

He turned to a couple of girls and a guy, carded them, and waved them in. They looked at me with pity or maybe scorn.

I put my hands on my hips. "Do you know how pissed he'll be if he hears that I got turned away?"

The bouncer rolled his eyes. "What's your name?"

"Kayla."

"Hold on." He yelled inside, "Jamie! Watch the door for a minute, would you?"

I stepped away from the door to wait and considered leaving. What if I got Remy in trouble? What if he got mad at me for coming to the front door?

The bouncer returned and waved me in, growling, "If I catch you drinking, your ass is cooked. I don't care who your boyfriend is."

Smoke engulfed me as soon as I stepped inside. I saw pool tables to either side, longhaired girls leaning on their cues, and guys with cigarettes dangling from their lips leaning far over the tables to take shots. Guys followed me with their eyes as I moved into the back, where the tables and booths faced a platform set up for the band.

People filled about half of the seats. Everyone seemed to be in pairs or small groups. Feeling conspicuously alone, I found an empty booth off to one side. My eyes watered from the smoke and my mouth was dry. I wanted something to drink, but I'd forgotten to bring any money. One minute I felt cool and grown-up. The next I wished I was back in my room making shoe castles for Elvis.

Remy came out of the back wearing a snug-fitting black T-shirt, jeans, and black cowboy boots. Over his chest hung the chain and brass key. He scanned the room, combing his long hair back with his fingers, putting it into a ponytail, until he saw me. I thought I'd be relieved to see him; instead, I felt more nervous. He walked over and kissed me on the cheek. His eyes ran over me so fast I wondered if I'd imagined it.

"Hey, foxy. You made it."

I tugged on a piece of hair behind my ear. "Almost didn't. The bouncer was a little concerned."

Remy grinned. "He takes his job too seriously. You want something?"

"No, thanks. I mean, sure. You know—a glass of water or something."

He called over to a guy serving drinks, asking for two glasses of water. A petite girl with short orange hair and a beaded black vest came over to us. "Rem, the sound system's still messed up. Could you get on it?'

He turned his smile on her. "I'm all over it."

She turned away, muttering, "Yeah."

A couple of guys called out to him and a lot of girls looked him over. One ran her fingers across his shoulders as she walked by and he caught her hand and squeezed it before letting go.

"Long time," she said.

He winked and smiled back.

111

Feeling awkward, I couldn't think of anything to talk about. He clasped his hands behind his back, stretching his arms out.

"Nice place," I finally managed to say—a stupid remark, I thought instantly. The joint was smoky as hell and definitely on the grungy side.

Luckily, he thought I was joking. "They don't get much finer than this."

We both laughed, and I wondered if he felt nervous, too.

"When do you start?"

"Ten minutes ago."

Orange-head crossed the makeshift stage, looking daggers at him.

"I should get on it," he said. He moved as if to take my hand but shoved his hands into his pockets instead. "The first set'll be good, but pay close attention to the second, okay?"

"Sure," I said.

"See you at break," he said.

Watching him walk away, I realized I'd probably have to leave before the second set. "Remy."

He turned.

"I have some stuff to do. I'm leaving at nine."

He looked disappointed, then brightened. "Got it."

I stopped feeling self-conscious once the band launched into its first song. The lights dimmed, and the darkness blended me into the growing crowd. Remy was awesome to watch. His body swayed with the music, and he sang as if his soul were turned inside out. His lyrics were full of poetry—"the kindred wind," "the palette of your moods," and so on. I didn't know much about music, but Terra Luna seemed pretty good to me. The crowd thought so, too, and it swelled to fill all the tables, extending back into the pool area, where a lot of folks were standing. About ten minutes into the set, Remy introduced the other band members: Eva, the orange-haired girl, who played drums;

Preston, a lanky guy with a dark mustache, on keyboard; and Tye, a blond and tattooed girl, on bass. A couple of guys joined me at my booth, drinking many beers and ordering for me. They didn't seem to notice that I pushed the beers they bought me to their side of the table, where they quickly downed them.

A song had just ended when I noticed that one guy's watch read nine o'clock. Working my way toward the door, I heard Remy announce, "Before we break, here's a new song for a new friend." The lights on the band dimmed, leaving only a spot on Remy and his acoustic guitar. He sang without any music.

"Kayla lights the sky with her arms open wide,
Runnin' with the beasts, coyote by her side.
Don't be afraid, that's her howlin' at the moon.
If she shows up in your life, it won't be a moment too soon."

The band now kicked in. Flattered and embarrassed, I forgot how late it was getting as Remy sang about peaceful rivers and stirring up wildfires and panic in the brush—it was sweet and probably silly and it made me feel way too warm. Thank goodness it was dark in there and no one knew me—though as soon as it ended and I pushed my way out, the bouncer raised an eyebrow at me. I hummed the beautiful melody all the way to New Horizons, where I pulled my flannel shirt over the sheer one and took off the long earrings. I could have run all the way home and would have liked to, especially once I noticed that my hair, my clothes, even my skin stank of cigarette smoke. I'd have to ride with the car window open and hope that my mother didn't notice.

Fat chance of that. Better not to pretend, I decided as Mom emerged from New Horizons. As soon as we got into the car, I said, "Boy, I really stink, don't I?" I held out one arm for her to take a whiff. "Lisa's brother and his friends smoke like chimneys!"

Mom was quiet.

I asked, "How was your class?"

"My class was excellent. In fact, the whole evening has been terrific until now, when you lied to me about where you've been."

I shifted uncomfortably in my seat. "What makes you think I lied?"

"This is a small town, Kayla. Bell knows Lisa. She happened to mention that Lisa's dad and brothers were killed in a car accident years ago."

My heart skipped a beat. "Okay. If you want to know the truth, I went to a bar."

"That's more obvious than you realize."

"I didn't drink." I breathed hard in her direction. "Believe me?"

She scowled. "Thanks for the proof. Okay, so you didn't drink. What bar did you go to, and why?"

If I told her I went to Billy's, she might find out who played there and put two and two together. I'd seen another bar near Billy's and I named that one.

"Did Lisa go with you?"

"No."

"How did you get in?"

I could have sworn she sounded more curious than upset now. "There was no bouncer."

"And the why part?"

"I don't know," I answered, trying to keep my voice even. "Boredom. To see if I could do it. There was some band playing. I thought they might be good." I paused. "They weren't."

Mom pulled in at our trailer. "Do you know how dangerous it can be for a fifteen-year-old to go into a bar by herself?"

If I said yes, I'd have to explain my complete disregard for my own safety. If I said no, I'd get a lecture. Either way, I'd look stupid.

"Maybe not."

She sighed. "Please don't do that again."

SEVENTEEN

Less than a week later, Remy asked if I wanted to go for a ride. I hadn't seen him since the night at the bar. I was just finishing up with Rebel, and Remy had been sitting on the couch, working on a new song. I hesitated long enough to think what to write on the stupid calendar for Mom. "Sure," I told him. I ran to the trailer, scrawled, *Doing errands. Home by six,* stuck a lip-gloss in my pocket, and flew back to Remy's, applying the lip-gloss on the way.

When I got into his VW bus, I couldn't help checking for a mattress. To my relief, there wasn't one. The back was carpeted and empty except for Rebel and some thick extension cords.

"Where are we going?" I asked.

The dog tried to lick my face, and Remy shooed him into the back. "It's a surprise." He peered at me a little anxiously. "Is that okay, to surprise you?"

I sure liked how considerate he was. "It's fine."

Rebel whimpered, and Remy said, "He thinks you're in his seat." I reached back to scratch the dog behind the ears.

We left the highway about half an hour north of Rio Blanco and took a two-lane road that wound through clusters of cottonwoods and past roadside stands selling ristras, long strings of red chili peppers. When I remarked how pretty they were, Remy pulled over at the next stand, bought a two-foot-long string of deep red peppers, and handed it to me.

"You are officially welcomed to New Mexico now."

I think my face turned as red as those peppers, but that was happening so often around Remy that I was beginning not to care, especially since he never mentioned it.

It grew a little cooler as we drove higher. The air hitting my face felt great. Rebel stuck his muzzle out my window, his nose cold and wet against my elbow. I told Remy how much I had liked his band the other night. Remy launched into his plans: bookings in bigger venues; selling his songs to well-known artists who would get them onto the airwaves. "It's all going to happen," he said, squeezing my shoulder. "I think you'll bring me good luck."

What a line, I thought. Still, it made me blush again, and laugh. He took my hand then and held it as he drove, and I could feel mine get sweaty. I really hadn't held hands with anyone before—my mother didn't count, and Hal sure wasn't a hand holder.

"How'd you like the song?" He asked lightly, but his face was serious.

I knew which song he meant, but I said, "That one you were practicing when I brought Rebel home?"

He started to explain, until he noticed I was smiling.

I took my hand away from his. "My mom would say you're fishing."

"Your mom's pretty smart."

"What do you want me to say?"

"That it's the best song anyone's ever written about you."

"How do I know it's about me?"

He glanced over. "Didn't you hear your name in it?"

"Maybe you know a dozen Kaylas." I looked away, trying not to giggle.

"I do."

"Hey!"

"But none have inspired me to write about them."

Oh, boy. I tried to let that sink in and didn't know what to say next. Remy drove into a tree-lined lot and parked. Pointing to a DOGS ON

LEASHES ONLY sign, he tossed Rebel's leash to me. Another sign said something about cliff dwellings, so I thought we were going to see birds that nested on cliffs. As we hiked up a sloping trail, I offered Remy the leash, but he wouldn't take it.

"He listens better to you," he said.

"But you should learn how to handle him."

"I'll learn by watching you."

That kicked my adrenaline level up a notch or two. I concentrated on walking slowly along the path as it curved past a sandstone cliff, our feet crunching on the gravel. We came to a turn where we could see a much higher cliff—maybe a hundred feet up—with many ledges. I saw small holes in the rock and figured that was where the birds nested, and I did see a few swallows swooping near them. Then I realized that along the ledges were stone walls, some with window openings, and that the walls formed rooms. Ladders and steps led up to some of the ledges.

"This is cool, Remy."

"Yeah. I love this place."

He went ahead while I read a sign telling a brief history of the Anasazi cliff dwellers—how they farmed, built their homes on cliffs, and then vanished about seven hundred years ago.

Remy climbed a staircase cut into a cliff, and I followed him, leaving Rebel tied to a signpost. The steps rose to a ledge high above the path where I'd left the dog. Remy stood near a rectangular stone with a shallow depression in the top and a smaller stone nestled in it.

"A metate," he explained. "For grinding corn."

I squatted and ran my fingers over the grinding stone, which was surprisingly smooth. We walked along the flat ledge to a wall made of sandstone blocks. Remy ducked through a small doorway and I followed him into a tiny room. Another small opening led to a second room and a third, where we sat on the hard-packed earth and gazed over the crumbling outer wall to the valley below. Cottonwood trees lined the arroyo, refreshingly green against the surrounding dry earth. Their leaves fluttered, and we could hear the river tumbling over rocks. I tried to imagine the people who had lived here, grinding their corn, hauling water from the river.

Remy studied me. "When are you going to show me the rest of your poem?"

I scratched the dirt with my boot. "It's not finished. Why do you want to see it, anyway?"

"Listen." He got up onto his knees and sat back on his heels, his hands spread on his thighs. Keeping his eyes on me, he cleared his throat and sang my poem to me in a melody I'd never heard before. The words rippled through me. When he came to the last line, he returned to the first: "Love isn't always what you want . . . ." and he kept repeating it, his hands now beckoning as if to say, *Come on, come on,* and we both burst out laughing. I don't know what got him—I was just nervous. He said, "Don't leave me hanging, girl!" Taking my hands, he looked me up and down. "Where's the rest?"

I dropped his hands and leaned away, a grin stuck on my face. "Maybe," I said, "there isn't any more."

He bent toward me and pressed his lips gently to my cheek. "I'll bet . . . ," he said, turning my face and kissing the other side, "I could coax it out of you."

I shivered, and my throat felt as dry as the stones at our feet. I stood and swept my arm through the air. "Imagine living here!"

He leaned against the back wall, a half smile on his face. "Sure. Cramped. Smoky. Freezing in winter and hot in summer."

"Didn't you read the signs? They had passive solar heating. And feel how cool these rooms stay." I pressed my palms against a wall.

"You read signs. I'll bet you follow directions, too."

"Depends on who's giving the directions," I said.

I swatted him playfully. He grabbed my wrist and pulled me to him. I expected a kiss, but he tickled me instead, and I broke loose, a little out of breath. I pretended to pick up a bow and arrow. Drawing the arrow back, I asked, "Did the Anasazi hunt with bows?"

"Beats me," he said.

I aimed straight for Remy's eye. He watched me calmly. Above us, a bird sent a cascade of notes into the air. Twisting toward the river, I let my arrow fly.

"I had a great time," I said as we jumped out of the bus at Sam's. It was nearly dark, and I wanted Remy to offer me a ride home, but he didn't. Not that I'd have taken it: I didn't want my mom to see us together. But I wanted him to offer.

"It's a magical place," he said. "I'm glad you could see it."

"Thanks." I stood there, feeling awkward. "Well, see you later." I turned away.

He caught my hand, put it to his lips, and kissed it. "At your service," he said with a broad grin.

On the dusty road to my trailer, it was easy to forget my occasional uneasiness with Remy. The first stars glittered in the dark indigo sky, and the early-night air felt like soft silk against my face. I imagined a photo of Remy and me on the cover of *Rolling Stone—Singer-Songwriter Duo Hit Top of Charts with "Love Isn't Always What You Want."*

At the trailer door, I remembered my ristra, still lying on the floor of Remy's bus. It was probably just as well, because I didn't know how I'd have explained it to Mom.

EIGHTEEN

Inside the trailer, Mom was filling four quart-size Mason jars with water and tightening the lids. I went straight to the sink, thirsty from another adventure without water, filled a glass, and drank it down.

"What's all this, Mom?" I pointed to the jars.

"You've been gone a while." She lined the jars up on the counter. "Where were you?"

I leaned against the counter and crossed my ankles. "The bank, Big-Time Bargains, the drug store"—I pulled the lip gloss from my pocket and waved it at her—"and the library. I found this cool book on the Anasazi. Do you know who they are?"

She shook her head.

"They lived here about a thousand years ago and they built their homes in the sides of steep cliffs." I refilled my glass. "There are ruins of their cliff dwellings all around here. We should go see 'em sometime."

"Sounds interesting." She stood near me and ran a finger across my cheek. "Was it sunny in the library? You got yourself a sunburn." She raised her eyebrows at me.

I put my hand to my face. It was warm. "I was out for a long time with both dogs, and I ate lunch outside. The sun was pretty brutal. What's with the jars of water?"

She studied me a moment before turning to look at her jars. "I got some information on detoxing today at the health-food store," she said. "I've got to start drinking at least four quarts of water a day. Purified would be best, but I hate paying extra for water. We're already paying enough. A few extra minerals can't be that bad."

"Detoxing?"

"Short for 'detoxification.' Cleaning out from years of digesting harmful stuff. Smoking, alcohol, pesticides on our food. You should do it, too, even though you haven't been polluting yourself as long as I have."

Opening the refrigerator for a soda, I was dismayed to find only rice milk and some weird green juice. "Mom, what the heck is *Apple-phyl?* It looks like juice for cows."

"Fresh-squeezed apple juice with chlorophyll and spirulina."

I knew what chlorophyll was, though I couldn't for the life of me figure out why I'd want to drink it. "What's spirulina?"

Mom scrunched up her face. "Let me see. Is it a fungus or an algae? Something full of vitamins, anyway. You add it to salads and juice and stuff. It enhances the nutrient value."

I put the green stuff back in the refrigerator, filled my water glass a third time, and took it to my bedroom. Elvis begged to come out of his cage, so I let him climb all over me for a while. Mom got busy in the kitchen making a big salad and a shake out of the green juice, an avocado, beets, and wheat germ. I put Elvis back in his cage and searched the kitchen cupboards, wondering what to make for my own dinner that night.

After a meal of scrambled eggs and baloney, I holed up in my room, leaving my mother to study a booklet titled *The Detox Cure: A Pure and Simple Way to Health and Happiness*. I found my unfinished poem, copied it into my notebook, and tried to think of an ending.

Lying back on my bed, I admitted to myself that I wasn't sure what was going on between Remy and me, but I figured he did since he was older. I wasn't about to ask him—*Hey, is this going to turn into a girlfriend-boyfriend thing?*—because what if it was the furthest thing from his mind?

Luz stopped by that night with Celie—a miniature version of Luz in a Skoal chewing tobacco T-shirt and rhinestone sandals—to hang out for a while. Celie squealed every time Elvis stuck his head out of his little house, and we gave her the rat to hold. She got so excited, she nearly strangled him.

I almost talked to Luz about Remy, but even though she was close to my age, she seemed—or tried to act—much older sometimes. What if she thought I was too young for Remy?

There was also my lie about being seventeen. I wasn't ready to tell anyone about that.

Cool air tinged with wood smoke and the fragrance of dry juniper needles surrounded me on my way to Sam's early in the morning. Only Remy's bus sat in the driveway, and Rebel barked at me from the end of his chain. I took him out back and let him run before I worked through his commands. He was completely obedient, responding quickly to everything I asked until he saw a rabbit twitching its whiskers next to a large rock. Rebel streaked after it as if he'd discovered the last bunny on earth. The rabbit bolted, zigzag-ging and darting under bushes, with Rebel scrambling behind. I yelled for Rebel to come back, but I might as well have been order-ing the moon to drop down to Earth. He ran crazily, scrambling right and left, trying to follow the rabbit's jagged path. Finally, the bunny dove under a boulder, and Rebel stopped just short of bash-ing his head on it. He barked and dug and wagged his tail. By the time I got there, he'd dug a large hole, but the burrow was deep. Poor Rebel didn't have a chance.

"He outran you, boy. Give it up."

He whimpered, dug a little more, then sat on his haunches, pre-pared to wait it out.

"Rebel, that rabbit is already miles away, laughing its head off. There are at least eight other entrances to this burrow. Now, *come*."

Reluctantly, he followed me toward the house, glancing back a couple of times just in case the rabbit happened to appear. "Fuzz for brains," I told him. "That's what you've got."

He took that as a compliment, running up to lick my hand.

"Learned that from Remy, did you?"

Remy stood in the open doorway when we got back, yawning and stretching his arms, wearing only cutoffs and the chain with the brass key. "Coffee?" he asked, rubbing his eyes.

I didn't like coffee. "Sure, I'd love a cup," I said, and followed him inside.

He disappeared and returned wearing a T-shirt and jeans, his hair tied back in a messy ponytail. He filled two mugs with steaming coffee and handed one to me. I added lots of cream and sugar.

He blew on his coffee. "It would be a shame if you didn't finish your song," he said.

"You mean my poem?"

"Your *song*, girl. Aim high." He sipped his coffee. "Love is a great topic, and you're definitely onto something. Gave me the shivers, first time I read it."

"Really?"

He nodded. Now I got a shiver. He set his mug on the counter and put his hands on my shoulders. "When you have a gift like yours, it's terrible—nearly a crime—not to use it."

"What gift?"

He leaned against the counter and took up his mug. "You're a natural lyricist, Kayla. I've never heard anyone put words together like you do."

He peered at me intently over his coffee. I felt like laughing. I sipped my own coffee, relieved to have something else to focus on, but the taste made me grimace. "You can't be serious," I said. "You've seen one poem. And it's not even finished."

He ran a hand slowly over the top of my head, his fingers working gently through my hair. "What will it take to convince you?" His hand slid down the back of my neck, his thumb tracing the top of my spine. "Or help you?"

I took a large swallow of coffee and winced as it burned my throat. He seemed genuinely interested in me *and* the poem. I shrugged. "I'm trying to finish it."

"Come," he said. I followed him to the living room, where he took the O'Keeffe book and patted the cushion next to him on the couch. I sat and he opened the book so it straddled our laps. I drank my awful coffee while he turned the pages slowly, commenting, "She did amazing things with shadows," and "Look how the bones contrast with the sky." I'd never heard anyone talk like that before, and I said so. He replied, "You would, too, if your dad were an art dealer."

I didn't answer. Remy stroked the top of my head. "Is that a sore topic? Your dad?"

"It's not much of a topic at all. Never knew him. Never will. End of topic."

Remy took his hand away. "I want to play something for you." He got his guitar case and sat in a chair across the room. He tuned the guitar and began to strum. "Close your eyes." When I didn't, he laughed. "I guess I was wrong about you following directions. *Please* close your eyes."

I laughed and swung my feet onto the couch and shut my eyes, hugging the pillow while I listened. I thought he might sing my poem again, but he picked a different melody on the guitar. I pictured the music like star trails through my veins. When he was finished, I hoped he'd play another. He did, and when that one was done, I waited for a third. I heard him set the guitar down and move onto the floor beside me. I felt him brush the back of my hand lightly. I peeked: he'd used his knuckles.

"Girl, are you still breathing?"

I exhaled loudly, and he laughed.

"Let me try that again."

I closed my eyes. He repeated the stroke, this time on the inside of my forearm. Butterfly light. And then he stopped. My arm felt like a rare and newly discovered thing.

"Songs come from this, too," he murmured, and did it again, a feather-light stroke. I sighed and he caressed and so on, moving to new places: my cheek, the side of my neck, my collarbone, the hollow of my neck. I wondered what this had to do with songs and if he was going to reach down into my shirt and what I would do if he did.

He didn't. He stroked my foot, my ankles, my shins, my calves, pausing between caresses. Each stroke painted another portion of me, gave it substance. For the first time, I was amazed at the existence of my limbs. My breath came a little fast and I felt soft, like a candle left on a sunny windowsill. I thought I should tell him to stop or not go past certain places—*Not into the jungle, leave the big fruits alone*—and I heard someone, couldn't have been my mom—*You know, one thing leads to another*—but I couldn't figure out where to end it, couldn't separate each stroke of his fingers from the wonderful shivers they sent through me that tapered off into his next touch. He wasn't going where I didn't want him to. There wasn't a darn thing wrong with this, and besides, he was making Hal and all the other heavy-handed lugs disappear.

I didn't want it to end. I didn't ever want him to stop.

He did, though, someplace around my knees.

He stood up and redid his ponytail and said he had to go. I felt a mix of disappointment and more than a touch of relief. He smiled—apologetically, I thought—and pulled me slowly to him. His embrace was gentle, and I tried not to hold him any tighter than he held me. I thought he might kiss me and he did, another soft, brotherly kiss on my cheek. That embarrassed me, and I wondered again if I was misinterpreting his touch.

"Gotta head out." He chucked me lightly under the chin and collected his things.

I checked the time and gasped—I was late for Cocoa. "Remy, can you give me a ride?"

"A ride? Where?"

"Big-Time Bargains."

He took his time packing up his guitar. "How about near there?"

He sounded wary. And cool. It made sense, though. He had to be careful. So did I. I shrugged. "Good enough." I told him to drop me at the drug store two blocks down from Shirley and Sherrie's. On the way there, neither of us spoke, and I wished I'd walked. My limbs bristled, and I needed to move.

I thought how Remy must have come from a whole separate species of boys. Of men. There were pawing, groping boys like Hal who acted like they were lost in the dark. There were hot and heavy breathers who thought if they stuck their tongue into your mouth far enough, you wouldn't notice their hands sliding under your bra or down your pants.

Remy was different. He didn't forget I was there.

Of course, I still wasn't sure where "there" was. Or what we were doing. The way he touched me, the way he tuned in to me, was a hot zone where I'd never been before. I was afraid to talk or ask questions about it. I felt as if I were under a spell, and to speak about the magic would break it.

NINETEEN

I woke at dawn with this revelation as bright and clear as the sun coming over the far mesas: Remy thinks I'm too fat. It made total sense, since he wouldn't touch the biggest parts of me. The girls he greeted at Billy's had that wispy, willowy shape. He liked my mind, my poetry, but the rest repulsed him.

I tried out my theory on Shirley and Sherrie that afternoon, after I'd bribed Cocoa into walking with dog treats only half-dipped in chocolate. Shirley was writing in her spiral notebook, Sherrie was unpacking a box of clothes, and they had me sticking price tags on a pile of new consignments. I waited until I had a good rhythm going with the work. "I know a girl—she's a lot older than me—and she's been hanging out with this guy in a band—Remy Coltan, he plays with Terra Luna—and he's really sweet and romantic with her but not exactly, you know . . ."

The two women stopped what they were doing.

"He does stuff like kiss her hand and kiss her on the cheek, but he doesn't, you know—" I could feel myself turning red, so I bent over the pile of tags and clothes in my lap.

"Jump her bones?" Sherrie interjected.

"Yeah. Nothing, you know, sexual. Except—"

"He's very sexy?"

"Very." I got really warm under my shirt, so I pretended to examine a price tag as if something might be wrong with it. "They've been seeing each other now and then for weeks," I went on, "and I just figured it out. I can't believe how stupid we are. She needs to lose ten or twenty pounds. That turns guys off, right?"

The women looked at each other. Sherrie took off her bifocals and cleaned them. I thought she was trying not to smile. Shirley folded her arms. "She's built like you, this friend?"

I could barely look at her. "Kind of."

"Big women are sexy," she said sternly.

"So are small women," added Sherrie.

"Tall, skinny, cross-eyed, one-legged—it doesn't matter. Nothing wrong with how you're built, Kayla."

I ducked my head over the pile of tags in my lap. "It's not about me."

"Tell your friend, then."

"I will," I assured them, wishing it were that simple. I should have known I'd get an answer like that from those two.

Sherrie said, "There could be another reason he's keeping his doggies tied up. I'm not one for gossip, but—"

"Then don't," Shirley interrupted. She turned back to her notebook.

I asked, "What, Sherrie?"

She held up both hands. "Shirley's right. It's just fifth-hand nonsense." She turned to Shirley. "You know, that might make an interesting twist in your book."

Shirley crossed something out and looked up. "What's that?"

"If Victor had a thing for big women. That's why he wants to be rid of Camille. She's thinner than a chopstick."

"Even though he feels so indebted to her for saving his life?"

"Sure," said Sherrie. "When his vision was blurred by temporary brain damage, her ravishingly beautiful face looked big to him, just the way he likes it."

Shirley clicked her ballpoint pen several times. "So he recovers, healed as much by her love as her surgeon's hands, and when he sees her clearly for the first time, he's shocked."

"Horrified," said Sherrie.

They prattled on about the book, but I didn't listen. What had they heard about Remy? Why were they suddenly so antigossip?

I slapped price stickers on a bunch of tags. Whatever they know doesn't matter, I thought. I just don't turn Remy on. Why did I ever think I would?

That night, Mom worked on her resumé for hours. Crumpled drafts lay on the floor at her feet like giant snowballs. I'd never seen her take job hunting so seriously.

Just as I found an old movie on TV, she said, "Kayla, be a doll and makes us a big salad for dinner, would you?" She crushed another sheet of paper. "I've got to get this done."

I counted back several nights. This would be the fourth dinner in a row I'd be making. "Isn't it your turn?"

"I really need your help, Kayla," she pleaded. "I have to get this typed in the morning to take to an interview in the afternoon. Please. There's spinach and avocado and sprouts and maybe a few radishes. See what else you can find to put in it, okay?"

Like a pizza? I thought, but that would be so fattening. I hated thinking that way. Some girls counted every calorie they put into their mouth, even carried calorie lists and little plastic calorie clickers. I asked, "What's the interview?"

"It's at a bank."

The circles under Mom's eyes were darker than usual. Waiting for my answer, she tapped one chipped, polished nail on the back of her chair. I noticed a hunk of quartz on the table, a cluster about the size of my fist, with inch-long crystals rising out of the base, pointing in different directions. It must have been covered earlier with her papers. I rose from the couch and lifted the quartz in the palm of my hand. "Where'd this come from?"

"I found it at a little boutique in town."

"It's pretty, but why'd you get it?" I wondered how much of my money she'd spent on it.

She crossed out a line on the paper before her. "The woman in the store explained how crystals have different qualities. Quartz is for clarity, for connecting to your soul's purpose."

I looked at the crumpled papers on the floor. "Doesn't seem to be helping."

She frowned. "Kayla, you're distracting me. Now, dinner?"

Nodding, I went to my room to let Elvis run. The phone rang and Mom greeted Bell loudly, then lowered her voice. I picked up Elvis and opened my door a crack.

"I'm a little worried about her. . . . No, it's not that. She's kind of uncooperative. And secretive. Sometimes she's gone long hours— they don't always match up to what she's telling me. . . . Ask what?" She laughed. "I'll think about it." She groaned. "Maybe I shouldn't have moved again. Everything's piling up. My credit card's maxed, I'm sick of interviewing. . . . What? . . . Oh, yeah," she said bitterly. "Easy for you to say."

When I heard the phone click in its cradle, I went to the kitchen to make dinner.

In the morning, Mom wore her new work clothes and waved freshly painted fingernails in the air. She looked so . . . regular. I took a deep breath. "Mom, about those clothes?"

"Do I look okay?" She smoothed the front of her skirt and fingered the second button on her blouse. "Should I button this one?"

I shook my head. "It's not that," I said, hesitating.

"What, then? The color? Too bland?"

"You got them on credit."

She stood up straighter. "It's nothing to be ashamed of."

"*My* credit."

She narrowed her eyes a little. "Kayla, we're a team."

"I know," I said, much too quickly, immediately regretting that I'd agreed with her. "Maybe you could check with me next time. If you think you might want to do it again."

"Check with you," she echoed.

"I might have plans for it. For the credit." I felt flustered, and I couldn't call it *my* credit any longer. I'd become unsure of whose it really was.

She turned her face away and chuckled, unsuccessfully trying not to laugh in my face. "Honey, how many pairs of jeans and T-shirts do you need?"

I couldn't answer. I'd blush if I said I wanted some different clothes now, sexier clothes, even. Something more flattering. She'd love that, and she'd try to take over, insisting I shop with her and try on all these ridiculous things, probably drag me down to Victoria's Secret. And what if she got more suspicious about Remy? Right then, I did not want her to have a shred of awareness about my feelings for him. Especially because they didn't matter anymore and never had.

"Forget it," I said, turning away. I grabbed a magazine and leaned against the counter, pretending to browse through it. "Will you be gone all day?"

She picked up a folder labeled *Resumé* and slid one arm through the strap of her purse, being careful not to touch anything with her nails. "It's all on the calendar. Open the door?"

I kicked the door open and stuck my face back in the magazine.

"Kayla?" She touched my shoulder lightly.

I turned a magazine page and didn't look up. "What?"

"You're my main girl. You know that?"

I just shrugged, but I guess that was a positive enough answer for her.

"You need a ride into town?"

"No. I've gotta do Rebel."

She ran the engine while she applied lipstick, craning her neck toward the rearview mirror. I took a deck of cards off the counter and laid them out for solitaire and remembered the poker games Hal had taught me in the back of his van. I used to shiver in my underwear on warm Dallas nights, waiting for him to bet. Hal liked to play for clothes, and, as with everything else Hal wanted, I'd played along. Mom wanted me to be her rock and her main girl, and Remy wanted me to be as thin as a chopstick. I shoved the cards into a pile. Who did *I* want to be?

Elvis had gotten used to riding on my shoulder or in my pocket as I moved around the trailer, and I'd even taken him with me on walks. I kept sunflower seeds in one pocket for him. Putting Elvis in my shirt pocket now, I headed down to Sam's, but when I saw Remy's bus in the driveway, I kept going. Rebel saw me and barked, and it pained me, but I walked faster. Maybe Remy would be gone later, I thought, and then he wouldn't have to see me. I'd walk the dog then. I kept going, but it was hard to ignore Rebel's barking.

When I got to Shirley and Sherrie's, they were in the middle of an argument. Shirley noticed me edging out the door and called out, "Hold on, Kayla, we're almost finished." Thirty seconds later, they'd agreed to disagree, and it was over. Sherrie left to do an errand, and I remarked, "You sure disagree on a lot of things."

"Comes with the territory," said Shirley. "When you live with someone for twenty-six years, you find plenty to disagree about."

"You've been roommates for that long?"

"I guess you could call it that," Shirley said.

Later, when Cocoa and I returned from his walk, they were apologizing to each other in the back hallway. Before they noticed me,

Shirley leaned over and gave Sherrie a kiss on the lips. They turned and caught me staring at them. Shirley said, "Here, I'll take Cocoa."

I gave the dog's leash to her, and she coaxed him into the Dog Palace. Sherrie joked, "For a while there, I thought she was going to move herself back into the Palace."

I followed Sherrie out to the counter. Embarrassed, I blurted, "Is that why you keep so much food in that room? So one of you can live there sometimes?"

Sherrie opened a box of jewelry and sorted the items. "Nah. Those are our emergency rations. The way the world is going, you just might need to hole up for a while—earthquake or fire or nuclear disaster, you know what I mean? And that's another thing Shirl and I don't agree on. She says if disaster strikes, we'll deal with it, but I like to be prepared."

"I wouldn't mind taking refuge there once in a while," I said.

"Oh, yeah?" Sherrie continued laying out pairs of earrings. "You and your mom ever straighten out that credit arrangement between the two of you?"

"Kind of. I guess she needs my help. She's just getting back on her feet."

"Huh," said Sherrie, holding an earring to her ear and looking in a mirror. "We're going over to Gallup to my niece's wedding this weekend. I've got two gals covering the shop, but I could use some help with Cocoa. Walk him two, three times a day, Saturday and Sunday."

"I can do that."

"I tried to get someone to stay overnight with him. He gets nervous by himself. Barks all night, bothers the neighbors."

"I could take him to our place," I offered.

She shook her head. "He hates strange places. He'll bark there, too."

I felt a rush of excitement. "I'll stay with him in the Palace, then."

Sherrie frowned. "You're kind of young to stay on your own."

"Not really. My mom has left me alone plenty of times."

She raised her eyebrows. "Oh?"

"It's okay, really. I don't mind. Please, Sherrie, I'll ask her." I thought about my mom and Redbone. "Sometimes she can use some time to herself, too."

"Well, see what she says."

Just then, Shirley came out of the Palace and set her keys and the black canvas bag she used as a purse on the counter. "Ask who about what?"

"Kayla's going see if she can stay in the Palace with Cocoa Saturday night."

Shirley gave Sherrie a dark look. "Whose idea was that?"

Sherrie glanced over at me and back at Shirley. "We both came up with it."

Shirley put one hand on her hip. "It's nothing about you, Kayla. But you're only fifteen."

"Nearly sixteen."

"Let's just see what her mother says, all right?"

"Sher," said Shirley, "can I talk to you? Alone?"

I couldn't bear to see my opportunity fizzle. "Please. My mom has this boyfriend. And our trailer's so damn small."

That stopped them in their tracks. I had no idea whether Mom and Redbone would go public with me this weekend, but Shirley and Sherrie didn't have to know that. Sure enough, although Shirley scowled, she relented. "See what your mother says, then. Sherrie, I'm going to find shoes to match my outfit. Nothing here works with it." She rolled her eyes. "Weddings."

While she went to get her outfit from upstairs, Elvis, who had been sleeping, poked his head out of my pocket. Sherrie saw him and smirked. She unzipped the top of Shirley's bag and held her hands out to me. "Give me the little love." She slipped the rat inside Shirley's large bag along with her keys, zipped the bag almost closed, and winked at me.

Shirley bustled out of the Palace, plastic-covered pants suit in hand, and seized her bag. "Where did my keys go?" she asked.

"I put them in your bag so you wouldn't forget them," said Sherrie.

"Since when do I forget my keys?"

Sherrie patted Shirley's shoulder. "Just trying to be helpful."

Shirley said, "You two are up to something."

I sucked in my cheeks to keep from smiling. Shirley swooped out of the store.

"Better follow her." Sherrie nudged me toward the door.

"Aren't you coming?"

"Of course. I wouldn't miss this for anything."

When Shirley dug into the oversized purse for her keys, it was Sherrie's name she bellowed at the top of her lungs. I ran to the car to take Elvis out of the bag, hoping he wasn't traumatized. As I reached for him, Shirley hissed, "I'll get her for this."

She looked furious, but I had a feeling it wouldn't last. I marveled at the two of them. I'd never seen a relationship like theirs.

TWENTY

"You want to sleep where?"

It was Saturday. I had waited until almost the last minute to ask about spending the night in the Dog Palace so that Mom wouldn't have time to change her mind once she said yes. I had given her one hundred dollars the day before, plus the usual fifty for rent—a huge portion of what I'd managed to save since asking Shirley and Sherrie to pay me mostly in cash—so that she didn't have to use the credit card or try to borrow more money from New Horizons for food. I had already explained what and where the Dog Palace was, but Mom wasn't listening. She checked the purchases she'd made with my money against a list someone at the health-food store had given her—a tiny bottle of brown liquid called St. John's wort, a box labeled *Liver Cleanse,* sandalwood incense, a CD of Gregorian chants, and another bottle labeled *Lavender Essential Oil.* She held up the last item and read, "Add two to three drops to the bath. Enjoy the relaxing vibrations of this pure essential oil."

"Shirley and Sherrie's Dog Palace," I repeated, picking up a receipt that had floated to the floor. $68.44. Damn. What was all this garbage?

She squinted at the bottle. "We don't have a bath."

"Mom, did you hear what I'm asking?"

She opened the bottle of oil and dabbed a couple of drops on her wrist. "Kayla, why do you want to sleep at their place?"

"I'm dog-sitting. They're going to Gallup for the weekend, and the dog gets scared when he's left alone overnight."

She held her wrist out to me. "Nice, huh?"

I sniffed obligingly. "Can I go?"

She rested her hands in her lap. "By yourself?"

"I don't mind. Plus, it'll give you a chance to have some alone time."

Screwing the cap onto the tiny bottle, she said, "I'm not crazy about this, but I guess it's okay." She opened the Liver Cleanse box and examined the contents. "Promise me you won't leave there until morning and you won't have anybody over."

"I'll only walk the dog."

She shook an instruction pamphlet at me. "*Call* me if you want to come home. Even if it's two in the morning."

Wake my mother to pick me up? It was hard to take her offer seriously. I'd rather wake a bear out of hibernation than try to rouse my mother out of a deep, possibly alcohol-induced sleep or tear her from the hairy arms of the latest object of her affection.

Impulsively, I kissed her on the cheek. "I won't need to call you. I'll be fine there."

Late that afternoon, I made myself a box of macaroni and cheese and took off for the Palace, leaving my mom to her incense and Gregorian chants. At that moment, I was so glad to have an evening in the Palace on my own, I wouldn't have cared if Redbone did join her.

Shirley and Sherrie had already gone. The roll-top desk in the Dog Palace stood open, and a note on it said to make myself at home and be sure to lock all the doors and windows when I left. A framed photograph on the desk showed the two women looking much younger, each with an arm around the other, standing by a sign for Grand Canyon National Park.

I made a nest of pillows on the floor and took a nail file, polish, remover, a blues CD that Remy had lent me, and a notebook and pen from my backpack. Cocoa sniffed everything, licked my hand, and returned to his bed.

I put on the CD and turned up the volume. The music exploded into the room, sultry saxophone and stormy piano and drumming that made me want to strut around the room and swing my hips. I listened to it as I did my nails, which took a while, because I'd never painted them before. When I was done, I danced, waving my fingers to dry the polish and moving whichever way the music lured me. Cocoa barked so hard, his whole body rose off the floor. After a while, he saw that I was just having a good time and lay down, only his eyes following me as I strutted and twirled.

When the CD ended, I flopped onto the daybed to catch my breath, and I opened the drawers underneath. Staples like canned beans and tuna crowded them, along with jars of more exotic fare like marinated artichokes and capers. The stuff must have been there awhile, because everything had a layer of dust on it. In the back of the right-hand drawer sat a tampon box, which seemed odd, because the two women looked old enough not to need those anymore. Then I saw the corner of a ten-dollar bill sticking out of the box. I opened it, and it was full of money—twenty- and fifty- and hundred-dollar bills—the denominations all mixed together. I dumped the money and counted it: three thousand dollars. It looked like a fortune, and I was tickled that the two women trusted me around it—or had they forgotten it was there? I replaced everything and closed the drawers.

I tried on my black tank top with short skirts and tight pants I borrowed from the store, eventually returning them to the racks and stepping into my own jeans. I found scissors, trimmed my hair a little, and applied styling gel to give my hair a spiky, windblown look. My reflection in the bathroom mirror said "just out of bed" more than "windblown," but that wasn't such a bad style, either. I added lipstick, then wiped half of it off.

I put on my sheer long-sleeved blouse over the tank, hooked Cocoa's leash on him, and slipped a small bag of dog treats—now only one-quarter dipped in chocolate—into my pocket. Just before

I left the store, I shrugged off the sheer blouse and left it behind.

Terra Luna was playing at Billy's, and I couldn't take Cocoa in there. Even without the dog, I wouldn't have gone in—I didn't want to get caught again stinking of smoke. I planned to ask the bouncer to let Remy know on a break that I was outside, but there he was, outside Billy's already, talking to a girl who was taking long drags on a cigarette.

Remy did a double take, walked over to me, and gave me a huge, gorgeous smile. I could just about hear my heart go *ping* as that little bubble of resentment I'd been holding burst into nothing. If he was upset that I hadn't walked Rebel the other day—if he'd even noticed—he didn't show it.

"You're working late," he said, nodding toward Cocoa, who sat squarely on my foot.

"I'm staying overnight with him while Shirley and Sherrie are off at a wedding."

Remy crouched down and rubbed Cocoa's head.

"I need to walk the dog again later. Want to come with us?"

Eva stuck her head out the tavern door, called, "Two minutes!" and vanished inside.

"There is something I'd like to talk to you about," Remy said. "Midnight's not too late?"

My heart lurched. "Just knock on the back entrance, off the alley."

When the knock came and I opened the door, Remy stood there holding a bunch of grapes. "For you," he said. "And me."

I smiled, trying to relax. "Thanks. You want to come in?"

"Can we walk?" he asked. "I'm kind of wound up from the gig."

"Sure." I got Cocoa and his leash. We ambled down the street, heading away from the center of town, popping grapes into our mouths. The air held a sweet tang that I couldn't identify, and we moved in and out of shadows. Sometimes, in the darkness, we bumped against each other. We kept apologizing at the same time.

Remy cleared his throat. Here it comes, I thought. He's going to come clean about what's wrong with me. Why he wants to stop seeing me, or why we'll never be more than friends. Suddenly, I wanted him to get it over with, and I felt a twinge of anger that he'd been stringing me along.

"My dad is throwing me out," Remy began. "He asked me to leave, anyway. Or pay rent. He knows I can't do that. I'm close to making a break, but he . . ." Remy stopped, wrapped his arms around his chest, and bit his lip.

I waited, still expecting him to announce that he was done with me, barely taking in what he'd said.

He shrugged. "It's tough when someone doesn't believe in you."

He was confiding in, not dumping, me? Telling me about his troubles? My heart went out to him. I was no stranger to being evicted, and he sounded genuinely distressed.

"I don't know, Remy," I said, so relieved that I wanted to hug him. "You sounded great the other night. Everyone in that room thought so. Maybe your dad just doesn't understand."

"That's for sure."

"Where will you go?"

He sighed. "There's always the bus. My home sweet home on the road. It wouldn't be the first time I've slept in it. Eva said I could park it in her driveway."

"What about Rebel?"

He made two fists and tapped one with the other. "Bingo. Eva's landlord won't allow dogs, and Rebel will go nuts if he has to stay in the bus." Remy rolled his eyes. "*He's* welcome at my dad's, if you're willing to keep taking care of him. The crazy thing is, my dad's going to Europe for three months, but he wants the house painted while he's gone. He said I could stay there if I did the painting."

Painting in exchange for a place to stay seemed like a good deal to me, but maybe that kind of work was the kiss of death for an aspiring musician like Remy.

"As if I have time for painting," he went on. "One minute he's nagging me to stay focused. The next he's trying to stick a paintbrush in my hand."

"Sorry," I murmured. "Hey, don't worry about Rebel. I can handle him."

"You're a sweetheart," he said.

Taking an awkward step toward Remy, I put a hand on his shoulder. Just to be supportive. Cocoa barked, and I turned to see what was disturbing him, but it was only the wind rustling a nearby tree. Remy slipped his arms around me, and with a shock, I felt his lips on the back of my neck. I pulled away. He turned me around, took my face in his hands, drew me gently toward him, and kissed me—a warm, moist, soft, lips-on-lips kiss.

I closed my eyes, confused and trying to think. I wondered if I should stop him, and I decided I would when he started groping. That was what always came next.

He didn't grope. He just kept kissing me. I dropped the remaining grapes and pushed him gently away.

"Is this okay?" he asked.

I wasn't sure. Energy buzzed through every cell in my body. Without waiting for my answer, he moved close again, this time spinning me around slowly as we kissed, almost as if we were dancing. This is so romantic, I thought, but part of me had flown up to the top of the nearby telephone pole and watched from above like some voyeuristic bird. I tried to keep my mouth soft like his, not sure what to do with my tongue, fighting an urge to press my lips together, trying to recall how people kissed in the movies. We spun and kissed until I bumped into an adobe wall and he leaned gently against me, and I kept trying to come up with an answer to his question: *Is this okay?* It had to be, because he kissed the way he touched—softly, unhurried, lightly touching my arm or my hair or running a finger along my ear. Hal would've been all over me by now. Rushing. Trying to see what he could get away with next.

I broke it off. "It's okay. *Too* okay." He took my hand and we walked back to the store. Thinking how I must have misjudged him, I burst out laughing.

"What's so funny?" he asked.

I couldn't stop grinning. "I didn't expect you to kiss me."

He scratched the back of his neck. "Yeah, well, I didn't expect you to show up tonight looking so good with that ridiculous little excuse for a dog, and then . . ." He leaned forward and kissed me again. I wasn't the Dog Shit Girl. He liked all kinds of girls. All shapes. A giggle rose inside me, forcing me to break off the kiss, and he laughed, too.

Right before Remy left me at the store, he said, "One more thing about Rebel."

"What's that?"

He grimaced. "Unfortunately, there won't be any more money for taking care of the beast. Dad's cutting it off, and I can barely feed myself right now." He took my hand as he spoke, massaging it lightly with his. Smiling apologetically, he asked, "Can you handle that, just for a little while?"

My hand is connected to my toes, I thought, and to everything in between. "It's okay," I said.

He kissed me again and left, but a few minutes later, I heard another knock on the door. Remy stood there, smiling strangely. I was thrilled that he wanted more time with me.

"Ran out of gas," he said. "I thought I had enough to get to Eva's."

I knew I shouldn't let him in. What if Mom came by to check on me, or Shirley and Sherrie came home early? Still, I stepped aside and made a sweeping, inviting gesture with my arm.

He laughed. "No, no, I just need a little gas money."

"Oh," I said, hoping I didn't sound disappointed. I dug a bill out of my pocket. I had a ten. I had planned to take myself out to breakfast in the morning. "That's all I have."

"That'll do."

I hesitated just a millisecond before handing him the money.

"You're an angel," he told me, pocketing the bill, kissing my temple, and walking off into the night.

I jammed my hands into my empty pockets, hoping there'd be something worth eating at our trailer in the morning.

TWENTY-ONE

When I got Rebel the next day, Sam was perched on a stool in the kitchen, talking on the phone. "No, he's gone," Sam said. "I asked him to leave." Rebel bounded over to me. "Yes, the dog only, Sarah," Sam said, sounding irritated. Sarah was Remy's mother's name. "I'm done with the rest. I thought we agreed it was time." He glanced at me. "Hold on." He covered the receiver. "Are you all set?"

I nodded. "Just getting the leash."

"Here." He held out a ten-dollar bill. "Remy asked me to give this to you for some extra work you did."

Without thinking, I blurted, "I haven't done anything extra."

Sam folded the bill in half with one hand. "You haven't?"

"He ran out of gas," I explained uneasily, feeling caught between the two of them, "and I loaned him some money. Maybe that's what he means." I hoped his dad would be pleased that Remy was paying me back so quickly.

Sam spoke into the phone again. "That was Kayla—she walks his damn dog. Now he's borrowing from her. And lying about it." He offered me the money again and I took it. "No, Sarah, I'm covering it for now, until he gets a piece of my mind."

Pocketing the bill, I opened the door and slipped out after Rebel. Maybe Remy had lied to his dad, but he'd paid me back right away. *Shady*, I imagined Shirley saying. Sherrie would add, *Watch out for moochers.* I fingered the money in my pocket. The bill was crisp and new. Whatever was going on between Remy and his dad had nothing to do with me.

The trailer was dead still, and I knocked on my mother's closed bedroom door. "Are you in there, Mom?"

"I'm in here." Her voice was full of defeat, and my stomach turned over.

"What are you doing?"

She didn't answer right away. "Celebrating," she said finally.

"Did you get the job?"

"I got a job."

"Hey! Congratulations."

She didn't speak.

"Mom?"

"What, Kayla?"

"Isn't that a good thing?"

She exhaled loudly. "It's not the bank job."

"So what? What is it?"

"Cashier. At the Circle K. Not part of my vision."

"Well, so what? At least it's a job."

"Now you sound like Bell."

"Mom?"

She didn't answer. I heard the bedsprings squeak and the snap and hiss of a pop-top can opening. I checked for the beer in the cupboard. Gone.

I imagined barging into her room, grabbing the beer, pouring it down the drain. I would yell at her—*What the hell are you doing?*

Instead, I stood in the kitchen, my feet stuck to the linoleum.

Don't make it any worse than it already is, Kayla. Don't make a big deal out of a few beers.

Four beers weren't that much. I could stop her if she went out for more. Better to let this blow over. The stakes were too high, and we were doing okay. She had a job. I wouldn't have wanted to work at the damn Circle K, either.

I opened our last can of refried beans and warmed some stale tortillas, but when I knocked on Mom's door, she said she wasn't hungry.

Redbone showed up at dusk, looking for Mom. For the first time,
he wasn't wearing a baseball cap, and he looked different. He kept
smoothing his hair over a bald spot.

"She's not feeling well," I told him. "She's lying down."

"Did she say how her interview went?"

I felt surprised that he knew about it, but maybe I shouldn't have
been. "She got a job, but not that one. Not at the bank."

"You tell her congratulations from me, okay?"

I nodded.

He headed for his truck. "I've got a new water heater. I'll bring it
over tomorrow."

"It's about time," I muttered, but not loud enough for him to hear.

Mom slept late the next morning. Worried that she would miss her
first day on the job, I made coffee for her, then knocked lightly on her
door. She didn't answer. My heart skittering, I peeked in.

The shades were down. She rolled over and blinked at me. "What
time is it?"

"Eight-thirty."

"Let me sleep. I'm not getting trained until ten."

She emerged an hour later wearing jeans, boots, and a short-
sleeved blouse and carrying her old fringed backpack. She'd pulled
her hair back and put on lipstick crookedly. She turned down my
offer of toast.

"Redbone's putting in a new water heater today," I said.

"That's good," she said, rubbing her temples. She took two aspirin
out of a bottle and swallowed them down with the last dregs of our
orange juice, making a face like it hurt to swallow. "Thanks for making coffee," she said. She started to write on the calendar but dropped

the pen and didn't bother to pick it up. "Kayla, I'm done at two. I'll be home after that."

"Could you get some food on your way home?"

"If you've got some change." Reluctantly, I took the ten from my pocket and gave it to her.

She dropped the money into her pack. "How's my lipstick?"

"Fine," I lied.

She turned to leave. "Hold on," I said. I got a tissue and wiped the part that made her bottom lip look lopsided. She kept her eyes down as I worked on her. As soon as I finished, I took off for Sam's, pretending I hadn't seen her hands shaking like cottonwood leaves on a windy day.

Rebel clicked after me as I peeked into the room where Remy had stayed. The bed was neatly made and the room looked as if he'd never been there. After walking Rebel, I chained him up and he barked at me. I wished I could keep him with me.

I was relieved to see the Escort gone. I'd been worried that Mom might not go to her new job. I found four empty beer cans in a bag under her bed, but I left them there. I didn't want her to know I'd been snooping.

When Redbone showed up a little later with a six-pack and no water heater, I met him on the porch.

"She's at her new job."

"I'll just leave this for her." He held out the six-pack.

I ignored it. "What about the water heater?"

He scratched behind one ear. "Had some trouble with it. I'm gonna have to fix it." He thrust the beer at me. "Just thought I'd bring a little something. 'Cause it's taking so long."

I almost said, *What are we supposed to do with the beer, take showers with it?* but I stopped myself. I knew I could hide the beer or pour it out, but he'd just keep on bringing more. "Redbone," I said, my voice halting, "she doesn't like to say so herself, but she's taking a break from drinking. It makes her sick."

He adjusted his cap. "Kayla, I haven't seen her turn down a drink yet. 'Cept for that first day I laid eyes on you two."

I glanced away. A couple of chickadees chattered in a nearby scraggly bush. "It's hard for her," I said. "But she wants to stop."

He looked at the beer, considering. "Okay," he said, rubbing his forehead. "That's good to know." Before he got into his truck, he asked, "Kayla, if I stop bringing beer around, will you get to liking me any more?"

I thought about it. "Maybe."

Nodding, Redbone got in his truck and drove away.

TWENTY-TWO

Circle K gave Mom the three-to-eleven shift. She grumbled about it, but she went. When I got paid the Friday after she started, I had to loan her another hundred and fifty for rent and food and the phone bill, since she wasn't getting her paycheck for another week. But I made her promise to use the money only for those three things. "And cigarettes," she said. I glared at her. "You don't want me trying not to smoke," she said, "not when I'm starting this shit job." By some miracle, I still had a hundred dollars in the bank, and I sure wasn't going to add anything this week. After Mom drained my pockets, I had only a few dollars left.

I started slipping out early for extra time with Rebel. Not that I was getting paid for it, but I didn't care. Up beyond the overhang where Remy first took me, the whole valley spread out at our feet, a gigantic sculpture in browns and reds and yellows. Sam's house looked small, our trailer appeared tiny, and I'd imagine my mom no bigger than a flea. Up on those hills with Rebel, all was right with the world.

The dog liked to investigate coyote tracks, rabbit trails, and deer droppings. He ran ahead and stopped often to wag his tail at me. He was obedient, too, except when he saw a rabbit. Lucky for the rabbits, they always got away. Even when he ignored my commands to come back, I loved the sight of him streaking across the high desert, his fur bright red-gold in the slanted morning light. When he finally gave up the chase, he'd come running back to me, a furry torpedo of joy. It was hard then not to wish he were mine.

Some mornings, I took my poetry notebook up with me, or one of the poetry books I'd saved. I came up with a dozen or more endings for "What You Want," but they were pathetic: *It's all the rainbow colors/after a raging storm. It finds you in the dark/when you're cold, scared, and lonely/or when you're buying oranges/or taking out the trash.* I tried writing other poems, but all I could get were fragments—lines about prickly pear cactus laden with purple fruit or hawks turning dizzying circles in the sky. I was sure it had all been written before.

When he could, Remy picked me up at the trailer around four o'clock on the afternoons that Mom worked. We'd get Rebel and drive someplace where the dog could go free again. We held hands, kissed now and then, or stopped to sit on a rock together, our arms around each other. After a while, we'd go back to the bus, where Remy now had a piece of foam for sleeping. The first time he took me there, I was nervous. Hal and the train came to mind. Remy got in, but I went and sat on a boulder. I couldn't go into that bus. I knew it would change everything between us, and I wasn't ready for that.

Remy came and sat next to me. "Have you been with other guys?"

Every guy wants to know that, but most ask it in the first two minutes. It took Remy two months, so I didn't mind as much answering. "No guys. Just some gorillas."

He threw back his head and howled.

I added, "You've been kind of different."

With a fingertip, he traced my hairline and behind my ear. "What do you mean?"

I thought hard about my answer. "You know what I like more than I do," I said. "And you don't seem to want anything for yourself. You know. Physically."

He stood up. "Kayla, when's your eighteenth birthday?"

I hesitated before lying. "In a few months. Halloween."

"Okay," he said. "I'll make a deal with you. From now until Halloween, I get to make up to you for all the heavy-handed gorillas you've been with."

"I don't understand."

"We keep our pants on. Nothing heavy. Nothing that could get you pregnant. If it doesn't feel good, you say so and I stop."

I couldn't picture what he meant. Impulsively, I asked, "So you're staying away from the produce?"

He looked puzzled. Embarrassed, I explained how my mom named body parts different fruits, vegetables, or kinds of terrain. He ran his eyes over me slowly, then looked away. "No exotic vacations, and I'm staying out of the store."

I was really confused. "So what are we going to do?"

"I'm an artist, Kayla," he said, smiling mischievously. "I make it up as I go along. You'll have to trust me."

I wrapped my arms tightly around my stomach. "Okay, let's say I trust you. Then after Halloween, what? You turn into a gorilla?"

He chuckled. "No, after that, we're equals. I tell you what I like, see if you like it, too."

I walked a few paces away. "This is about my age, right? You think it matters?"

"I don't. But the State of New Mexico might."

"You're afraid we might get in trouble?"

He looked down at the ground and rubbed the dirt with his sneaker. "There was a time when another girl's parents and I didn't see eye to eye about my relationship with her."

"What happened?"

"We got involved. They got upset."

"My mother doesn't even know about you."

"And why doesn't she?"

I wasn't sure where he was going with this. "Well, you haven't come around."

"I don't get the feeling you want me to."

"She might think you're too old."

"What do you think?"

I shrugged and tried to keep my voice even when I answered. "I don't think age has to matter."

"Will you tell her about me when you're eighteen?"

I swallowed. "Maybe. She's kind of unpredictable."

"In what way?"

"She's overprotective." I sat down near him. "Or she's drunk."

"Oh." He put an arm around my shoulders.

"Remy, with that other girl, did you get in trouble with the law?"

"Briefly."

"They care even if it's a two-way street? If both people agree?"

"Even if it's a two-way street or a six-lane east-west highway, some people get their hackles up. The law isn't enforced the first time. Trouble is, I've been down this road once before."

I felt a little queasy. "How old was she?"

"Fifteen."

He looked kind of anxious, and I had to walk away again. My stomach was doing a dance, and I held myself, trying to settle it. "Did you hurt her? Physically, I mean."

He looked me in the eye. "Honest to God's truth: no. I would never do that."

I had a lot more questions, but mostly for the girl. Maybe I should have walked away right then—I had half a mind to—but we were miles from town, and the truth was, I wanted to believe him. Nothing he'd ever done gave me reason not to.

I told him, "You have a deal." He held out his hand, and he led me to the bus. I climbed into the back and sat on his makeshift bed. After closing the door, he sat on his knees and looked at me for a long time. He rummaged in a duffel bag until he found a small plastic bottle, set it aside, and told me to lie back. I took a deep breath and did. He pulled off my boots and socks and sat cross-legged so he could put my feet in his lap. He poured something from the bottle into his hands—it looked like oil—rubbed his hands together, and smoothed the stuff—it was oil—over my ankles and feet. He spread it between my toes and under the arches. As he massaged each foot, his thumbs rolled over the small muscles, his fingertips probing every spot.

At first, I got really relaxed, but after a while, a tight feeling spread across my chest. I closed my eyes. Outside, a wind came up and whined, and once, I felt the bus sway from the force of it. I thought about Hal, and the tightness became sadness that rolled up from my belly, and even though I tried not to cry, it spilled out as tears.

Remy watched me. He saw me wipe my eyes and didn't say a word. When I started to cry hard, he stopped massaging but still held my feet. I had to curl on my side. He curled up behind me and held me.

"Sorry," I whispered.

"It's okay," he said. "It's just your own poem. Your own song." I wasn't sure what he meant by that, but it sounded nice. "What's it about?" he asked.

Too many things, mixed up, I thought. It was Hal and my mother and my no-name father and a dog that was mine but wasn't. "I can't explain."

When I was calm and the windows of the bus had darkened with the sky, I rolled toward Remy and planted my mouth on his. He kissed back briefly. "Time to take you home."

I started spending time with Remy whenever I could, squeezing in visits between my jobs and his trips to play gigs out of town. When we got into the back of his bus, it was always more of the same—I don't think a girl's limbs have ever been more lovingly touched. I got more foot massages, plus hand, scalp, and ear massages, neck and shoulder and lower-leg rubs. We also hiked or found places to sit out-doors while I read or tried to write poems and he worked on songs. Sometimes we lay on our backs while Remy named the clouds: big fluffy story clouds, rippling mackerel skies, wispy mares' tails that answered questions by pointing in one direction or the other. When-ever Remy asked me how my "song" was going, I'd say, "I'm working on it," and we'd leave it at that.

Mom went out with Redbone more often, and sometimes she didn't come home until after midnight, so I slipped out to hear Remy play when Terra Luna did local gigs. When he saw me coming, the bouncer at Billy's scowled, but he looked the other way.

Mom and I crossed paths briefly in the morning or right before she went to work, and sometimes not even then. The day I noticed that the quartz crystals were gone from the table, I went investigating. I found the beautiful rock under Mom's bed with the empty beer cans, except now there were more cans, plus an empty bourbon bottle. My heart sank, but Mom was getting to her job each day, and between walking the two dogs, working occasionally in Sherrie and Shirley's store, and seeing Remy, everything seemed to be working okay.

One day, I got home from walking the dogs and found Mom sleep-ing in her room. Her shades were drawn, the room smelled sour, and I was tempted to open the window, but I didn't want to wake her. A couple of bags of clothing with tags on them sat on the floor.

On the answering machine was a message from Bell: "Marilyn, I'm worried about you. I've left three messages you haven't returned. Please call me." Then Redbone's voice came on: "The water heater's finally ready. When I bring it by tomorrow, how about a cup of coffee together?"

I found a couple of half-smoked Marlboro Lights on the kitchen table next to a copy of Mom's resumé. A nearly empty glass of soda sat on top of the resumé, and when I lifted the glass, it left a brown ring on the paper. I was about to toss it when I noticed the smell of rum. I groaned. Mom used to get sick as a dog from drinking rum.

I was hungry, and there was nothing to eat in the house, even though I'd given her thirty-five dollars for groceries the day before. I had seven dollars left, and I'd just learned from Shirley and Sherrie that Mom had helped herself to more than half of the hundred and twenty-five dollars I'd built up in credit, telling them we'd talked about it and I was cool. I threw the towel onto the counter, stormed back to my mother's room, and pushed the door open. "I need you to get up!"

Mom sat up and raised one hand, as if my words were arrows she had to fend off. "Stop yelling!" she hissed. "Just stop! Jesus, Kayla, can't you see I'm sleeping?"

She flopped back onto the bed, covering her head with the pillow. I grabbed it and pulled it off. "What did you do with the money I gave you yesterday?"

She lay there with her hands on her head. "Kayla, I am so dizzy. I can't even sit up." She burped loudly. "Kayla . . ."

I knew what was coming. I ran to the bathroom for the trash can, shoved it into her hands, and left the room, slamming the door behind me. The sounds of her vomiting carried down the hall of the rickety trailer.

By the time Mom got up, over an hour later, I'd let Elvis run loose for a while, feeling grateful that rats cannot vomit—I'd read that in the rat-care book. I'd fumed about my mother: I hated her, but she was *sick*, right? Wasn't that what the social worker had told me the year I stayed with the Patellas? That Mom was alcoholic and sick and needed treatment? And then she got that treatment, a whole year of it, while I got a year at the Patellas. Maybe there was something else wrong with her.

She appeared, rubbing her head, her face pale and pinched.

I said, "You look like hell."

"Thanks for the compliment." She laid one hand on her belly as if it hurt.

"How much did you drink?"

She stared at me. "You don't need to concern yourself with that."

"If you aren't going to, that pretty much leaves me, doesn't it?

She fished in her backpack for cigarettes. "Kayla, I'm on my feet all afternoon and evening at this shit job, and I don't need you giving me a hard time or prying into my business."

"Mom, you didn't get any groceries yesterday. There's nothing to eat in this house."

She tapped a cigarette on the table and stood up, opening and closing the refrigerator and cabinets. "Here are some canned pears."

I buried my face in my hands. "For dinner?"

"And here's a can of corn. Go ahead—I'm too sick to eat."

"You got drunk."

"I'm just sick. Shouldn't have eaten that burrito at work yesterday. God knows how old that thing was."

"You don't think it has anything to do with the rum and Coke?"

She looked me straight in the eye. "No."

I put on my jacket and opened the door.

"Where are you going?" Mom asked.

I walked over to the calendar and wrote *Out*.

"It's on the calendar," I said.

I walked around town for a long time, first just wandering, then looking for Remy's bus, frustrated that I had no way of knowing where he was. I went by Luz's, but she wasn't there. I ended up at the thrift store, asking the women if they had something for me to do.

"There isn't much, is there, Shirl?" Sherrie was filing her nails. Shirley had her pink notebook open but wasn't writing.

156

"Pull up a stool," Shirley invited. "Victor just discovered that he's got the clue to a murder that's been all over the news, and he doesn't know how he came by it. You want to listen while I read it? I could use a little feedback."

I shook my head. "I'm not really up for that, Shirley. Sorry."

She closed her notebook. "How's your friend whose boyfriend keeps his hands to himself?"

I couldn't help smiling. "Oh, he warmed up to her. I guess there wasn't anything wrong with her."

Sherrie sniffed. "I don't doubt it."

I ducked my head and scratched my scalp. "There might be another problem, though."

"What's that, honey?"

"He's a little bit older than she is."

Shirley asked, "How much of a little bit?"

"Maybe eight or nine years."

"You said she was a lot older than you."

"I thought she was. Guess I was wrong."

The women exchanged glances. Shirley said, "Well, my grandmother wasn't more than sixteen when she married a thirty-seven-year-old logger. They had five kids, married for fifty-eight years. Can you imagine? Sixteen with a thirty-seven-year-old? But I guess it was more common then. They lived in Idaho. Weren't a lot of women in those logging camps."

"Was she happy?" I asked.

"Happy?" said Shirley. "I have no idea. She used to put hard-boiled eggs in the meatloaf, and Grandpa hated that. Fifty-eight years of hard-boiled eggs in the loaf. Every time she made it, he'd complain, and she'd always say, 'That's the way it's made, Franklin.'"

Sherrie came over to the counter where I was standing. She leaned her elbows on it. "Kayla, does your friend know about the trouble he got in a few years back?"

I felt my ears getting hot. "It didn't amount to much," I replied. "They dropped the charges when the girl wouldn't cooperate."

Sherrie said, "Well, she might've had good reason not to."

Shirley scowled. "What the heck are you talking about?"

"He's awfully cute," Sherrie said. "I think he's the next Elton John."

"He doesn't sound anything like Elton."

"You know what I mean. He's gonna go far."

"If he ever gets out of this town."

They both looked at me. I'm sure I was blushing furiously.

"He should probably get out soon," Sherrie said.

"For your friend's sake," added Shirley.

I moved toward the door. "I need to go."

"This friend of yours," said Sherrie. "She wouldn't be named Kayla, would she?"

I laughed at Sherrie's question. "I wish it *were* me."

TWENTY-THREE

From Big-Time Bargains, I went by Billy's to ask the bartender where I might find Remy. He told me where Eva lived, said Remy might be there.

To my relief, he was. Sounds of the band practicing drifted out of the small stucco house. As soon as Eva answered my knock, she said, "You probably want Remy," and she called for him. He came quickly and stepped out of the house, closing the door behind him.

"What's up?"

I was afraid I might start crying. "Can we walk?"

He hesitated, and I bit my lip and looked away. I really didn't want to cry right then. I didn't want to be such a baby.

He cracked open the door. "Guys, I'll be back in fifteen."

I heard groans and Eva's exasperated voice: "Remy, we're right in the middle."

"I'll be quick," he promised.

I managed to collect myself, and waited to speak until he'd shut the door. "It's okay. You should go back. I just wanted to see if I could hang out with you for a bit."

"I can swing by your place and pick you up in a couple of hours."

I shook my head. "Remy, I can't go home right now."

"Why not?"

"My mother's a mess. I just need some time out from her." Please, I thought, but I didn't say it. I didn't want to beg.

Putting an arm around my shoulder, he drew me toward him. The hug felt good.

"Come on in."

The others looked relieved when Remy rejoined them. He introduced me, saying, "Everyone, this is Kayla." They all said hi except Eva. "I guess every group needs its groupies," she said. "Come on, guys. Let's get this thing right."

They spent the next hour working on a blues piece about a gold miner who leaves his family to seek his fortune and winds up losing everything but his one-eyed mule, and then he loses her, too. Listening to Remy draw out the beautiful melody almost made me cry again. He sang it low and sweet, the deep tones vibrating through me. He swayed to the music and sometimes he looked at me as he sang.

They played it a number of times, stopping and starting as different band members interrupted to suggest a new riff here or an added harmony there. Once, Remy got into an argument with Eva, and he turned to me. "Which way did you like it better?" I liked Eva's way, and I said so, which surprised her. On a break a few minutes later, she told me that if I wanted anything to eat or drink, I should help myself.

After the practice, Eva went to pick up pizza and beer. Preston and Tye went out. Remy, Eva, and I drank beer and ate popcorn and watched a movie, the three of us sitting on the couch together, Remy's leg pressed against mine. I drank only one beer, but it made me a little lightheaded. Around ten o'clock, I called my mom.

"Where *are* you?" she asked.

"With friends," I told her. "In a safe place. And I'm staying out for the night."

She didn't say anything.

"You don't have to worry about me."

She spoke slowly. "Kayla, I need to know where you are."

"I'll call you tomorrow," I said, and hung up. Remy and Eva watched me. "I need a place to crash."

Eva stood up. "The couch is available," she said, looking straight at Remy. "There's a sleeping bag in the closet." She left the room.

Remy and I sat close on the couch. He started to kiss me but, I didn't feel like kissing. "Doesn't feel good," I mumbled, and he stopped, as quickly as if I'd pressed a magic button. Amazing. Hal hadn't ever seemed to know the meaning of the word "stop." Remy stayed close, and I felt like a sponge soaking up his warmth. He kissed my hair and my ear. I was confused. Part of me longed to stretch out next to him and feel that comforting closeness all night.

Instead, I pushed him away gently. "Still doesn't feel good," I said, needing some time to think. He moved a few inches away from me, putting his elbow on the back of the couch, resting his head on his hand. "What's going on?"

I told him about Mom, about her drunkenness and her lying. "I can't even tell anyone," I said. "If she gets in trouble, I'm cooked. I can't do more time in some stupid foster home." As soon as I'd said that, I realized my mistake.

He picked at a fingernail. "Kayla, if you're turning eighteen on Halloween, why would anyone try to put you in a foster home? Aren't you free at eighteen?"

I tried to laugh. "Of *course*. I'm so stupid sometimes. I keep forgetting. Everything will be different then." Agitated, I paced the room. "But it's not that simple, Remy. How can I just leave her when she's so sick?"

He locked his fingers behind his head. "What are you? Her mother?"

While I tried to think of an answer, he got the sleeping bag from the closet and spread it out on the couch. Without another word, he kissed the top of my head and went out to his bus. At first, I thought he went to get something. When he didn't come back, I got up to find him, and I heard the VW engine start up. By the time I opened the door, he was driving away.

I lay awake for a long time, listening for the bus and wishing I could sleep in the Dog Palace. I felt too lonely on this strange couch. Eventually, I dozed, but I slept fitfully. At dawn, Remy's bus was back, the curtains drawn. I wanted to go to him, but I wasn't sure I'd be welcome at that hour—or at all. He'd left so abruptly, I was certain he was upset. He had to know I'd been lying—or maybe being involved with me and my soap-opera family was just too much trouble.

In spite of my worries, I fell back to sleep. When I woke again, it was full daylight and the bus was gone. I found Eva drinking coffee in the kitchen. "There's plenty," she offered.

"No, thanks. I should go. Do you know when Remy will be back?"

She put her mug down and wrapped both hands around it. "I don't have a clue. Remy's kind of his own man."

Fortunately, Shirley and Sherrie were busy with customers when I picked up Cocoa, as well as when I dropped him off. Using the phone in the Dog Palace, I called to check on Mom, who acted as if there was no reason for me to be checking on her about anything. She asked, "When are you coming home?"

"When I'm ready," I said.

The walk to Sam's felt long. I sat in the doorway and let Rebel lick my face.

Redbone's truck faced the road, parked next to the Escort. A hot-water heater sat in the back. When I got near the trailer, I heard arguing. Redbone's voice carried out of my mother's bedroom window, and it scared me. He was practically yelling. Who did he think he was? My heart pounding, I ran inside.

Redbone stood in the doorway to Mom's room, his back to me. I started down the hall, but Mom's voice stopped me. She was crying, and while I couldn't make out most of her words, I heard my name.

Redbone spoke again, his voice low and bitter. "You got a kid, you got a job, what the hell are you doing?"

Mom let loose with more weepy, garbled words. I sagged against the wall, listening.

"How long do you think I'm gonna keep collecting from a child?" Redbone growled. "You're a disgrace like this. I gave you a break. You didn't even have the decency to tell me what was going on. Your daughter had to tell me. A kid!"

Redbone turned, holding a half-full whiskey bottle. He saw me, stopped, and went back to my mother. "Take it," he said, holding the bottle out to her. "You gotta decide. I'm not gonna tell you what to do. And I sure as hell hope your kid doesn't have to, either." He set the bottle on the floor next to her bed. As he passed me, he shook his head, saying, "I feel like an idiot. Should have seen this coming." He walked out to his truck, and I followed him to the porch.

"Redbone."

He leaned out of the truck window.

"She has been trying."

He started the engine. "She's going to have to try harder." He drove off, taking the new hot-water heater with him.

In our annoyingly quiet trailer, Remy's questions—*What are you? Her mother?*—repeated in my head. Several times, I headed for Mom's room, but I felt so repulsed at the thought of seeing her— weepy and sour-smelling and self-righteous—that I dropped back down on the sofa. I could handle the headaches, the nausea, the fragile appetite, the million and one complaints. I'd busted my butt to take care of her before, could do it again, but what for? I knew where this was heading.

Of all people, I thought, Mom should know how I feel. She hadn't wanted to take care of her mom, either.

I curled up and dozed, and when I woke, it hit me that I hadn't given Elvis a minute's attention in days. I found his water bottle empty. Tapping on the cage, I peered into his little house, relieved when he crept out. I filled his bottle immediately and he sipped frantically for a long time. With my door closed, I let him out. He ran as if he'd lost something and was trying desperately to find it. I slipped out of the room, leaving him loose to explore.

Luz called, wanting to get together. "I've got another Celie-free day tomorrow," she said. "Let's take Elvis out again. Or leave all of our creatures behind and go by ourselves."

I wanted to see her, but I didn't know what kind of shape Mom would be in and whether I should leave her again. Plus, I was hoping to hook up with Remy. "Can I call you back in the morning, Luz? I might be busy tomorrow."

"No problem," she said. "But grab me when you can. My free days don't come often."

I hung up, tempted to call right back. I'd had such a good time with her. While I debated what to do, Mom shuffled out of her room, one hand on the wall to steady herself, the other shielding her eyes from the light.

"Who was on the phone?"

"Someone for me."

"Good." She pulled a pack of cigarettes and a lighter from her robe pocket and stepped outside to smoke on the front porch, leaving the door open. Some of the smoke drifted in on the evening breeze. Disgusted, I got up and slammed the door. I listened to a phone message from Bell beseeching Mom to call her. I erased it.

When Mom returned, I told her that Bell had now called at least four times.

She said, "I know," and then she told me she had a new work schedule. "Seven to three, starting tomorrow."

We were doomed. She'd never get out the door in time for a seven o'clock start. That job was as good as over. The only way she might be ready for work at that hour was if I woke her, made coffee, and prodded her to dress and get out the door. I'd have to stop taking Rebel out early, and that was the best part of my day—the one good part I counted on. She opened the refrigerator, stared inside, and closed it. "Would you make me a piece of toast and bring it to me, Kayla? That would be a big help." Without waiting for my answer, she swayed back to her room.

The first piece of toast burned black while I sat on the steps outside resenting that I was making it for her. After successfully toasting the second piece, I discovered we didn't have any butter. I took it to her plain. If she was unhappy about that, she didn't say, and I wouldn't have cared if she did.

I decided to call Bell myself, but I vowed that if calling her led to some social worker telling me I had to go into foster care, I would leave. I had a little money saved, and maybe I could borrow more from Shirley and Sherrie and repay it later, after I'd set up a new pet-care business elsewhere. Or maybe I could go off someplace with Remy, if he wasn't angry with me.

Having a plan calmed me. Mom would have to be okay by herself, and if she wasn't, surely Bell would have a pack of social workers all over her.

There were a couple of other hitches—Rebel and Elvis—but that was more than I could plan for right now. If I had to leave, maybe I'd just take them both with me.

Bell came over right after I called her. She marched straight back to Mom's room and closed the door. Their muffled voices rose and fell for over an hour, Bell's like a steady river, low and continuous under Mom's higher-pitched outbursts. I wondered if I should have called Bell sooner.

Leaving a note on the table, I took myself down to see Rebel. He was excited about the unexpected nighttime walk. At the lower end of Sam's property, I lay down on a smooth stone slab and looked up at the stars. Rebel tried to lick me, but I pushed him away. Just when I started to get cold, a shooting star streaked across the sky. It happened so fast, I barely saw it. I waited, and after a while I saw another, and a few minutes later, a third. I remembered reading that meteor showers happen in August. Rebel came and went, his feet padding lightly on the soft earth. Solid rock below me, fleeting star trails above, I watched the sky and hugged myself to keep warm. I wished Remy were with me, but it would have been different, and for just a few minutes I wasn't sorry to be alone.

TWENTY-FOUR

Miracles do happen. Mom got up early the next morning, before my alarm rang, and took off for her job.

In the late afternoon, Remy showed up at our door, after I'd done all my pet care. Mom hadn't come home yet. He was grinning from ear to ear, and he hugged me hard.

"What's up?" I asked, relieved that he was glad to see me again.

"We got a sweet gig in Denver. Two weeks at a great club, and it's an awesome jumping-off point to bigger and better things." He hugged me again, and as he started to tell me more, I heard the Escort pull into the yard.

"Remy, that's my mom."

"Isn't she supposed to be at work?"

"New schedule."

"Listen," he said. "I came by because I want to take you up to the ruins."

Mom came in with a bag of groceries. She looked tired and pale, but her movements were steady. She stood for a moment, observing Remy and then me before setting her bag down.

"Remy." She nodded to him.

"Hi." He seemed almost shy.

"How've you been?" she asked.

"Great," he answered.

"What brings you over here?"

I got a soda from the refrigerator, popped it open, and took a swig. My jaw felt tight.

Remy cleared his throat. "I'm taking Kayla up to the ruins. Just for a look around." He cleared his throat again. "Have you been up there?"

Taking her cigarettes out of her leather backpack, she sat down heavily. "No, I haven't."

"Soda, Remy? Mom?" I offered.

Remy shook his head. Mom asked him, "What time will you bring her back?"

I felt so embarrassed. She acted as if I were ten years old. "Remy," I said, "why don't you just wait in the bus? I'll be right out."

He ignored me. "It's Marilyn, right?" he said to my mother.

"Yes."

"If it's all right with you, Marilyn, she'll be back after dinner. Eight or nine."

My mother tapped the cigarette pack against her hand until she could pull one out.

Remy asked, "Do you need us to pick up anything for you?"

Mom shook her head. "No, thank you."

"Remy." I glared at him. "I'll be right out."

"Okay," he said, and stepped outside.

I went to my bedroom to get my jacket and leave food for Elvis. When I returned, Mom asked, "How long have you been seeing him?"

"It's none of your business."

She scowled. "Do you know he had another girlfriend your age? Bell told me. It was all over the papers a couple of years ago."

"Bell is just a fountain of useful information, isn't she? Can she see into the future, too?"

"You don't know what you're getting into. What if you get pregnant?"

I was dimly aware that I wanted to hurt her more than I wanted to make any sense. "At least I know his last name."

She slammed the pack of cigarettes on the table. "Kayla—"

"Mom, you might not believe this, but I'm not sleeping with him. We're just friends."

She fumbled with a lighter, then lit her cigarette and drew deeply on it. "That's reassuring, especially since you've been lying for weeks."

"Have *you* considered that I'm not like you? That maybe I don't have sex with any jerk who leers at me—or offers me booze?"

For a long moment, she stared at me, and then she blew smoke at the ceiling. "You do not have my permission to go."

I laughed. "That's a joke. You should have my permission just to take one little baby step." Without waiting for her reply, I walked out.

As we drove away, my insides boiled. "Remy, what the hell were you doing?"

He glanced at me. "Just didn't want her to worry about her little girl." From behind the seat, Rebel tried to lick my hand. I fumed silently. Remy sang as he drove, and his voice took the edge off my anger. When he did the song he'd written for me, it was hard to stay mad at him.

At the ruins, we wandered up and down the ladders and staircases, sometimes separately, sometimes holding hands. We didn't say much. Remy had brought a bag of tortilla chips and salsa, and we ate them and licked the salt off our fingers while watching a glorious sunset from one of the ledges. As the sky blazed deep pink and purple, he gave me a long, salty kiss.

"Think the Anasazi kissed like that?" he asked me.

"Did they have salt?"

We watched as the colors in the sky faded to one strip of fiery orange-gold.

* * *

It was dark when we climbed into the bus and Remy told me that he and the band were moving to Denver. They would share an apartment, play their stint at a club called Gracie's, and start work on their first CD. This was great for him, but my insides sank. I asked, "When?"

"Preston and Eva have already gone up there to find other work and a place for all of us to live. Tye and I go as soon as we scrounge up gas money. We are so broke, it's scary. I may have to sell one of my guitars." He shrugged. "It'll be worth it."

I tried to smile. He drew me onto his lap, saying, "I wish you were coming with us." I nodded. He pulled me into a hug. "One more year of school and then you could join us."

"Us"? I thought. Why not "me"? Was I just a groupie, as Eva suggested?

He ran his fingers lightly up and down my spine. "Next best thing would be for you to send me off with the rest of that song you're writing."

Up to now, I'd liked the idea of giving him the rest of the poem, but the thought of his taking it to Denver bothered me. I'd always imagined us as a duo, collaborating on songs, sharing the glory when we got a hit. He hummed the melody he'd put to it in my ear. When he stopped, I asked, "What if it has no ending?"

He nibbled on my ear. "It has one. You just have to find it."

I had no idea my ears were so sensitive and so directly linked to every other part of me. My questions vanished. "Okay," I murmured.

He held me away from him, his fingers drumming on my shoulders. "Let's go celebrate."

"Where?"

"There's a good dance band at Billy's tonight—but I did tell your mama I'd get you home." He pulled out his watch. "About an hour from now."

"So? She doesn't run my life."

He adjusted his ponytail. "Maybe not, but I'll bet she could put a big crimp in mine."

I leaned into him again. "Remy, that time you got in trouble—why was it in the papers?"

His hand lightly smacked the steering wheel. "The girl's dad's a bigwig in local government. What should've been no more than a two-line blurb buried in the middle of the paper got blown up into a front-page feature. The charges were dropped. His daughter was furious at him. She left town as soon as she got together enough money."

"Were you embarrassed?"

"No. Pissed as hell, but not embarrassed. I didn't do anything wrong."

I looked into his handsome face, and then I kissed him. Underneath me, he was getting aroused, and I moved back to the passenger seat. "Forget my mother. Dancing sounds like fun."

Remy nodded, started the engine, then shut it off. "Kayla?"

"Yeah?"

"If we're going to keep this deal we've made, I'd better take you home."

"Maybe we don't need to keep the deal." I was scaring myself, but I felt sick about his leaving. Plus, I was feeling kind of worked up myself. And the last person I wanted to be around was my mother.

He crossed his arms on top of the steering wheel and leaned his head on them. "Kayla, I might be a fool for not agreeing to end the deal, but I'd be a bigger fool if I did anything to screw up, right when I'm making a break. And that mama of yours?" He started up the engine. "She's got daggers in her eyes."

"Okay, but don't take me home yet. You told her nine, and it's only seven-thirty."

"Fair enough," he said.

* * *

I knew Shirley and Sherrie were out. Telling Remy to park in the alley behind the store, I unlocked the back door and led him through the hallway to the Dog Palace. Cocoa stopped barking as soon as he heard my voice. When I opened his door, he sniffed Remy's ankles and trotted back to his sheepskin. Remy stood in the Palace doorway and whistled.

"Come in," I said. "It's my refuge."

With a wry smile, he shook his head. "Kayla, I can't go in there with you."

I didn't know if I was more disappointed or embarrassed, and I wasn't sure what I'd been expecting. A long, dizzying kiss and the two of us tumbling onto the daybed? A game of hide-and-seek behind the many curtains? Snuggling and whispering about our happy future together? Probably all of the above. Certainly not that he'd refuse to step into the room.

"Okay," I said slowly. "Close your eyes, and wait here."

I dashed into the dark store, finding my way by memory and the faint glow from the streetlights. I located the gold sequined top and a slinky skirt. Glancing back to make sure he hadn't followed, I shed my own clothes and put on the sequined tank and skirt. Then I found a French beret and, taking it back to Remy, set it on his head. Slipping past him, I scooted back onto the daybed and leaned against the pillows. "Now will you come in, Mr. French Hat?"

Pulling the beret off his head, Remy opened his eyes and grinned when he saw what it was. Then he saw me. He stood stock-still, and then he leaned against the doorframe. Burying my face in the one of the pillows, I heard him clear his throat.

"You're beautiful," he said. "You're stunning. And I've still gotta go."

I peeked at him. He held the beret out to me.

"Halloween," he said. "Right?"

Halloween felt like a long way off, and Denver might as well have been on another planet. Is this love? I wondered. And if so, how would I keep it going? "Wait," I told Remy. "Close your eyes again. Don't move."

He hesitated, but he obeyed. Shutting the door between us, I opened the right-hand drawer under the daybed. I took out a hundred dollars in twenties and replaced the box. I went to Remy and said, "I can't give you the rest of the poem yet, but I have this." I pressed the bills into his hand.

He stared at the money. Wrinkling his brow, he counted it. "Is this yours?"

"It's okay," I lied. "They pay me in cash or credit, and I've got a bunch of credit."

"It's a loan?" he asked.

You can have it, I almost said but stopped myself. "Yes. A loan."

He was quiet. He leaned over and kissed me on one cheek, then the other.

"Is that all?" I asked.

"Are you trying to buy me?"

I was glad the light was dim, because my face grew hot. "No."

"I'll pay you back," he promised, giving me back the beret.

I nodded.

"C'mon." He stroked my cheek. "I need to drive you home."

173

TWENTY-FIVE

Remy was true to his word. A week after I'd given him Sherrie's money, he sent me one hundred dollars in cash, folded inside a card with a drawing of a pumpkin on it. He'd written, *Sometimes love is what you want and where you want it. Yours in Denver, R.* The saying "Absence makes the heart grow fonder" may be a cliché, but to me it contained more than a shred of truth. I felt smugly, secretly satisfied all day. When I got to Big-Time Bargains to walk Cocoa and return the hundred dollars, I grabbed a tiny silver crown with fake rubies off the counter and made the women promise to stay put. After I snuck the money back into the drawer, I put the crown on Cocoa and paraded him out for the women to crow over.

Maybe good things were in the stars, because all that week and the next, I didn't see my mom get drunk once, and she went to her job every day. She started buying our groceries, and she chipped in fifty dollars every week toward the rent. She was making enough to cover all of it, but she asked me if I'd keep paying also so she could pay off some of our huge credit-card debt. It burned me, but I did it. When we were alone together in the trailer, we circled each other like two sharks.

Redbone came for dinner every few nights. Sam was still in Europe, so I'd eat quickly and escape down to his house, where I'd let myself in with the hidden key and take Rebel for a late walk. When I returned, I'd run the fan in my room and write poems. Or try to, anyway. Over the fan's hum, Mom's and Redbone's bursts of laughter poked at the loneliness I felt in Remy's absence.

When Remy had been gone two weeks, Mom asked if I'd mind Redbone coming over to watch a movie. She'd found a used VCR for ten bucks and picked up some dumb romantic comedy that Redbone had raved about but that looked awful. She asked with her back to me, keeping busy at the stove. She'd never asked me about a man coming over before. They'd just show up. Maybe I should've been glad she was trying to be considerate. Instead, her question just rankled.

She said, "You're welcome to watch with us."

"Won't that be cozy," I said, picturing three of us crammed on our funky little couch. "Then what? Tarzan and Jane in the jungle?"

Mom actually blushed. "He's not staying over."

I'd have hung out at Sam's, but someone else who worked for him had a key to the house and occasionally slept there. I called Luz to see if she could come get me, but Celie had a high fever and Luz couldn't leave her. Next, I tried Shirley and Sherrie. I got Sherrie at the store and asked if she thought Cocoa would like some company for a few hours that evening.

"What's up, hon?" she asked.

Mom sat at the kitchen table, slicing stalks of celery.

"It's going to be kind of crowded here," I said.

Mom started to speak but clamped her mouth shut and kept chopping.

"Hold on," Sherrie said. A minute later, she asked, "Will you need a ride?" I told her no. "Okay," she said. "It's our bingo night, so the place will be quiet."

After I hung up, I got myself a plate of crackers. Mom and I moved uneasily around each other in the kitchen. It wasn't just Redbone coming over that bugged me. Except for our year apart, it had always been just Mom and me—plus her guy of the moment. They came, they went, they didn't pay much attention to me, and vice versa.

Redbone took some notice of me. I didn't miss having a father—

you can't miss what you've never had—but I wanted to know more about Mom's relationship with him. Maybe because I had a relationship of my own now. Or maybe because Redbone seemed bound and determined to be a permanent fixture in our lives, and Mom blushed when she talked about him. Or maybe, to keep moving forward, I just needed her to fill in some of the gaps in our past.

"Where did you meet Desmond?" I asked, taking my time slicing cheese to go on my crackers.

Mom took hold of the broom and began sweeping our small living room and kitchen.

"If you have to know, in a bar."

I laid the cheese in a semicircle on the plate. "What kinds of things did you do together? Take walks? Go to movies?"

"None of that." She bent to sweep a pile of dirt into the dustpan. "Maybe we took a walk, once."

"Once," I repeated. I scratched at a sticky mark on the tabletop left from a piece of tape. "Was he kind?"

She hesitated. "Yes."

"Did he help you out? Give you money or anything?"

She dumped the dirt into the trash and banged the side of the trash can with the dustpan harder than seemed necessary. "If you're asking did he give me money for sleeping with him, it wasn't like that." She yanked the plastic liner out of the trash can and tied it shut. "I didn't have a job then, so he paid the rent and bought our groceries."

"Why don't you ever tell me about him?" I helped myself to some of her celery stalks.

She sighed again, almost a groan. "There isn't much to tell."

It seemed to me there was plenty. For the first time, I considered that the sleazeball who fathered me might have been a nice guy. This made his leaving even worse. It's one thing when an asshole walks out on you. It's another when the guy has the potential to be cool but chooses not to be. I suspected Mom actually cared about him, so it must have sucked when he left. My sympathy for her having been abandoned rose a notch or two—though nowhere near enough to think of Redbone as a qualified replacement. He might have parked our trailer on a lot with million-dollar sunsets, but a slumlord was a slumlord.

"Are you done interrogating me?" she asked. " 'Cause I've got half an hour before Redbone arrives and I haven't showered."

"Don't let me stop you." I got up to leave but paused by the door, hoping Mom would offer me a ride.

"What about dinner?" she asked.

"I'll get something."

"You don't have to go."

I stepped outside, calling back over my shoulder, "And you wouldn't, in my shoes?"

Luz called the next morning. She had finished her summer classes, and she invited me to go with her and Celie that afternoon to meet two of her friends. At first, I was a little anxious about fitting in, but I realized quickly that a seventeen-year-old with a toddler doesn't hang out with the kind of regular kids I never could relate to. While we lay around on blankets next to a river with a great swimming hole, Celie made piles of rocks and gleefully knocked them over. Luz and her friends got into a conversation about what they wanted to do with their lives. Tanya wanted to do research on cancer. The other girl, Fran, hoped to be a writer—she was already sending her stories to publishers—and Luz talked about going to law school so she could fight for women's and children's rights.

"How about you?" Fran asked me. "What do you want to do?"

Her question embarrassed me. I could barely think about next week, never mind the next ten years. What could I say? That I couldn't decide between finishing high school and following the guy who might be my boyfriend while he made a name for himself in music? Compared to their plans, mine sounded pathetic.

"I'm not sure," I said.

Luz threw an arm around my shoulders. "Don't sweat it. You're only fifteen."

"Sixteen, in a week."

"Happy almost birthday," Tanya said.

"Yeah," added Fran. "I thought you were older."

"Kayla is great with animals," Luz said. "She's going to be a world-famous veterinarian."

"She could be a circus trainer."

"Or run a dog obedience school."

"No, cat obedience school. She'll figure out what nobody else has been able to."

"I've got it!" Luz said. "You could be a pet psychiatrist. You know, the ones that get a hundred fifty an hour to tell Fifi's worried owner why her precious puppy pees in the owner's high heels?"

The afternoon distracted me from missing Remy. When he called that night, I had a problem. The only phone—an old corded thing—wouldn't reach from the kitchen to my room. I covered the mouthpiece and asked Mom if she'd go into her bedroom so I could have some privacy.

She gave me a look. "Privacy to talk to the guy you aren't sleeping with?"

Exasperated, I hissed, "Yes, Mom. There's been a nuclear explosion in my lonely desert and thousands are perishing. We're working out a top-secret emergency rescue plan."

"What's that supposed to mean?"

"It means *go!*" I glared at her. Slowly, she scooped up her papers and left the room.

Remy raved about the Denver gig—a slow starter that got packed audiences after a local rag reviewed their act. They worked on their CD in a recording studio most mornings, and everyone but Remy held down a part-time job to make ends meet.

"How did you get off the hook?" I asked.

"I'm the main man," he said. "I'm working twenty-four- seven as songwriter, manager, and booking agent. It's frying my ass, but it's great."

In the pause that followed, I waited for him to ask me how I was doing. Or about Rebel. He didn't, but he did say he missed me.

I asked, "Are you coming back here for anything?"

"No way," he answered. "We can't step an inch out of Denver till this CD's done. I can't even drive my bus except to go to the club and back, we're that tight."

I chewed my lip.

"How're things with your mom?" he asked.

That was almost like asking about me. "Okay, I guess. I start school next week." Damn, that sounded juvenile. I didn't mean to remind him what a schoolgirl I still was. "And Rebel's doing okay," I added. "He's kind of lonely, so I try to walk him a few times a day."

"You're his angel, Kayla. Hey, I should keep this short. Eva will kill me if I blow our phone budget. You take care, okay?"

The phone call made me miss him more. He hadn't asked much about me—not anything, really—but I figured he was swept up in all the stuff happening in Denver.

Mom came out of her room and wanted to talk about him, but I told her that he was on the road and likely to be off for a long time, maybe for good, so there was nothing to talk about.

Elvis looked mournful, so I let him out. He scurried around as enthusiastically as if it were the first time. Meanwhile, I wondered if Remy hadn't asked about me because he was falling in love with Eva. I pictured the no-nonsense girl in leather pants, leather boots, tank top, and earrings that dangled to her bare shoulders, and Remy reaching for her. She had to be twenty-two—the *perfect* age for him. I worked up such a jealous fit that I didn't notice until too late that Elvis had chewed through one of my bootlaces.

A week later—the Friday before school started—Mom insisted on going with me to register for school. On the way there, she apologized for not being able to buy me new school clothes.

"That's okay," I told her. "I'll get what I need at Shirley and Sherrie's."

"Maybe we could swing one new outfit—"

"Save it, Mom. Since when do I wear *outfits?*"

She shrugged. "I thought you might like some new clothes. And I could take you to the salon to get your hair styled. It's cute how it's growing in."

My mother drunk was a horror, but her perky, sober mission to make me presentable was as welcome as a splinter. "Mom, how about keeping your fashion ideas to yourself?"

"Your hair just needs shaping, that's all."

At the high school, a new cement-and-glass fiasco that resembled a prison more than a school, Mom reached out for the registration forms a woman handed us, but I grabbed them first. I took a seat between two other people, where Mom couldn't sit near me.

"Why don't you give me part of it to fill out?" she asked.

I glanced around the room. A couple of girls and one boy each sat with a grownup, the pairs of heads nearly touching as they went over the forms. "Just chill, Mom. Go smoke or something. I've got it under control."

She clicked her pen against her chin. "I think you need my signature," she said.

Bending my head over the forms, I replied, "I'll let you know when I do." She waited a moment, then finally walked away.

Two years to go, I thought as I filled in my name, address, phone number, last school attended. I liked school well enough, though it was hard when I was always playing catch-up. I'd started over too many times, in too many places. I'd made a career of walking into classes midyear, weeks or months after everyone else had adjusted to the teachers and the piles of homework and had more or less caught on to each subject. Under different circumstances I might have been happy to start this school year with everyone else. In any case, Mom hadn't finished high school, so graduating was another way to be different from her.

Mom started reading over the forms I handed her to sign. "Just put your name on the bottom and let's go," I insisted.

"Don't rush me," she said, but she scanned to the end and signed.

The next day—one day before my birthday—I met Luz at Big-Time Bargains. She was standing with the two women, and she announced, "Kayla needs a birthday suit."

"Doesn't she already have one?" Sherrie asked.

"She's got a fine one, but she needs to enhance it with something to wear over it."

We wandered through the store together, holding up clothes for the other to see.

"How come you didn't tell me about your boyfriend?" Luz asked, browsing through a rack.

"My boyfriend?"

"Remy Coltan?"

"Luz, he's not my boyfriend."

"That's not how your mom tells it to Bell."

Sherrie was nearby, pulling shirts off a rack. She turned and looked straight at me.

"Sherrie," I said, "you stay out of this."

"What do you know, Sherrie?" urged Luz.

"Ooh, he's been courting her for some time, from the little I've been able to gather. But Kayla's as secretive about that boy as she is about her birthday suit."

"Stop, you two."

"Boy?" said Luz. "When he played at my high school dance two years ago, he was already going gray."

"Give me a break," I muttered, grabbing a couple of pairs of jeans off a rack and diving behind the curtain of a dressing room.

"Kayla," Luz called after me. "You already have six pairs of jeans."

"I need to get away from the two of you."

"Don't think we're going to let you off so easy." She laughed, and I could hear Sherrie chuckling with her.

They were just teasing me, but I felt cornered. I put on the first pair of jeans. They were huge, slipping off my hips like some homeboy's. The second pair was so small I couldn't get a leg into them. In the mirror, I saw a tall, serious girl with grapefruit-sized breasts, a little extra weight around her middle, long, strong-looking legs, and short dark hair that—Mom was right—needed shaping. I twisted to look at my butt and realized I was trying to come up with the name of a fruit or vegetable that accurately described it. *Her butt was like a pumpkin.*

Luz shook the dressing-room curtain. "What are you doing in there, admiring yourself?"

"Yeah, I am."

She handed me an armful of skirts. "You'll look even better in these."

"Seriously, Kayla, why didn't you tell me?" Luz sounded angry, but she looked hurt.

"I don't really know what's going on between Remy and me," I said, feeling defensive. "And if I had told you I might be getting involved with a twenty-four-year-old guy, wouldn't you have said I was nuts?"

We were sharing a banana split in her car outside the Dairy Queen. I'd spent forty dollars of my two-hundred-dollar credit at Big-Time Bargains, and I'd asked for another twenty dollars from the women in cash. "I don't tell people anything anymore," she mumbled, her mouth full of ice cream. "So many folks said I was stupid when I was pregnant with Celie—and what did they know? Now I'm going to college. No one in my family has done that." She licked the back of her spoon. "On the other hand, you are kind of nuts." She pointed the spoon at me. "Kayla, what do you want to do with your life?"

I groaned. "Not this again. Remember, I'm not even sixteen."

"Seriously. Just right now. Finish school?"

"Sure." I looked down and took another bite of the split. "But sometimes I want to go to Denver and finish school there, or go to college early, like you."

"So, hit the road with Remy, do your groupie thing, *and* go to school?"

She made it sound stupid—and impossible. "Maybe."

She lifted the rest of the whipped cream off the split. "Has he sent you anything for your birthday?"

"He's broke. And it's not until tomorrow."

"Hallmark is cheap. And tomorrow is Sunday—no mail delivery. He should have sent you something by today."

I jiggled my knee nervously. I could let her think he was a selfish jerk, or I could tell the truth. "Luz, I hate Hallmark. And he doesn't know it's my birthday."

She raised an eyebrow. "Why not?"

I didn't want to say, and she must have read my face.

"Kayla, what *did* you tell him?"

"Don't you need to pick up Celie?"

"No, I've got plenty of time. *Talk.*"

"He thinks I'm seventeen—almost eighteen."

She winced.

"I *feel* like I'm at least seventeen."

She rolled her eyes. "You're acting more like fourteen."

That burned. Luz wasn't much older than me. Where did she come off acting like my big sister?

"You know his history?" she asked.

I nodded. "It was nothing, right?"

"Oh, it wasn't nothing. I know the girl. She never wanted him to get in trouble. Said he was awfully good to her." Luz smirked.

"Well, he's good to *me,* Luz, but we're taking it slow. He's not looking for any more trouble. The thing is, he thinks we can speed up as soon as I turn eighteen."

"Which he believes is . . . ?"

"Halloween."

"Why Halloween?"

"I don't know. I just picked it. I wasn't thinking straight."

"You sure weren't. Most girls don't, around him. When're you going to tell him the truth?"

"I don't know. I'm working on it."

She frowned. "What about condoms?"

"I told you. We haven't gotten that far."

"Now I know what to get you for your birthday." She handed the split to me. "You've been seeing him since when?"

"June."

"And he hasn't pushed you to give it up?"

"Nope." I smiled at her, but she was frowning.

She asked, "So what's he been wanting instead?"

I opened my mouth to tell her how he was encouraging me to write, how great we got along, and how sometimes I imagined the three of us—Remy, Rebel, and me—as a family, maybe not rich but successful enough and happy with each other and music and living

184

on the road—but I was afraid that my words would fall flat before my future-lawyer friend's scowling face. I took a big bite of banana with chocolate sauce and shrugged. "Nothing," I mumbled. "He's just being cool."

She folded her arms. "I wonder what that's all about."

TWENTY-SIX

Mom worked the early shift on Sunday—my birthday—and Remy called while she was out. I'd been practicing telling him the truth in the bathroom mirror all morning, and as we talked, I looked for just the right opening. It never came, especially not after he said that we should pool any spare money we had on Halloween so I could take a bus up to Denver to see him. I agreed. I could break it to him then.

I fell asleep in the afternoon, waking when I heard a knock on the door and Redbone's truck pulling out of the yard. He'd left a bouquet of chrysanthemums on the porch, still wrapped in cellophane with the price tag on it, and a small card that read *Have a sweet 16th, Kayla. Redbone.* That night, there was a series of knocks on our door as first Luz and Celie, then Bell, then Luz's friends Fran and Tanya, and even Shirley and Sherrie showed up for my birthday. Mom and Luz had arranged it. I was still angry with my mom, but I tried to shove that aside for the evening.

Luz's friends brought me a candle with a full moon on it. Celie wished me a garbled "birdday" and gave me a slimy kiss. Luz made me put on the skirt she'd convinced me to buy the day before, and in my room she slipped me a small package that crinkled.

"This is not an endorsement," she whispered, "but, dammit, take care of yourself."

Mom gave me a beautiful embroidered tank top from Mexico, apologizing that it wasn't new, and Sherrie exclaimed, "Badmouthing our goods, are you?" which made everyone laugh except me. I wondered if Mom used my credit to buy the shirt. Shirley and Sherrie gave me earrings and a matching necklace, and Bell, who'd brought along tarot cards, offered to do a reading. We ate enchiladas that Luz made and rice my mom cooked and a lopsided pink heart-shaped cake that Shirley and Sherrie said was a real pain in the butt to make but was worth it because it was for me.

After dinner, Bell told me to ask a question for the tarot cards. Silently, I asked about Remy, but out loud, I said, "What's it going to take for me to get a dog?" Bell laid out three cards: a fiery, wild-looking woman called the Six of Wands, a jester-type fellow called the Fool, and a man hanging by a noose—the Death card. She interpreted the cards to mean that I should express my deepest desires, take everything with a good dash of humor, and be willing to let go of someone, something, or some idea I held about myself.

Luz said, "That death card is freaky," at which Bell insisted that it wasn't about a literal death but some symbolic ending in my life. Luz whispered to me, "Here's my interpretation: wear 'em down with your demands, don't do anything foolish, and knock out anyone who gets in your way." That was pretty good advice, whether I was going for a dog or a guy.

All evening, Mom sent me hopeful, happy looks, and once, she tousled my hair and asked, "Are you having a good time?"

I responded, "What do you think?" I wasn't ready to be her buddy so fast. After the last guest left and I helped her clean up, she asked if I wanted to share the last of the sparkling cider with her. I told her I was going to walk Rebel and not to wait up for me. I said it more harshly than I'd meant to. She bit her lip and turned away.

All the way down to Sam's, I felt my insides shriveling from guilt. I could see how hard she was trying. Trying again to stay sober. Trying to be a good mother. Why did I feel as though every time she jumped through a new hoop, I had to raise it just a little bit higher?

A light shone inside Sam's, and a blue Suburu sat in the driveway. I started back to the trailer, hoping Mom had gone to bed, but I could see her still in the main room. Checking to make sure I had the key to the store in my pocket, I headed down the road toward town.

Cocoa barked when I let myself into the Dog Palace, and Shirley came down to investigate, as I knew she would. Her eyes widened at the sight of me.

"Is it okay if I crash here tonight?"

Sherrie appeared alongside Shirley. Sherrie wore a huge purple nightgown, and she'd washed off her makeup. Shirley had on plaid flannel pajamas. They both looked tired.

"Did you and your mom have a disagreement?" Sherrie asked.

I was tempted to lie and tell them she was drinking or being mean or something. "I just like it here," I said. "I wanted to be alone. Kind of a birthday present to myself."

The women studied each other's expressions for a moment, and then Shirley said, "Do you know your mom hasn't had a drink in over three weeks?"

I started to protest, then counted back. I hadn't seen Mom drunk or hung over since that day Redbone chewed her out and I called Bell—at least three weeks earlier. "Sure," I lied, "but how do you know?"

"She told me tonight, just as tickled as anything. You're not the only one who's got something to celebrate."

"What's the big deal?" I burst out. "She never keeps it up."

Shirley said, "Since it's your birthday, why don't you take thirty, forty minutes to yourself. Then I'll give you a lift home." She turned and climbed the stairs to the apartment.

"Sherrie, please," I began.

But she said, "Sometimes, when you get a bunch of gifts, you've got to give some back." She patted my shoulder before hauling herself up the steps.

I sat on the daybed, wondering what I was supposed to return. Redbone's flowers? I still didn't like the man. Was it wrong to accept them? Did they want me to return the jewelry they'd given me? Why didn't they just say so? As for returning something to my mother—what for? This was supposed to be my day, not hers.

Whatever they meant, clearly I wasn't welcome in the Dog Palace that night—maybe ever. I felt impatient waiting for Shirley to come back. We didn't speak all the way to the trailer, until she stopped the car, leaving the motor running.

"Sometimes you've got to go home, Kayla," she said.

I stood outside the trailer after Shirley drove away. A pack of coyotes howled off in the distance. The neighborhood dogs joined in, mournful and frustrated. The living room light glowed, and the windows in Mom's bedroom were black. Reluctantly, I went inside. Mom lay on her side on the sofa, her arm dangling over the floor. I thought she was asleep until I noticed the bottle of rum, can of Coke, and empty glass beside her. She wasn't asleep. She was passed out. I ran to the porch, but Shirley was gone. I swore and kicked the door shut.

When I could bring myself to go back inside, I noticed a wrinkled piece of paper under Mom's hand. I picked it up, stepping back from the stench of alcohol that rose from her, and silently read the first lines: *Stayed at Janice's when I knew Mother needed me at home to make her lunch . . . Swore at Mother when she wet her bed . . . Left Mother in her wheelchair on the porch after dark . . .*

Mom's gravelly voice made me jump. "Read it to me," she ordered, slurring her words and peering up at me from under half-closed lids. Outside, the dogs whined again and went still.

I felt sick. "What is this?"

"My amends," she said, pushing herself to a sitting position and holding her head in her hands. "To your grandmother."

"Why are you hanging on to this?"

189

"I don't know." She burst into a shrill laugh that sent chills through me. "Maybe she'll hear it if you read it. She can't hear my voice."

I wanted to run outside, into town, catch a bus for Denver, for anywhere, stick out my thumb, anywhere, anywhere. I wanted to be far away from this crazy, fumbling woman.

"I'm tired. I'm going to bed." I dropped the paper in her lap.

She shook her head violently. Wisps of hair fell into her face. "Please. You're such a help to me. The words are too jiggly."

"I'm not going to read it. Read it yourself. Do it tomorrow, when you can see straight."

She attempted to smooth the creased paper on her knee, but her jerky movements tore it. She looked up when I opened the door, and I could see that she was crying. "You're going out?"

I slammed the door behind me and ran into the smoke-tinged night. The cool air hit my face and I gulped it and nearly lost my balance hurrying down the uneven dirt road. At Sam's, the Suburu was gone and the house was dark. I let myself in. Rebel wagged his tail furiously and licked every inch of skin he could reach. Taking off my boots and jeans, I crawled into the bed where Remy used to stay. My heart thudded too quickly to let me sleep. The dog turned a couple of circles and settled down next to the bed with a sigh.

Early in the morning, I called Bell and woke her up. She said she would meet me at the trailer, but after I hung up the phone, I spent hours roaming the hills with Rebel, returning only when I was too thirsty and hungry to continue. Bell's car was parked at the trailer, making it easier to go inside. She sat in the kitchen, and Mom's bedroom door was closed. There was dried vomit on the couch and on the floor.

"Where have you been?" Bell asked when she saw me.

"I had some stuff I had to do."

She watched as I collected Mom's vitamins, incense, CDs, and bottles of powdered green stuff and threw them into the trash. I emptied the Mason jars filled with water and chucked those, too. "A lot of good all this has done for her," I said.

"Did you think those things would keep her from drinking?"

"She thought so."

Bell was quiet.

I looked in the refrigerator and found leftovers from the party. I put cold enchiladas and a slice of cake on a plate and sat down to eat.

Gently, Bell asked me again, "Kayla, where did you go?"

I tapped my fork on the side of the plate. "Okay, I shouldn't have left her."

Bell shook her head. "I'm not saying that. On the contrary, sometimes leaving is the right thing to do. I'm just wondering how you took care of yourself last night and today."

I took another bite of enchilada. The congealed red chili sauce made it look like some kind of dead thing on the plate. I set down the fork and told her where I'd slept and where I'd been all morning. She listened, and then she stuck around for a few hours, urging Mom to get up after a while and standing by while Mom cleaned up her own mess.

I was grateful for Bell's presence. I think it would have been hell without her, and I would never have had the courage to stand around while Mom did all the dirty work. Bell offered to fix us dinner, but I told her I could do that much. After she left, I found a box of macaroni and cheese and a bag of frozen peas. Mom barely spoke. At least she didn't drink any more.

Telling me she was exhausted, she kissed me on the top of my head and went to her room, closing the door. It had been so long, I felt that kiss for minutes.

I wanted to call Remy, but I didn't want his Denver phone number to show on our bill. I tried Luz, but she didn't answer. After the light went out in Mom's room, I walked Rebel again, and then I took him home with me. I didn't want to be alone in the trailer with Mom. He curled up on my bed, taking up most of the space where my feet usually went. Just before I dozed off, I heard Mom open my door. Rebel's tags jingled as he lifted his head, and his wagging tail shook the bed, but I pretended to be asleep. After a moment, she quietly closed the door.

The next day, my last before school started, I walked each of the dogs, grateful that Sherrie and Shirley were too busy with customers to talk to me. I felt a little satisfaction at getting Cocoa to obey me with plain dog treats as his reward, but those feelings didn't last long. When I got home, Mom was still at work. Her bed was unmade, and clothes were strewn across it and on the floor. Under the bed I saw two paper bags. One held a dozen or so empty beer bottles and an empty whiskey bottle; the other held two full bottles—one whiskey, one rum.

Luz thought I was an immature idiot. Shirley and Sherrie were taking Mom's side against me. Remy was probably in love with Eva. And Mom was drinking again. With that stash of booze under her bed, she sure didn't have plans to stop. She could drink herself into oblivion for all I cared, but I wasn't going to stick around to watch—or get dumped back into foster care as a result. Let Bell take care of her. At least I had someplace else to go. And someone else to go to. I almost went down to Sam's to call Remy right then and tell him my plan, but I decided to wait until I was completely ready to take off.

TWENTY-SEVEN

Mom left for work the next day convinced I was going to school, but I took Rebel for a long hike instead. Afterward, I treated myself to a $5.99 breakfast special of huevos rancheros at the Piñon Diner and showed up at Shirley and Sherrie's close to noon to walk Cocoa. I'd decided to forgive them for throwing me out the night of my birthday. They must have had their reasons. I knew they might be upset that I wasn't in school, but I had a solid rationale ready—one that didn't include Mom's getting wasted. I wasn't sure whose side they'd be on.

As soon as I walked into Big-Time, I could tell they were not pleased. Sherrie's brow wrinkled with concern, and Shirley looked downright pissed off. Sherrie excused herself from a customer. "Why aren't you in school, honey?" she said to me. "Doesn't it start today?"

In the most optimistic tone I could manage, I said, "Regular high school is such a waste of time. I've decided to get my GED or take some of those accelerated high school/college classes instead."

"I see," Sherrie said.

Shirley pegged me with the same question, and my answer didn't satisfy her at all. "Well, you can't do a stitch of work here until you either get yourself into the regular school or start up those other programs," she said. "I won't be aiding and abetting a dropout." She wheeled around and stalked back to her work behind the counter.

Sherrie nodded slowly, looking impressed. "She has a point there," she said. "I guess we'll have to take care of Cocoa ourselves until you get this straightened out." She, too, turned and walked away, casting a worried look over her shoulder.

I felt like a fool. Who the hell did they think they were, trying to control me? Making decisions about what I should or shouldn't do?

Fuming, I walked out, but I didn't know where to go. I wandered around town, fueled by my anger, hearing all the advice people were giving me—*You've got to go to school; Sometimes you've got to go home; Sometimes you've got to leave*—and seeing over and over again my mother handing me her list of amends, her voice cracking, ordering me pathetically to read it aloud. I ended up in front of the ugly high school, my mother's *Take her, take her* echoing in my mind. I strode into the school, made an excuse for being late, and got my schedule. Throughout the day, I wrote down every assignment and the title of every book I was supposed to read. I took detailed notes, covering pages and pages of borrowed notebook paper, got my name on the attendance lists, and counted the minutes until the last bell rang. I'd go to school, but only to keep up appearances until I could get myself to Denver.

When that first day of school ended, I walked Cocoa and afterward returned my store key to Shirley and Sherrie. Showing them my many homework assignments, I told them I'd be much too busy to help with the dog, at least at first, until I got into a rhythm with my home-work. Looking relieved, they thanked me for everything I had done with him and told me to stop by anytime and to let them know if I wanted to work again. I took Cocoa back to the Palace, closed the door behind us, hung up his leash, and checked all the windows. They were locked, as usual. I moved the latch on one of the windows just enough so that it was no longer locked. Returning to the store, I told the two women I'd see them around. Shirley opened the cash register. "Here's what we owe you," she said, putting $175 in an envelope and handing it to me. I got a lump in my throat. Before Sherrie could hug me and I lost it, I turned away.

In homeroom on my third day of school, the loudspeaker

squawked my name, telling me to report to the guidance counselor's office. The counselor had a folder with my name on it. He said he'd spoken to my last school in Dallas and he wanted to make sure I got off to a good start in Rio Blanco. I almost asked him what they'd said about me but decided it was better not to know.

He leaned his elbows on his desk. "One of your previous teachers indicated that you have a talent for writing poetry. Do you like to write poems?"

"Sometimes," I replied, shrugging.

He said, "I'd like to change your regular English class to Mrs. Ramirez's poetry class." He waited for me to say something.

I wasn't going to be in this school much longer. "I don't care," I said.

He dropped his pencil and tipped his chair back. "Would you like to tell me why you don't care what classes you take?"

I backpedaled. "I meant that it's fine. I don't care if you make the change, because the poetry class sounds good."

I was relieved when he nodded and gave me a new schedule, along with a pass. "Is there anything else I can help you with?"

"Nothing I can think of. Thank you."

I couldn't wait to get away from him, but he insisted on walking me to Mrs. Ramirez's room, making suggestions about joining the school newspaper or the photography club. I half listened and agreed to try everything. I must have sounded convincing, because he looked really pleased with himself, and I relaxed a little more.

Mrs. Ramirez's class had already started when I gave her the pass and found a seat. About half the class was writing, and the others were chewing on pencils, doodling, or looking out the window. The teacher, a stout woman with a long braid, came over to me and told me that the class was writing what she called "minute poems"—taking one simple image and quickly brainstorming a few lines about it.

I went to work. When Mrs. Ramirez asked for volunteers to read their poems, I folded my paper in half.

A tall blond girl stood and read:

> *"Dust bites*
> *Car headlights*
> *Stricken like a deer*
> *What's to fear?"*

She sat down, whipping her long straight hair behind her. Other kids glanced at her admiringly or smirked at each other or continued staring out the window. A few erased furiously and rewrote their lines.

Mrs. Ramirez asked, "What did you like about Kelly's poem?"

No one spoke. Finally, someone asked, "What do you mean, 'Dust bites'?" Several kids snickered.

The blond girl blushed. "I don't know; it just came to me."

A girl raised her hand, and Mrs. Ramirez called on her. "Taylor?"

"I think she feels like a deer caught in headlights at night, but can't really acknowledge it." The girl said more, but I was distracted by her left arm, or by the lack of it; it ended right below her elbow in a stubby hand with only two tiny fingers. Since the rest of the class seemed to have gone to sleep with their eyes open, Mrs. Ramirez and Taylor continued their analysis for a while, and I decided grudgingly that Taylor was pretty smart and that Mrs. Ramirez wasn't bad for a teacher. When the bell rang, everyone jumped as if they'd been jolted with a cattle prod. They tossed their poems on the teacher's desk and left before I'd even collected my stuff. I took another look at my poem:

> *mama sips*
> *mama slips*
> *biding time till*
> *mama flips.*

Mrs. Ramirez straightened up her desk. "Did you have any difficulty writing a poem?"

I crumpled the page into a ball. "No. No difficulty."

I stuffed my books into my backpack and chucked the poem into the wastebasket by her desk. Then I realized that was stupid. She might take it out and read it. Too embarrassed to go back and pull it out of the trash, I walked away as if I didn't care.

I expected her to stop me, but she didn't, and I resisted the urge to see if she was watching me walk away.

I went to school all that week and the next in body but not in spirit. I was already on my way out of there. Everyone else raised their hands in classes, signed up for intramural this or that, huddled in noisy groups by the lockers. I had a plan that took up most of my attention. In study hall, I got a library pass and went on the Internet to check out bus fare to Denver and browse apartment rentals (in case I needed to move on from Remy's), and I wrote up several budgets—best case based on having a booming dog-walking business, and worst case based on flipping hamburgers at some minimum-wage fast-food joint. A couple of times, teachers called on me and I didn't even know what the question was. Some idiots laughed, but I didn't care. Their callousness just gave me one more reason to get out of town.

Mrs. Ramirez's poetry class, on the other hand, sucked me in every time. Once she read a poem by someone named Sarton that compared love to spider webs. It ended with these lines:

> *Spiders are patient weavers*
> *They never give up.*
> *And who knows*
> *What keeps them at it?*
> *Hunger, no doubt,*
> *And hope.*

Then she had us all write a short poem about spiders, and this time I was tempted to read mine aloud. I didn't, though I did leave it on her desk.

I didn't realize until I was already sitting down for my history class and it was too late to get it back that she hadn't even asked us to turn our poems in.

When she gave the poem back to me the next day, she'd written *This is delightful. I look forward to reading more of your poems.* That sent a rush of warmth through me.

Still, I kept planning my escape. Mom was now staying sober, but that meant nothing to me. She'd been sober before. Lots of times. I knew it wouldn't last. Like Bell said, sometimes leaving is the right thing to do.

Saturday evening—Shirley and Sherrie's bingo night—I made up a story for Mom about going to meet Luz, and she offered to drive me. "No, thanks," I said.

"I don't mind."

"I said *no,*" I snapped at her, more harshly than I'd intended. "I just feel like walking. It's nice out."

"There's a storm coming."

She was right. Dark clouds had gathered overhead, threatening rain. I found an umbrella and pushed the door open. "I'll be fine. I want to walk." She didn't say anything as I left.

I wasn't meeting Luz. I went to Big-Time Bargains instead. On my way there, I decided that if the window was locked, it was a sign to leave Rio Blanco with the money I had and trust that it would be enough. And if it wasn't, I should take some of the money that was hidden in the Palace.

Though I almost wished it wasn't, I found the window unlocked. I slid it open and climbed inside, talking soothingly to Cocoa and slipping him several dog biscuits. Taking out the box with the money, I counted it. Still three thousand dollars. My hands shook as I counted out half of it. Nearly choking on guilt, I put five hundred dollars back.

I stood up and tried to calm my breathing. For an instant, I got the crazy idea that the women wanted me to take the money—or at least wouldn't mind. Maybe they knew I took that first hundred, and because I replaced it, they trusted me. Now they would trust me with this new amount. Plus, why would they have let me stay in the Dog Palace in the first place with that much cash if they didn't trust me with it?

Either way—whether they knew what I took or not, whether they found out or not—I'd make sure the money came back. It would be okay.

These thoughts didn't stop my heart from racing or sweat from breaking out on my upper lip as I folded the bills and stuffed them into my pocket. Replacing the box, I gave Cocoa another handful of treats and climbed out the window, shutting it all the way.

As soon as I heard Mom leave for work on Monday morning, I jumped out of bed. I called Remy from his father's house and told him I wanted to come to Denver to see him. Now. That I had enough money for the bus and things weren't good here and I needed to talk to him.

"Hasn't school started?"

"I'm not going."

I heard him moving around. "Kayla," he began.

"Things are really bad here, Remy. I can't stay."

"What do you mean?"

"I'll tell you when I see you. Please."

He was quiet for so long, I wondered if he'd hung up, but then I heard him clear his throat. I expected him to tell me not to come, but he said, "When will you get here?"

"I'm not sure. I'll try to call you from the road. And I have to bring Rebel. There's no one else to take care of him."

I thought I heard him swear under his breath.

"Remy, are you—"

"Never mind," he said. "Just . . . come. I'll figure something out."

I called the bus station and learned that pets weren't allowed on the bus. Not inside, not underneath in a kennel with the suitcases, only guide dogs. I briefly wondered if I could put a harness on Rebel and pretend to be blind but quickly put that idea aside. I had no choice. I'd have to hitchhike.

Dumping the schoolbooks out of my backpack, I replaced them with as much clothing as I could fit. Elvis poked his face between the wires of his cage. It was hard to look at him. I filled his water bottle and gave him lots of food. I took him out and held him in my hand, but he wanted to explore, so I stuck him back inside the cage.

I had about $130 of my own money, which I pocketed along with the cash I'd taken from the women. I'd been planning to take the hundred in my savings account with me, but now that I didn't have to waste any money on bus fare, I just wanted to get going.

I yanked back the covers on Mom's bed and laid all the empty beer and liquor bottles, along with the full ones, on her pillow and mattress. Booze was her first love. She could sleep with the bottles.

When I stepped outside, the air seemed too thin, the sun too bright. The leaves of a cottonwood down at the bottom of Sam's land gleamed yellow. I dropped my pack and carried Elvis's cage outside, placing it under the trailer in back. I put out an extra bowl of water, poured all his dry food into the cage, and, feeling kind of sick, opened the door. Hurrying away, I forced myself not to look back. He might not last outside, but it seemed better for him to die there than inside the trailer, a certain victim of my mother's drunken neglect.

Rebel thrashed his tail when he saw me. I wrote a note for Sam, who wouldn't be home for a few more weeks. Outside, Rebel tried to head for our usual haunts, but I had him on the leash, and I tugged him toward the highway.

TWENTY-EIGHT

It seemed important not to look back. Once I saw the highway on-ramp curving ahead, I breathed easier, but before putting my thumb out, I felt like a small kid sitting at the top of a big slide, scared to push off.

We got a ride to the Exit 290 truck stop with a young guy in a shiny blue pickup who was reluctant to let Rebel ride in front, but I insisted. I wasn't taking any chances that he might jump out. At the truck stop, I led Rebel away from the diner and the many cars around it, searching among the big rigs parked separately. Most of the cabs were empty, and the drivers I asked said they weren't going to Denver or they didn't take hitchhikers or they wouldn't take a dog. I hung out in that lot all day, watching semis come and go, asking every driver for a ride. Occasionally, I grabbed something to eat at the diner. By evening, I was tired and discouraged. I tied Rebel to a tree where I could watch him from inside and ordered the meatloaf and mashed potatoes special and a hot cocoa. Counting my money—I had blown nearly twenty dollars on food that day—I felt more desperate about getting a ride.

While I was eating, I saw a purple and black semi roll in. The driver came into the diner, sat two booths away from me, and ordered dinner. He had on a Denver Broncos cap. He looked maybe forty or so, but it was hard to tell because his longish hair was practically white. He had blue eyes and a weathered, friendly face. I couldn't help smiling at him a couple of times. When he paid his bill and left, I followed him out to his truck, slipping Rebel the hunk of meatloaf I'd saved for him.

"Excuse me," I said. He turned. "I'm Kayla, and this is Rebel, and we have to get to Denver. Are you going there?"

He chewed on a toothpick. I held my breath. "I'm going there. My name's Barlow," he said, offering me his hand. He had a warm, firm grip. "You know this is against the rules, right, Kayla?"

I nodded.

"So you have to follow my directions, otherwise we could both get in trouble."

"Okay."

"The main rule is, anytime I have to stop to get the truck weighed or I run into anyone else from the company I work for, I have to hide you and your dog in the bunk."

I shrugged. "That's okay."

He offered to take my backpack, and he stowed it in a corner of the bunk, which was separated from the seats by a curtain. I coaxed Rebel onto the bunk and soon we were putting miles behind us. The walls of the cab were covered with stuff: postcards, photographs, tiny stuffed animals, sports pennants, statuettes of the Madonna and child, and a pair of tiny baby booties that looked as if they were woven out of strips of aluminum foil. Barlow asked me where I was headed and who I was going to see. I said my mom was sick and I was going to stay with friends. "We don't have much money," I said, as if to explain why I was hitchhiking.

"You're lucky you got a ride from me," he said. "Not all drivers let you ride for free."

"Thank you." My voice came out smaller than I'd intended.

"Your mom know you're hitchhiking?"

"Yes."

"Is that how she wanted you to get to Denver?"

"She can't take care of me. That's why I have to go." I hadn't meant to sound as if I needed to be taken care of.

"What's the address?"

I told him.

"That's not too far from where I'm going. I have to make one stop, but I'll have you there by early morning."

"Okay."

He turned on the radio. "What kind of music do you like?"

I relaxed a little. His one stop was just a couple of exits up the road, but because of some delay—another trucker he was supposed to connect with was late—it took several hours instead of a few minutes. I had to keep myself and Rebel hidden the whole time. After that, we stopped at a diner, where I let Rebel out to run, and Barlow bought coffee for himself and brought a burger back to the truck for me. I ate the bun and the fries but gave the meat to the dog.

By the time we got back on the road, it was nearly midnight, and I was tired. I thought it best to stay awake, but the adrenaline kick that had launched me out of the trailer had long since worn off. Barlow asked if I wanted to sleep on the bunk. I said no, but when I started falling asleep in the seat, I gave in. I figured it was safe: what kind of funny business could he try while steering thousands of pounds of tractor-trailer down the highway doing seventy? Plus, I had Rebel with me. Of course, the dog might just make friends with someone who tried to mess with me, but I liked to think he offered some protection.

I climbed in back, nudging Rebel over. It was cozy on the bunk, and the motion of the truck and the whine of the engine lulled me. Every time I started to doze, though, Rebel shifted around, and his tags jingled and woke me. I took off his collar and stuffed it in my pack. Stroking his silky head, I whispered to him, trying to settle him down. It must have worked, because soon we were both asleep.

I woke in the dark. The truck was stopped near a diner, and Barlow was stretching his arms over his head. Rebel jumped down to the passenger seat, whining to go out. Through the windshield, I could see dawn just starting to light up the eastern sky.

"We're close, but I need some food and coffee," Barlow said. "I can't take you in there, but I can bring you something. What'll you have? It's on me."

I dug a ten out of my pocket. "You don't have to pay for me."

He wouldn't take it.

"Okay," I said, thinking of sharing with Rebel. "How about a cheese omelet, toast, hash browns, sausage?"

When Barlow jumped down from the cab, Rebel followed him, desperate to pee. I followed the dog along the perimeter of the rest stop, where he left his mark on a dozen shrubs. Nearing the highway, I called Rebel back, but he caught sight of a rabbit and lit out after it. The rabbit darted across the wide interstate and disappeared into a big depression between the north- and southbound lanes. I yelled, "No, Rebel! Come!" but he bolted across the highway right in front of a barreling pickup that barely missed him. My heart leaped into my throat. Still chasing the rabbit, Rebel dropped out of sight. I ran to the edge of the road, scared that he'd get hit trying to cross back.

Cars and trucks whizzed by, throwing grit into my eyes. When a gap opened up, I dashed across the three northbound lanes, hoping Barlow wouldn't take off without us.

In the weak dawn light, I could barely make Rebel out, about a hundred yards off, still on the wide center strip. He wove in and out of clumps of scrubby trees and brush, and he seemed to have lost the rabbit. I ran and kept yelling for him, but my voice got drowned in the highway roar and carried the wrong way by the wind blowing into my face. When he was still too far away to hear me, I saw him gallop back across the highway in front of a small green car that blared its horn, swerved, and hit its brakes. The tires squealed. I covered my eyes.

When I dared look up, the car was parked on the shoulder. A woman, a man, and a small boy jumped out. Miraculously, Rebel was okay. He ran over to them wagging his tail, the idiot. He was still too far away to hear me, but I screamed his name and "Hey, you! That's my dog!" I ran along the highway, looking for a hole in the traffic so I could get across. They didn't hear me. They didn't even look my way. Keep charming them, Rebel, I thought. Stay near them until I get to you. I had a stitch in my side and my lungs burned. Sweat rolled into my eyes and stung.

Suddenly, they all piled into the car. *All* of them—Rebel included. That stupid, brainless dog. I thought, Maybe they've seen me coming and they're keeping him safe, but I didn't like the looks of it. When the taillights flashed and a small cloud of dust appeared behind the tailpipe, my throat jammed, my stomach flipped. The car pulled forward and built speed, swerving onto the highway. I could see Rebel in the back. I jumped up and down, waving my arms, screaming "Stop!" They kept on going. I couldn't believe what I was seeing. How could they just drive away? With a dog that wasn't theirs? I watched the car get farther and farther away.

I startled Barlow in a booth inside the busy diner, waving my hands and pointing toward the highway. "The dog's gone. Please. Come!"

"Hold on," he said. "I have to pay."

I ran to the register and threw a twenty onto the counter. "That's for him!" I said, pointing to Barlow. "Hurry!" I cried. Heads turned toward me. I grabbed Barlow's arm and tried to get him to run. "Rebel took off. A rabbit—he chased a rabbit. He got away—and someone picked him up. They took him. They took the dog! They can't be that far ahead yet. We can catch them."

"Hold on, Kayla. Which way did they go?"

I pointed north. "Please, we have to hurry!"

"They're miles away already," he said, shaking his head. "What kind of car was it?"

I stared at him. "What kind? Shit, I don't know. Green. A station wagon. Small. A small green wagon with yellow plates."

Maybe five minutes passed before we were heading north on the highway, but it felt a lot longer, and I fought back tears. I kept calculating: sixty miles an hour, they've been gone ten minutes, how far is that? Six miles? Ten? No, more—everyone's doing at least seventy, eighty. Barlow got on his CB radio and his cell phone and called truckers ahead of us. He gave descriptions of the car and the dog, but no one reported seeing them. We got calls back from miles up the road, but it was as if the car and the dog had been swallowed by the earth.

"He has ID tags, right?" Barlow asked.

"Yes. No!" I groaned. "They're here."

We watched the road in silence. In less than an hour, we reached the outskirts of Denver. Reports over the scanner came less and less frequently. Once, I thought I saw Rebel running in the sparse brush out of the corner of my eye, but it was only dry grasses and occasional shrubs tilting in the wind. Finally, Barlow said, "Sorry, Kayla, but that dog's just plain gone."

I couldn't answer. I hated myself for taking off his collar, for not putting him on the leash. I wiped tears from my blurring eyes. I had to keep watching. Just in case.

Any fantasies I'd clung to of spotting the dog thieves walking Rebel on the streets of Denver vanished once we left the highway to work our way through the labyrinth of quick marts, shopping malls, and housing developments that made up this part of the city. After winding through the endless sprawl, Barlow pulled over next to a plain beige apartment building. White painted rocks and scraggly shrubs in need of a good watering lined the walkway to the front door. Laundry, bicycles, plastic toys, and plants cluttered the tiny balconies.

"Here's where to find me," said Barlow, holding out a card. "Tuesdays and Fridays I usually make the run back to Albuquerque. I pull out of this depot at seven in the morning."

I took the card. "I appreciate what you did."

"No problem. I'm just sorry it didn't turn out better."

I pulled my backpack onto my lap. I felt dead tired, and I set the card on the dashboard. "I'm not going back. But thanks."

He took the card, turned it slowly in his fingers, and offered it again. "It's no skin off your nose to take it."

I put it in the pocket of my backpack along with Rebel's collar and leash. When the semi drove off, the sound of its whining, stepping-up gears fading, I wanted to run after it, ride the highways, hunt for Rebel. Why did it have to take this for me to get it? Rebel was more mine than Remy's or Sam's. I had to find him.

It was early, only seven A.M A sloppily scrawled sign on the elevator inside Remy's building read *Out of Order.* I climbed two flights of steps in a windowless stairwell, planning what to say: Rebel got lost on the way, but I'm going to find him. I'll search the shelters and the lost and found ads, place some myself, find a job so I can support us both after I've brought him home.

I'll be cool, I'll be grown up, I'll be confident, I told myself.

Standing before Remy's door, I stared down the stale-cigarette-smelling hall, hoping, expecting, willing Rebel to come bounding miraculously around the corner. The arm I finally lifted to knock on #26E felt heavier than concrete.

TWENTY-NINE

I couldn't help it. When Remy opened the door, my carefully planned speech turned to smoke and vanished. He was dressed only in jeans, his hair messy from sleep. I threw myself against his chest, sorrow cracking my resolve to be confident, sobs breaking out of me in a wet, noisy eruption. He eased us into the hallway, closing the apartment door. "Shh, shh," he murmured, stroking my head. "Are you okay?"

I nodded and gasped, "Yeah." I tried to breathe deeply, to slow down my crying. "R-Rebel," I managed to say.

Remy glanced down the hall. "Where is he? Did you leave him outside? I'll get him."

I shook my head hard, overtaken by a fresh spurt of tears. Remy steered me back to the stairwell, where my sobs echoed loudly against the concrete walls. "Sit," he said, reminding me of the way I spoke to Rebel, gently pressing on my shoulder. I sank onto the steps. I was a mess, my eyes and nose streaming. "Wait here," he said, going back to the apartment, and I cried harder. By the time he returned with a roll of toilet paper, I was almost under control, though I lost it again when he sat close and put both arms around me. When I thought I could talk, I said, "He was with me when I hitched out of Rio Blanco. We got a ride with a really nice trucker, but at a rest stop—"

"Hold on." He looked dismayed. "You hitchhiked? I thought you were taking a bus."

I buried my face in my hands. "You *can't* take pets on the bus," I moaned. "He chased a rabbit, got really far away. A car stopped, picked him up. . . ." I hugged myself. "They took off with him."

"They took him? He's gone?"

I nodded.

Remy rubbed my shoulders. "Well," he said slowly, "at least he didn't end up all over the pavement."

A huge lump blocked my throat. "I'm really sorry," I whispered. "I tried to stop them."

"It's okay," he said. "I'm just glad you're all right." He chuckled. "Ol' Rebel. Always had a mind of his own."

A sob made me shudder. I said again, "I'm so sorry," more to the dog than to Remy, as if the words might escape this dim stairwell and fly to wherever Rebel had been taken.

Remy cupped my face in his hands. "Kayla, stop worrying. He was just . . . a dog. I probably shouldn't have gotten him in the first place. It would have been hell for him here." He pulled me forward, pressing his forehead against mine. "I'm not angry."

I twisted away. He didn't get it. I wasn't worried about him. A torrent of sadness rose in me, and I pressed my fist to my mouth.

He pulled my fist away and kissed it. "Kayla," he said, "it might even be better this way. Maybe he's found a home with whoever picked him up."

Better? I couldn't look at him, fixing my gaze instead on the frayed knee of my jeans. How could this be better? Rebel could be hurt or scared, chained in a filthy yard where nobody gave him food or water for days.

Remy pulled me to my feet and led me into the apartment, past band instruments, sound equipment, and a couch where Preston lay sleeping, to a bedroom where a sheet and an unzipped sleeping bag covered the narrow foam mattress from his bus. Beside the mattress were a messy stack of papers, a scratched bureau, and a few books. "Preston camps in the living room," Remy said. "Tye and Eva share the other bedroom." He dropped onto his mattress and patted it. "Take a load off, Kayla."

At least I could relax about where Eva slept. I walked over to the window. It wasn't much of a view: the busy, wide boulevard, other plain apartment buildings, a doughnut shop, an auto-parts store. A pang of missing the mesas around our trailer hit me. Remy came up behind me and gently rubbed my arms, neck, and shoulders. I leaned against him, fighting back more tears.

Someone knocked on the bedroom door. "Yo," Remy called, jumping away from me.

Eva burst in, scowling. "Rem, this phone bill's huge." She did a double take when she saw me. "Whoa. Kayla. You're a long way from home."

I sniffed and wiped my nose on my sleeve.

"You okay?"

I nodded.

"Is this a bad time?" she asked Remy. " 'Cause I've got to get this in the mail soon."

"Go ahead."

"Who's calling Nashville, L.A., New Orleans, and New York?"

"Your booking agent, drummer girl. Did you think we'd work forever in this cow town?"

"We can't pay this bill."

"You've juggled worse."

I left them alone, wandering through the living room and onto the balcony. Bits of conversation drifted out to me in tense, hushed tones.

"How long . . ."

"She's not staying. She only came to bring me the dog. . . ." Remy's words stabbed an already tender spot. Only to bring him the dog? Not staying? Where was I going to go?

". . . the other issue?"

"Eighteen, next month."

A minute later, Eva came out to the balcony. "Whatever you heard, don't sweat it. We're all a little cuckoo around here."

"I can help."

"That's what the man says, and it's noble of you, but we gotta do our own thing." She leaned on the railing. "Kayla, shouldn't you be finishing high school or something?"

I tried to chuckle. "Do I look that young?"

She sighed. "It isn't how you look. It's how you *look,* if you know what I mean." She stood up straight. "C'mon, kid. You could probably stand to shed a few layers of road dirt. I'll show you where you can shower. Did you bring a towel?"

I followed her back inside, smarting from being called a kid, grateful for her kindness.

Remy, Eva, Tye, and Preston went off to a recording studio. I slept most of the morning, waking midday with a heavy, disoriented sensation that kept me flat on Remy's mattress for a long time wishing I'd woken in the trailer and Rebel was waiting on the end of his chain for me to walk him. Hunger finally drove me down to the street to buy a late lunch.

While the band practiced that evening, even though they'd turned down the amps, hoping none of the neighbors would complain, I felt like climbing the walls. The music I usually loved ricocheted inside the small apartment, pummeling me. I retreated to the girls' room, the quietest and nicest in the apartment, with a Mexican blanket on one wall, a mobile made of tiny ceramic birds, and two cactus plants by the window. When Tye popped in to grab a sweater, she narrowed her eyes at me. "What are you doing in here?"

I mumbled, "It's kind of noisy out there."

"We're a *band*," she retorted.

I slipped out of the apartment. The harsh neon lights of the surrounding businesses irritated my eyes, still raw from crying. I shivered in the cool air and wished I'd put on my sweatshirt until I remembered that I hadn't brought one to Denver. I wandered up one block and down another, wondering where Rebel was, afraid to go back and ask to borrow a sweater, as directionless now as I'd been full of determination and purpose just twenty-four hours before.

A pay phone stood in the shadows of a convenience mart. I fingered the bills in my pocket and went inside to get change. I would just let Mom know I was okay. She couldn't find me if I called from a pay phone. I'd done her a favor by leaving, but I didn't want her to worry unnecessarily. That was how I thought of it now: my leaving was as much for her as for me, maybe more so. She could do what she wanted without me looking over her shoulder and being a burden. It would be simpler now with this distance between us.

My fingers betrayed me, jerking awkwardly as I punched the wrong numbers and had to start over.

She answered after one ring. "Yes?"

"It's me, Mom."

I heard her fumbling with something. "Where the hell are you? I've been worried sick."

Worried enough to drink? Or worried enough not to? "I'm with friends. In Denver."

"Christ. How did you get there? And who do you know in Denver?"

"I just wanted to let you know I'm okay."

She waited. "That's all you're going to tell me?"

"I need some time."

"For what? Kayla, I'll come up there and get you. Just tell me where you are."

The edge in her voice was a black hole, pulling me in. "I'm not ready to come home."

"Jesus."

I bit my thumbnail. What had I expected? That she'd be happy about my leaving?

Mom said, "Look, we've had a hard time, but we'll get through it. We always have."

I didn't trust myself to speak. I might bawl again.

"Kayla, please tell me where you are. At least give me the phone number."

A wave of tiredness came over me, and I leaned my head against the phone.

"Kayla?" Mom's voice was low. "What if I never see you again?"

I twisted away, and the receiver on its short cord nearly jerked out of my hand. She's overreacting, I thought. I never said I wouldn't see her anymore. She's trying to frighten me because she didn't get to see her mother again. It's not the same.

"Kayla! Are you there?"

"I'm right here." I cradled the receiver between my head and shoulder and jammed my hands into my back pockets.

"You're scaring me," she said.

Good, I thought, but my stomach felt icy.

"Are you doing this to punish me?" she asked.

"No," I said, but I wasn't sure.

"What did you do with Elvis?"

My throat constricted. "He's behind the trailer."

"You just let him go?"

"I put all his food out there, too." That didn't sound as good as I'd hoped.

"Just like that?"

I rubbed a tight spot on the back of my shoulder. "I've gotta go."

"Wait! Promise you'll call me tomorrow."

I held my breath. I didn't want to promise her anything. *Was* I punishing her? Was it wrong to punish your mother?

213

"Kayla?"

I cleared my throat. "I have to go."

"Call me tomorrow," she pleaded. Her voice was tight and uneven.

What if she couldn't handle my being gone? My eyes filled, and hot tears escaped.

"*Call* me," she repeated. "Kayla, did you hear me?"

I hung up the phone and leaned against it, baffled and frustrated. I'd only wanted to reassure her, but it had gone all wrong. I'd crumbled. I practically needed *her* to reassure *me*.

On my way back to the apartment, each step felt jarring. As I climbed the stairs, I tried to imagine shedding Mom like a snake sheds its skin.

Remy, Eva, and Tye were putting their instruments away. Preston stood in the kitchen doorway. "What's wrong with pasta?" he asked.

Remy said, "We've had pasta the past three nights. I'm turning into semolina."

"I can cook something," I offered.

They looked at me. "What can you cook?" Tye asked.

"Have you got any canned refries and tortillas?"

Tye groaned. "I thought you said you could *cook*." She picked up her jacket. "I think my aunt is roasting a turkey or a pig or something. I'll see you later."

Eva jumped up. "Tye, your aunt likes me. Wait up." The girls left together.

"Remy," I said, "I have some money. We could go out."

Remy clapped Preston on the shoulder. "You're on your own, buddy." He winked at me. "You saved the day, girl. Let's go."

THIRTY

Souped-up Mustangs, Chevies, and lowriders raced each other on the busy boulevard. Remy slipped his arm around my waist, now that we were by ourselves. In Rio Blanco, our secrecy was a bond, even a thrill: Remy and I against Mom, against all odds, against the world. Here, having to hide our closeness made me uneasy.

We ended up at a pancake house, where I thought I might be able to stomach some eggs and toast. I couldn't stop thinking about Rebel, but the dog seemed to be the furthest thing from Remy's mind. The band had one more day of work on the CD, he told me, and then he was taking it to L.A. "Most people mail their discs," he explained. "But I'm going to hand-deliver ours. We'll make a much bigger splash. The CD's solid." He kissed his fingertips. "Preston is brilliant, Eva smokes, and Tye is as good a bass player as you'll hear anywhere."

"And you?" I asked, trying to get out of my funk, into the spirit of things. His things.

He played with the hair that curled over the back of my neck. "I am absolutely hot."

Service was slow, and the rubbery eggs didn't exactly fire up my stalled appetite. Remy chatted happily and nearly nonstop over his Cowboy Special: three eggs sunny-side up, sausage, biscuits with gravy, and a side of corned beef hash. He ate as if he hadn't had a good meal in a week.

"This is terrific," he said between bites. When I pushed my half-eaten food away, Remy asked if he could take it to Preston. "He'll love you for it."

He asked the waitress to pack up the food, and then he turned to me. "Let's talk about you, okay?" Immediately, my eyes filled with tears. I turned from him, trying to blink them away. "What's wrong?" he asked, his dark eyebrows knitted with worry.

"Aren't you worried about Rebel?" Though I tried to stop them, a few tears slid down my face. I brushed them away.

He dropped his head, tapping his fingertips together, then smiled reassuringly. "People who pick up strays usually care about them. I'm sure he'll be fine." When I didn't respond, Remy bent toward me and whispered, "Kayla, I can't have him here. And you can't have a dog, either, remember?" He reached for my hand. "C'mon. I've got a lot to do tonight. We should go."

I blew my nose in my napkin. What happened to talking about *me?* While I paid the bill and struggled not to cry, he left the restaurant. He was standing by the door when I stepped outside. He put his arm around my shoulders, and we started walking. "Kayla, you look really tired," he said, "A good night's rest, you'll feel better in the morning." I took that to mean I could stay at least one night at his place. I nodded, relieved that he wasn't turning me out right away, that I'd have a night to sleep and figure out a plan.

The rest of the way back, he rambled on about the latest issue of *Rolling Stone* magazine. I kept waiting for him to ask why I'd come to Denver, but all he wanted to know was whether I had enough money to take the bus home. Inside the apartment, music drifted out from the girls' room, and Preston was nowhere in sight. Remy told me he needed to change some lyrics to the song they were recording tomorrow.

"That's okay," I said. "I'll just read or something."

"Great," he said.

I followed him to his room to borrow one of the books I'd seen there. He turned abruptly in the doorway and I nearly bumped into him.

"Kayla." He scratched behind one ear, looking uneasy. "I know I've written around you before, but here I'm on a different track, with deadlines and all. I can't have any distractions, you know?"

I felt like I'd been slapped. "No problem," I said, backing away, embarrassed. I closed his door, wrestling with the notion that I was a distraction. I knew how to be quiet. I could be practically invisible, too. Years with Mom had made me an expert.

I looked around the living room for something to read. There wasn't a printed page in sight, unless you counted the Lotus Blossom takeout menu or the classifieds section of the *Denver Post*. In the kitchen, the clock on the stove said 10:12. Muted guitar chords drifted through Remy's closed door. He seemed more than a couple of rooms away. I missed Rebel. With his company, I wouldn't have minded being by myself in the apartment. I pictured Mom alone in the trailer. Serves her right, I thought. Probably what she really wants, anyway.

I washed a pile of dishes, put Preston's leftover spaghetti in the refrigerator, and scraped dried strands of it off the counter. When there was nothing more to do, I got out my notebook and stared at the unfinished poem Remy used to want, wondering if he still did. Fighting sleep, I laid my head on the notebook and closed my eyes.

Remy's whisper woke me: "Hey, sweetheart, we can find a better place for you to sleep."

It was eleven forty-five. Remy noticed the half-finished poem, but he didn't say anything when I closed the notebook. I followed him like a sleepwalker. Eva and Preston sprawled on the living room floor, giggling. They looked up when Remy said, "It won't be the Ritz, but it's a place to sleep." He took me to a hallway off the entry. On one side was a closet, on the other a second door to his room. The hall dead-ended at a wall with boxes stacked against it. In front of them,

Remy laid out a thin camping pad, the half-inch lightweight kind backpackers use. Over that, he put a sheet and a Mexican blanket that looked familiar. We were out of sight of the others now, and he pulled my hips close and kissed me. It was comforting and bitter at the same time. If I closed my eyes, I saw Rebel running. If I opened them, I saw Remy watching me intently. I broke off the kiss and rested my head on his shoulder.

"I'm sorry to stick you back here," he said quietly. "The others are worried. If your mom makes a stink, it won't matter if you're sleeping up on the roof and I'm in the basement. Everything that's happening for us will come to a screeching halt."

"She's not going to make a stink."

"How do you know?"

I didn't, of course, but it seemed far-fetched. She'd never really stopped me from doing anything. "She just wants to know that I'm safe—not out on the streets or something."

His arms tightened around me. "I'm glad you're safe, too." I knew he was thinking of how I'd hitchhiked, and my eyes welled up. "Sleep tight," he said, and kissed the top of my head. He let me go, went to his room, and closed the door.

I couldn't sleep. My makeshift bed was hard, and the blanket wasn't warm enough. Why hadn't Remy taken this lousy bed and given me his? *Different track, deadlines, distractions.* I put on every layer I had, but I still felt cold. I wanted Remy to hold me. When I finally drifted into an uneasy sleep, I dreamed that Rebel slipped out of my grasp and ran down a hole that was way too small for me. I stuck my head into it, calling him. The hole suddenly widened, and I fell.

I woke in a cold sweat. Feverishly, I made plans. I'd spend the morning filling out job applications, and in the afternoon I would call every animal shelter and pound in the city. Outside the city, too, if I had to. Finding a place to live would have to wait. I had plenty of money. I'd check into a motel, maybe, one I'd seen around the corner.

I took off my extra layers and tried to smooth my wrinkled shirt. In the bathroom mirror, I worked my fingers through my matted hair. My eyes were puffy and lined underneath with dark circles. I found Remy in the kitchen, eating toast and drinking coffee. "Big sleep," he said. The clock read eight-thirty. "Feeling better?"

"Much," I lied, but it put a smile on Remy's face. "Where are the others?"

"Out already," he said, catching my hand, pulling me onto his lap, kissing the back of my neck. "I've got about three seconds before I need to go." He nuzzled behind my ear. "Too bad, huh?"

Now I smiled. "Can I use the shower?"

He pressed his face into my back, breathing in deeply. "Why? You smell good to me."

I twisted to face him. "Aren't I *distracting* you?"

His smile faded. "Yes, as a matter of fact you are."

I rose from his lap, confused.

Remy glanced at the clock. "Shit." He stood and picked up a worn leather bag with a shoulder strap. "Hey, where did you go last night while we were practicing?"

Without thinking I replied, "To call home."

His shoulders stiffened. "What did your mom have to say?"

I shrugged, kicking myself for mentioning home. "She's cool," I lied. "Just glad to hear I'm doing fine."

"She's not worried?" He looked pretty concerned himself.

"She's actually okay."

He adjusted the buckle on his shoulder strap. "Does she know I'm here?"

"No," I said, relieved to answer honestly. "She has no idea."

His face relaxed a little, and he gathered up papers and slid them into his bag. "Do you know the schedule for buses going to Rio Blanco?" he asked. "I could drop you at the station."

I took a deep breath. "I'm staying in Denver."

He said quickly, "I thought you were going back."

"Remy, for weeks we've dreamed about seeing each other, and now all you talk about is me going home."

"It happened so fast," he said. "Until your birthday, I just think it's best."

Best for whom? "I haven't even told you why I came here," I said, not sure how I would explain. An edge of pleading had crept into my voice.

He rubbed his head as if it hurt. "I know you haven't," he said, "but Kayla, I've met your mom. She can't be that bad—not for just the few weeks left till you can be on your own. You should go home and work things out."

What could I tell him, without revealing my age? And what did he know about working things out with anyone? He barely spoke to his father, and his mom lived thousands of miles away.

I shook my head. "I can't go back. She doesn't want me there."

A muscle on the side of his jaw moved. He came over to me and laced his fingers with mine, our palms together. Brought my knuckles to his lips. "I'm so sorry," he said. "I wish I could help, but the others are counting on me. We've sunk everything we have and more into launching the band, and every time they look at you . . ." He pulled me into a gentle embrace. "You have to see it through their eyes. To them, you're more than a distraction."

"And to you?" I pushed back so I could see his face.

He hesitated. "To me, you're a lot of things."

"Tell me." I was pleading again, and I hated myself for it.

He shook his head, closing his eyes for a moment. "Two months from now, everything'll be different, right?"

I forced myself to smile at him. "Sure. Don't worry about me. I'll find a place to stay. And a job."

He nodded and gave me a key. "Do me a favor. Lock up and leave this under the mat when you go."

He slid his hand behind my neck and kissed me again, his lips not quite as soft as before, his warm mouth almost making up for the fact that he was throwing me out.

I knew what I had to do—track down work and a place to live. I fixed toast, found a phone book, and carried both to Remy's room. The sleeping bag bunched at the foot of the mattress still held a bit of his warmth. I pulled it over my legs, propped his pillow behind me, made a list of all the animal shelters in the city, and started calling. There were eight shelters plus the city pound. Two, I learned, had golden retrievers. One was a male brought in early that morning, missing his collar.

"Red-gold?" I asked anxiously.

"You could say that," the woman at the shelter replied.

"Friendly?'

"Overly."

"Could you see if he answers to the name Rebel?"

"Hold on." I dug my nails into my palms while I waited. A few long minutes later, she returned. "He responds to 'Rebel,'" she said, and my breathing quickened. "But he also responds to 'Pooch,' 'Big Red,' and 'King George.'"

I refused to let that dampen my hopes and told her I'd get there as soon as I could. I packed my few things and locked up the apartment, tossing the key under the mat. I couldn't wait to see the dog. I had no idea what I'd do or where I'd go after collecting him. Once he was safely with me, I could think clearly and make a new plan.

It took me nearly two hours, walking and taking one wrong bus, to reach the shelter. Anxiously, I followed a man in a white coat to a long room reeking of dog pee and disinfectant and lined with kennels full of barking, whining, jumping dogs. The awful racket made me want to cover my ears. Even though the red-gold retriever there was too golden and hardly red, too white around the muzzle, and too heavy, my mind played tricks on me, trying to fashion this not-Rebel dog into him: maybe he gained weight, ate something that changed his hair color, aged from the trauma of being lost. He acted like he knew me—but so did a dozen other hopeful dogs in that awful room.

I turned away. The guy in the white coat said, "Sorry." My backpack straps dug into my shoulders. I found my way back to Remy's building and around the corner to the High Point Motel. It was ugly and needed paint but promised single rooms for thirty-six dollars. A large woman watched television behind the front desk, and I told her I wanted a single room.

"You got ID?" she asked.

"No," I said.

"I can't rent without ID."

I hadn't expected this. I took out my wad of bills. "I can pay extra—"

"You want to get me in trouble?"

"Never mind," I mumbled. "I'll go someplace else."

"Nobody's going to give you a room," she called after me. "Not without ID."

I hurried back to Remy's apartment and let myself in with the key he had told me to hide.

The band was off recording, so I had the place to myself. I ate some leftover food and did the dishes again, a bigger pile than before. I called all the shelters for the second time and left my name, Remy's phone number, and a description of Rebel. I stood on the balcony and watched traffic and women with strollers and men who walked with purpose or with the aimlessness of being unemployed. I'd heard that people were flocking to Denver faster than they could be hired, and I wondered what kind of work I'd find. Nowhere had I seen the kinds of houses where I might get ten or fifteen dollars an hour to walk a dog. I wrote up a flyer on the back of a discarded sheet of Remy's music paper, but I didn't have the heart to copy it, find the ritzy neighborhoods, and post it around. The only dog I wanted to walk was Rebel.

Around three o'clock, the sidewalks flooded with high school kids—groups of girls and boys sauntering with new-looking back-packs or messenger bags and cool hairstyles, their chatter punctuated with shrieks of laughter. Envy rose in me, as I imagined that each of those kids had loving families and safely tied-up, coddled pets. How else could they look so confident, so carefree?

Remy woke me from a nap by lying down beside me on his bed and stroking my back. He looked worried.

"What time is it?" I asked.

"Six o'clock."

I ran my fingers through my hair, wondering if I looked like a wreck. I sure felt like one. "I was going to check into a motel, but the ones around here are totally sleazy."

"I could have told you that," he said softly. His fingertips outlined my collarbone.

I sat up, took the money out of my pocket, and peeled off three hundreds. "When you leave tomorrow, what if I stay in your room for a few days, just till I find a job and my own place? I can help with the rent. Please."

He stared hard at the money. "Where'd you get that?"

I shrugged. "I've had two jobs, remember? No minimum wage, either."

He cracked a knuckle. "No, thanks. Keep it for Halloween."

"You sure?"

"Positive. Put it someplace safe."

I rolled up the money and stuck it inside my sock. "Is that safe?"

Trying not to grin, he pulled the sock off my foot. "Nope."

I slipped the money under my sleeve. "How 'bout there?"

He got onto his knees and lifted the neckline of my long-sleeved shirt, peering at the tank top underneath, pulling the long-sleeved shirt over my head. The money fell between us, the bills spreading out. "Not safe at all," he said, running his hand along my arm, wrist to shoulder.

I rerolled the bills and tucked them under my tank top, inside my bra. "Safe?"

He sucked in his cheeks, his gaze resting on my breasts. Keys rattled in the apartment door; voices tumbled into the living room, Tye and Eva and Preston arguing about pizza toppings.

Remy's eyes jumped to mine as he shifted onto all fours, not touching me, the air between us thick, electric.

"Safe," he whispered, and sprang up, opening the side door that led to my crummy bed. "It's right here," he said, loud enough for the others to hear, while he rummaged in one of the boxes in the hallway. I closed my eyes, spinning in the shame of being shoved aside, hidden again.

Try to understand. See it through their eyes. Until Halloween.

I didn't know what he told the others, but he let me stay a second night in the back hallway. He also let me hang out in his room while he packed for his trip, keeping his door open as the others moved about the apartment. He played a new song for me and wanted to know what I thought of it. All good things, I consoled myself as I lay awake again that night. I still had most of the cash I'd brought, and as soon as I found work, I'd be able to send money back to Shirley and Sherrie before they even knew theirs was missing. And hadn't Remy said I meant "a lot of things" to him? Some of those had to be pretty good.

I turned on the hall light and worked on a poem that had come to

224

me while Remy was messing around on his guitar, but I got stuck after the first five lines:

> *Looking for signs in a mare's tail cloud*
> *or which way a beetle flies.*
> *If the dust blows east instead of west,*
> *you might have to close your eyes.*
> *And then what will you decide?*

I kept recalling keys in the door, the band's voices, Remy springing away from me. He's better than Hal, I told myself silently, he's different. But I was still the hidden girl, the invisible one, an extra, expendable appendage. Eventually, my eyelids drooped, and I fell into a ragged sleep.

I woke in the dark. Remy moved around in the next room, getting ready to leave for L.A. I pulled on my jeans and met him at the door as he was hauling stuff down to his bus.

"Is there more?" I asked.

"In my room."

I grabbed a duffel bag and his guitar and followed him down. The sky was blue-black, the air softer and sweeter than in the harsh light of the traffic-filled day. I set his guitar behind the driver's seat, where I knew he liked to keep it. By the bus's overhead light, I studied a map of the western states while Remy stashed his duffel, briefcase, and mug of coffee. "Twelve hundred miles," Remy said. "Two days to get there, two days in L.A., and two days back." He leaned against me, looking at the map. "I wish you could go with me."

Blood rushed to my face, and I felt like a fish on a line. It sure didn't take much for Remy to reel me in.

"I can pack in two minutes."

"Don't you dare," he said, and we laughed. I felt a little sheepish because I had mixed feelings about going with him, about being in his shadow. If Remy knew I was pretending to be so eager, he didn't say so. He glanced up at the band's dark living room window and pulled me close. His good-bye kiss was surprisingly long and juicy, and it made me wish I could go, that jumping into his van would solve everything.

Eva's voice broke us apart. "Cowboy, muzzle it for a minute, would you?" She stalked over to us. "You two are leaving separately, right?"

"Yes," Remy answered for me.

Impulsively, I said, "That depends," pulled my big roll from my pocket, and counted out three hundred dollars. I thrust the money at her. "If I stay in Remy's room while he's gone, would this help?"

She searched my face, then Remy's, and ran her fingers through her hair. "Rem?"

"I don't know," he said. "I told you, she earns good money."

Taking the bills, her eyes widened. "That's a lot of rent money for just six days."

Had I given her too much? I said, "It's about what a decent hotel costs for the same amount of time."

Eva glanced at Remy, who rubbed the back of his neck. "You're the money manager," he said to her. He took a deep breath. "You decide."

"Okay," she said. "While he's gone, I guess it's okay. But then you gotta go."

"You still want to talk to me?" Remy asked Eva.

"Just get out of here," she replied, walking away. She turned at the door to the building. "Rem, you got enough for the trip?"

He grinned and waved her off. "Just barely. Don't worry about me."

My mom and I had traveled often with "just barely." It was never enough when the car broke down or we needed a motel room on a rainy night. I took his hand and wrapped his fingers around another five hundred dollars. "Just in case," I said, ignoring the misgivings surging through me. He'd see how much I cared about him, that I didn't have to be a drain on him or the band. "You don't have to spend it," I said. "Just take it with you. I know you're good for it, and I still have enough to tide me over until I find work." *If* I find it pretty soon, I thought, curling my fingers around the remaining $253 in my pocket.

He spread the bills. "Wow," he said, folding the money into his wallet. He handed me a key to the apartment, and he pulled me into a hug. His solid warmth was deliciously comforting. He kissed me again, but I broke it off, resting my head on his shoulder, doubts jumping inside me. I considered telling him the truth about the money, and I almost asked for three of the five hundred back. But with Remy pressed against me, his lips on my hair, I dropped both thoughts, not wanting to spoil the moment.

THIRTY-ONE

After Remy drove off, I walked a few blocks until I found a pay phone. Mom answered after two rings. "Goddammit, Kayla. Are you okay?"

"I'm fine."

She swore again, clicked something. A lighter, maybe.

"Kayla," she said when I didn't speak. "You haven't phoned me in two days."

I was suddenly sorry I'd called.

She said, "I need you to call me every day."

"I don't care what you need." Anger flooded me, blocking her demands. The distance I'd put between us wasn't enough. "And I'm not coming home."

She exhaled—or sighed. I couldn't tell which, but I pictured smoke rising from her lips, curling in the air above her flyaway hair.

"Please tell me where you are."

"No."

I heard a bang, like she kicked something or knocked over a chair.

"Kayla, what if something happens to you? How will I know? Who will help you?"

"Nothing's going to happen. There are plenty of people here to help if I need anything."

"You're with Remy, aren't you?"

I hesitated. "No." Not at the moment, anyway.

"I don't think you're telling the truth. People who know him say he's in Denver. And I went by Shirley and Sherrie's. They said you'd been talking about him."

"So?"

"So, honey, you're just sixteen."

"You were younger than that when you left."

She sucked in a long breath. Exhaled. I pictured her in a cloud of smoke. Foul habit.

"I *had* to leave," she said.

"So did I." I bit my lip.

More silence.

"Kayla!" she exclaimed. "You're not being reasonable!"

I traced the heads of the bolts holding the pay phone together. My throat was tight. "I'm looking for work," I said.

"What about school?"

"To hell with school," I shot back, trying to sound tough, be tough, but something broke in me and the tears started again. Pressing the phone to my stomach, I wiped my eyes on my sleeve. With the phone near my ear again, I heard her calling to me, practically shouting.

"—you there?"

I cleared my throat. "Mom, you wanted to start over. Now you really can. That's all I'm doing. Starting over." Now, *that* was reasonable, and saying it made me feel a little stronger. "You can have more than a year this time. Decades. The rest of your life. It'll be much easier."

"No," she said. "No. This is much, much harder."

"Weren't you just a little bit relieved when I went to the Patellas'?" I asked. "Maybe more than a little?"

"What are you talking about?"

"You told that social worker to take me. The day I went to the Patellas'."

"No."

"I remember it clearly. I sat outside your hospital room and you told that damn social worker, 'Take her.' She's probably got it in her records. You want me to get it in writing?"

"Oh, God," she whispered. "Kayla, I had no choice. I couldn't take care of you. I was too sick."

"And you're so much better now, right?"

"Now," she said slowly, "now, Kayla, honestly, I want a drink more than anything, more than I've ever wanted one before. But I haven't had one. Not since your birthday."

I felt sickly triumphant. "You want it more than me coming home, right?"

"In a way," she said. "Yes. More than you coming home."

My voice turned shrill. "So, bottoms up, Mom. Party on. I'm hundreds of miles away. What's stopping you?"

"I think . . . ," she began, and stopped. "I think if I can not drink long enough, that feeling of wanting to get drunk more than anything else will go away."

My head pounded. "What makes you think that?"

"I've heard it works that way. From people who know. People who drank."

"Well," I said, "you might discover that what you really want more than anything is a Harley or a house with a swimming pool."

"I might," she agreed, her voice low and hoarse. "But I don't think so."

The operator butted in, asking for more money, giving me time to breathe. It would have been so easy to hang up, to walk away. She was telling me to come home, but she didn't really want that. She wanted to drink—she admitted it, and nothing, nothing and no one— including me—mattered as much. I shoved four more quarters in, and when the connection came back, I said, "I'll send you my address sometime—"

"Dammit, Kayla! Listen!"

"Why should I?"

"Because—when they took you into foster care, you were too young to choose for yourself. Now you can—not legally, but still, you can. I'm asking you to choose *us,* even if it's not what you most want, like I'm choosing today not to take a drink."

There it was again, I thought, another twisted reason for me to come home. She doesn't *want* me. She thinks she *needs* me—but I'm done bowing to her every need. A woman stood nearby waiting to use the phone. She crouched at eye level with a little girl in a stroller, grinning and cooing and tucking in her blanket.

"Kayla," Mom said. "Please, come home."

Take her. Take her. I'm a fish on a line once more, unhooked and tossed, reeled in again.

"Why?" I asked again. Nothing made sense to me except the anger curling my hands into tight fists.

She cleared her throat. "Because I love you."

No, you don't.

The woman waiting for the phone leaned over and kissed the top of the child's head. *I love you.* Hollow, hollow words. "Yeah," I said. "I love you, too." I hung up, angrily wiping my eyes, and hurried away, avoiding the soft gaze of the woman with the child.

It was too early for my daily calls to the animal shelters. I stashed my backpack in Remy's room and set out in search of hot cocoa, ending up at a restaurant called the Grand Corral. In the window was a HELP WANTED sign. I sat at a table underneath spurs and horse tack and phony kerosene lamps. When a cheery woman maybe ten years older than me took my order, I asked what kind of help they wanted. She said to ask Pony, the cook and manager. I drank the cocoa slowly, taking in its warmth, and then went back to the kitchen. Pony barked questions at me while he grilled sausages and flipped pancakes. When I couldn't produce any ID or proof that I was at least sixteen, he told me to get lost.

Standing straight, I told him evenly, "I'm over sixteen, I work hard, and I need the job."

He tossed slices of ham on the grill as if he were dealing cards. "I can give you five an hour, under the table. Delia will get you started. You got questions, ask her. Been here six, seven years. She knows everything."

Confused, I asked, "Who's Delia? And when do you want me to start?"

He pointed his spatula at the woman who'd brought my cocoa. "Now."

"Right now?"

"You don't want the job, I'll hire someone else. Plenty of people around with ID."

"No—you just haven't told me what you want me to do."

He turned his back on me. "I already said, Delia'll get you started."

"Can I get some breakfast first?"

He pointed to a pot of oatmeal. "Help yourself. One meal a shift, my choice. No steaks, no shrimp, no sausages. Understand?"

Five an hour was a comedown from my own high-paying business. I scooped a little oatmeal and a lot of brown sugar and raisins into a bowl and found Delia, who put me to work prepping salads and desserts for lunch, filling bowls with jam packets and jars with maple syrup, and scrubbing pans. In my spare time, I had to bus and set tables. She helped me while the breakfast crowd was small, but eventually she said, "You're getting the hang of it. I've gotta do my own stuff now."

I thought I was managing okay until one of the waitresses brought a fruit salad back to me with a fly in it, acting like I'd put it in there on purpose. Pony yelled at me often, even when I was doing things right, and I cut my finger slicing a banana for someone's oatmeal.

During a lull, Delia pulled me out back and offered me a mint from a roll she kept in her pocket. I took one.

"You new in town?" Delia asked, popping two mints into her mouth.

"Very."

"Got a place to live?"

"For a few days."

"You got family?"

I shook my head. "Not around here."

She took a compact and a lipstick out of her purse. "You could share my place for a while," she said. She ran the lipstick over her lips. "Till you find your own." She wrote down an address and phone number, and I took them, grateful for my good luck. "Come by after work if you want to see it," she said.

As soon as my shift ended, I went back to Remy's and called all the animal shelters. No news was bad news, and I had to drag myself over to Delia's apartment to check it out. The neat one-bedroom had a kitchenette, a tiny back bedroom, a foldout couch in the living room. "How does three forty a month sound?" she asked. "I pay seven fifty, but with you just getting the couch, it doesn't seem fair to ask for half."

Three hundred and forty a month wasn't a lot less than half, but I decided not to point that out to her since I felt lucky to find a place so quickly that I could afford. I offered her two weeks' rent, but she really wanted the whole month, and we compromised on $240, with me promising to pay the rest as soon as I could. I pocketed my remaining thirteen bucks and told her I'd move in the next night.

Over a $3.99 burrito and chips at a taqueria near Remy's, I silently congratulated myself. At my age, my mother was homeless, probably scrounging food out of Dumpsters. I had a full-time job, a place to live, and a friendly roommate. My one regret was that I'd given Eva so much money and then needed to stay at the band's apartment only one more night. If I was going to be on my own, I had to learn not to panic so easily and throw money at every little dilemma in my path.

From now on, I reassured myself, I'd be okay. Mom wasn't here to screw things up. I needed to relax and trust that little by little I would work everything out.

THIRTY-TWO

I moved into Delia's apartment after work the next day—a Friday—right after Pony paid me only thirty-five dollars. "What about yesterday?" I asked. "And today, I worked eight hours."

Pony scraped the grill while he talked. "I don't pay to train," he said. "And I take out five dollars for your meals. Didn't charge anything for what you ate yesterday."

"That doesn't seem right," I said.

He fixed me with a questioning look. "I can take out another five for yesterday's meals, if that's what you want."

"No, I mean —"

"Did you find your ID yet?"

I shoved the money in my pocket and walked away.

Delia took me to her apartment when our shift ended. She cleared a couple of shelves in the living room for my clothes and gave me sheets for the pullout, and a towel. "I'm going out for a couple of beers with some friends," she told me. "I'd invite you, but I have a feeling you're not quite old enough."

"Not quite."

"Help yourself to the TV in my room," she said. She glanced at my small backpack. "Do you know anybody in town?"

"My boyfriend lives near here, but he's away this week." I busied myself putting clothes on the shelves. I'd never described Remy as my boyfriend to anyone. Saying it aloud made me wonder if that was the right word to use. I added, "I'll get the rest of my stuff once I'm settled into my own place."

After Delia left to meet her friends, the silence drove me out onto the street. I found a pay phone, confident that this call would be better, given my new situation. Still, I paced in front of it for several minutes before I felt steady enough to call.

"It's me, Mom."

"God. I know, honey. How are you?"

"Pretty good." Instantly, I wished I'd said great, or excellent. "I've got a job," I said, trying to sound more enthusiastic. "And an apartment."

She was quiet for a moment. "I hope you're not expecting me to congratulate you."

"I don't expect anything," I said quickly, trying to ignore a jolt of disappointment. This proved that the whole "I love you" routine was just a ploy to get me home.

"Where are you working?"

Did she think I was stupid? That I'd let her track me that way? "In a restaurant," I said.

"I don't want to play guessing games."

"Then don't ask questions you know I won't answer."

She sighed. "Kayla, try answering this: what do you know about the money Shirley and Sherrie had in their back room? What's it called—the Palace?"

I took a deep breath. "I don't know anything."

"Some money they hid there is missing."

Even though I'd expected this might happen, my heart flapped wildly.

"A thousand dollars," she added.

My hands felt clammy.

"Kayla? Are you there?"

"Yes. I'm just . . . thinking." I tried to keep my voice even. "Did they call the police?"

"No. They're hoping to deal with it themselves. They say you're the only person who might have known about it. They also say you couldn't have taken it because they counted the money after you returned their key. Was it you, Kayla? You've got to tell me the truth."

I bit my lip so hard, it brought tears to my eyes. "Like they said, I gave them back the key."

"This is a nightmare," she said. "Kayla, for chrissake, tell me where you are. Whatever's going on—with you, with this money—we'll work it out. Just tell me."

"There's nothing to tell."

"Shit," she muttered. "Then *don't* tell me, and I won't ask questions when you come home."

When I come home? I heard noises on her end, and it frustrated me that I couldn't tell what she was doing. Pouring a shot? Reaching for a tissue? Why did I want to know? A hand closed around my throat. I can do this. I can stay away.

"Who said I'm coming home?"

"Dammit, Kayla."

"Have you been drinking?"

"No."

"But you still want to?"

She hesitated. "Yes, Kayla. It's not going to change overnight!"

"Just let me know when it has changed, okay? I don't need to be around you before then."

"You asked," she said. "You wanted the truth. At least I'm telling you the truth. That's more than you're giving me."

I started to say, *I've given you too much already,* but suddenly even that seemed too generous. My truth. A piece of me. She didn't deserve it.

I hung up.

* * *

237

I told myself I didn't need to freak out—or run home. Mom wasn't drinking—or so she said. At least Shirley and Sherrie hadn't called the police. As far as I could tell, they had plenty of money, so I shouldn't worry that missing a grand was causing them any hardship.

I had my own life now. I would pay the two women back. I just needed time.

Hoping to make more money, I asked Pony the next day if I could add some evening shifts. With Remy out of town, I didn't have anything to do in the evenings, anyway. He said no, that since he was paying me under the table, I could only work days, when he was cooking. Another guy cooked at night. I started to argue with him but stopped when he glared at me.

I spent the second evening at my new place eating a frozen dinner of meatloaf, mashed potatoes, and peas—I'd picked up four of them for six dollars— and watching television with Delia, who was addicted to anything with hospitals or cops. The public television station had a show on Australian sheepdogs and other working dogs that I wouldn't have minded watching, but Delia hung on to the remote all evening, and she didn't ask me what I wanted to see. During commercial breaks, she leafed through a community college catalog, trying to decide which nursing courses to take. She circled several possibilities in red pen, tossing the catalog aside when her show returned. My feet ached from being on them all day, and my toes hurt; my boots were getting too small. Several times I dozed off.

"I came to Denver alone, like you." Delia's voice woke me. "About your age—seventeen, right?"

"Almost," I said, rubbing my eyes. On the TV, a nurse injected something into a patient's IV and nervously glanced over her shoulder.

"You'll do okay," she said, as if I weren't already. "Look at that. You think she'll get away with it?"

"I don't know." It annoyed me that Delia was offering opinions about my future. The TV patient went into cardiac arrest, setting off alarms and buzzers. Delia muttered, "He deserved it, don't you think?" I told Delia goodnight and left her room before she could make more predictions about the likelihood—or not—of my success.

By my fourth day at the Corral, I was already settling into a mind-numbing routine: up and into work by six-thirty, prep meals and bus dishes and dodge Pony's bad moods, buy myself a snack after work, check on the lost dogs listed in the paper and at the shelters, then go back to Delia's and heat another frozen dinner. Afterward, for lack of anything better to do, I put up my aching feet and nodded off in front of the TV. One night when Delia went out, I watched a show on grey-hound racing. Those dogs and I had some things in common: racing to a finish line—mine was payday—and running in circles. Only, they seemed to love what they were doing.

I spent my day off checking the shelters and picking up some food for the apartment because Delia had frowned at me when I helped myself to her juice and cereal that morning, and she asked me if I planned to get any groceries of my own. I wished I could ask Mom to send me the clothes I'd left behind and the ATM card. In my rush to leave Rio Blanco, I'd left the card in one of my drawers, and without it I couldn't withdraw any money. I still owed a hundred for rent, the next payday was four days off, and I was down to eighteen dollars. I'd breathe easier when Remy gave me back the emergency money I'd loaned him. Even if he'd had to use some, whatever remained would help.

Spending so many hours by myself that day, it was hard not to think about Mom. I hadn't called her in four days. Not talking to her was a load off my back, but the effort it took not to call had been almost worse. A woman at the grocery store reminded me of her, and I wondered if I should tell Mom about Shirley and Sherrie's money. A pet shop I passed reminded me of Elvis. Had Mom found him? Was he alive? The bars in my new neighborhood—three between the apartment and work, one across from the Corral—sent me into a tailspin: What if she goes on a binge and can't stop? Why do I need to know? Why should I care?

That afternoon, on a back shelf in Delia's front closet, I found more college catalogs like the one she kept browsing, but these dated back five to seven years. She'd folded down page corners and circled a few courses. I set the catalogs carefully back on the shelf, wondering if she'd finished high school. Would I be like Delia six or seven years from now? Dreaming of one thing and doing another? Maybe regretting that I hadn't finished high school?

Opening one of the catalogs again, I scanned the poetry classes, and then the sciences. What if I made a decision about school that had nothing to do with Mom? What would I need to become a veterinarian? A dog trainer? An overpaid pet psychologist, like Luz and her friends joked about?

Twice that night, I walked over to Remy's to check for his bus. The third time—nearly ten o'clock—it was there. Eva let me into the apartment. "He's unpacking." She nodded toward Remy's room. "Hey, thanks for the second batch of dough. You saved Rem's hide. Everyone's, really."

Preston came out of the kitchen with Tye close behind. "Let's go, Eva," he said. "I'm starving." As their footsteps echoed down the hallway and stairwell, I gathered the courage to knock on Remy's closed bedroom door.

"Hey, there," he said, drawing me into a snug embrace. "*Mmm.* This beats screaming down the highway in a self-destructing van. Are you the welcoming committee?"

"Sure." When he let me go, I kicked off my boots and sat on his mattress, tucking my feet under me. "How was L.A.?"

"Unbelievably awesome." His face flushed. "L.A. *loved* us." He went on about L.A., but I was so anxious to hear what had happened to the money, I barely listened and almost didn't notice when he changed the subject. "Eva said you moved out after one night."

I tried to smile. "I got a job and a place to live in one day."

"Cool."

"Rem, that money I loaned you—do you still have any of it?"

Under other circumstances, the warm smile that bloomed on his face would have melted me. "How did you know I'd need that much?" he asked. "You must be psychic. I wasn't going to use it, and then there I was, stuck on the shoulder of I-70 with a dead fuel pump. Nearest VW dealer? Eighty miles away. The most amazing thing was the guy who towed me knew about Terra Luna. He'd heard us at Gracie's and only charged me half what he should have."

"So you have some left over?"

He dropped down beside me, gently knocking me over. "Not a cent," he whispered into my ear, and then he kissed it. "But it was just enough. You are a lifesaver. I got to L.A. in time for all my appointments, thanks to you."

I tried to think straight while his lips worked down the side of my neck. "You think it'll be a while before you can pay me back?"

One of his hands made circles on my back. Under my shirt. "You want the truth, right?"

Hadn't my mom said something similar? "I guess."

"Let's just say I need some time," he said, moving in to kiss me, then giving me one of his sweetest smiles. "Welcome to the world of struggling musicians." Another kiss, slower, wetter. His hand crept up my spine. "Kick-ass, up-and-coming musicians."

The heat of his hand against my skin, his euphoria, the tip of his tongue finding its way between my lips, none of that was enough to counter the sinking in my gut, the persistent feeling that he didn't really see me, didn't really think about me.

Why didn't he say *Are you managing okay without that money? Is there anything I can do to help in the meantime?*

He's excited. He's had a breakthrough. See it through his eyes.

Not even *I'm sorry I can't pay you back.*

I wanted to untangle myself from him, but he did it first, pulling away, snatching a copy of Terra Luna's demo CD from the bureau. "Want to hear us? Knock your socks off?"

"How about tomorrow?" I straightened my shirt and reached for the door. "I've got the early shift in the morning."

"Tomorrow? If you insist." He grinned. "Though I'm not sure how you can wait."

He didn't say *I'll walk you back to your apartment.*

I waited maybe five more humiliating seconds, but he didn't offer, and I was not about to ask.

THIRTY-THREE

Delia called out from her room as soon as I let myself in. "Did your boyfriend pay you back?"

I walked slowly to her room, choosing my words carefully. "He couldn't. His bus broke down. I'm sorry." I offered her my last eighteen dollars. "This is all I have until payday."

She took the money, frowned, and gave it back to me. "Ask Pony for an advance, would you? I've got a dentist appointment tomorrow, and the rent's due."

As I unfolded the sofa bed, I wondered for the millionth time where Rebel was and whether he was okay, and that made me think of Mom. Having not heard from me in four days, she might be frantic by now. Her problem, though. She'd have to get over it. I certainly was. What had I been expecting, the sky to fall?

I got into bed, but I was restless. The sky *hadn't* fallen, so why not call? For all I knew, she might be just as amazed. Or a little embarrassed. *Sorry I rode you so hard, Kayla. You've done a courageous thing. Now I know what you went through. I didn't understand before, because I'd never been abandoned . . .*

And then I remembered Desmond, who did abandon her. Oh, what the hell.

Reluctant to dress and go out again or spend what little cash I had at a pay phone, I stuck my head into Delia's room and asked to use her cell. "It's kind of late to go out on the street, and I could pay you for it," I offered. A cell phone call had to be cheaper than the pay phone.

She barely took her eyes off the TV screen. "Sure, but don't make a habit of it, okay?" She dug the phone out of her purse. Feeling my face grow warm, I took it into the other room, closing her door behind me, and sat on the floor against the couch.

"Jesus, Kayla," Mom said when she answered. "Christ almighty. Why haven't you called?"

Here we go again. I took a deep breath. "I've been busy. Working. I just wanted to let you know I'm fine."

"Hell of a way to do it, not calling for a week."

"Just four days."

"Feels like a month. Where are you?"

"Same place. Denver."

"But *where*, Kayla? Where exactly are you?"

"Mom," I said, trying to stay calm, "it's none of your business."

"Hold on." Her voice got muffled for a moment while she talked to someone else. "Kayla? Listen to me. Listen carefully. Redbone and everyone else has been telling me to call the police, that I'm crazy not to."

Redbone is a traitor, I thought. If the cops come after me, the social workers will be right behind them. I got to my feet. "Why are you listening to Redbone? He's not my father."

"He's here, and he's been a big help."

"My real dad might have been a much bigger help, if you hadn't run him off."

"Don't change the subject," she said, her voice wavering slightly.

"This *is* the subject," I blurted, sensing that I'd hit a sore spot. My mind searched frantically for the right words to hit her harder. "I bet he couldn't get away from you fast enough."

"If I have to call the police," she said slowly, as if she was talking to a little kid, "they'll be all over Remy. Is that what you want?"

A chill ran through me. "Remy doesn't even know where I am. Leave him out of this."

"You're not giving me much choice."

She had me backed into a corner. I was furious, and I no longer cared if I made sense. I just wanted to hurt her, and I knew how. "Admit it," I said. "Desmond couldn't stand to be around you, right? Just like I couldn't."

"This isn't about Desmond."

Her avoiding the question made me bolder. "Answer me!" I demanded.

"It wasn't like that."

"What *was* it like, then? If you were so damn wonderful, why did Desmond walk out the door?"

I heard tapping, rustling, a soft thump. My insides churned, a prickly mix of anxiety and rage.

"Your father wasn't the one who walked out," she said.

"You told me he did."

"I never said that."

Was that true? Had she never said he left? "Are you telling me that you left him?" Blood pulsed in my temples.

More silence. Then, "Yes."

The air felt thin. "Did he know you were pregnant?"

"No." She paused. "Maybe he suspected."

"But he loved you, right? He gave you money, he begged you to stay. Why did you leave?"

She was quiet for so long, I asked again, "Why?"

"I didn't love him," she said.

I moved to the window. Across the street, a woman walked two small dogs.

"Why not?"

Mom cleared her throat. "I didn't love anybody then."

Not even me, I bet. I felt nauseated. The small, lurking idea that she loved me now was an arrow I had to dodge. I began to pace. Four steps from the kitchenette to my sofa bed. Four steps back. "So you want me home so you can have another opportunity to dump me?" She started to speak, but I cut her off. "Let's count the people you've left. All your boyfriends. Your mom—twice. Desmond. And me, for a whole damn year, with strangers."

"I didn't leave you on purpose, Kayla. And I came back, remember? I came back to you. I haven't left since."

I squeezed the phone so hard my hand ached. "It feels like you leave every time you drink."

She groaned. "I'm sorry. I'm really sorry."

"Big deal."

"Kayla," she pleaded, "come home."

I tapped my fingers on the receiver. "I've got a whole new life here. Something you always aspired to. Only, I did it." Gunshots on the TV drowned out my mom's next words. I took the phone into the bathroom and closed the door. "What?"

"I said, congratulations on your new life. That's what you want to hear, right?"

I sat on the lid of the toilet and spun the roll of paper. "Whatever."

"Kayla, for now, I won't call the cops, but only if you phone me every day. If you miss one day, I'll call. Do you understand?"

I stood. The girl reflected in the mirror was pale, with dark circles under red-rimmed eyes, scruffy hair, a scowling face. An urge to slam the phone into the mirror swept upward from my feet, and I gripped it tighter. *Come home. I love you.* Who did I love? A lost dog. A guy who loved himself. I slid down the door until my butt hit the floor. Why *didn't* she call the cops? Why was she was offering me one more chance to disappear from her life? "Whatever," I said. "Fine."

"Okay." Mom's voice was hoarse. "Kayla, please, what can I say to make you change your mind about coming back?"

I closed my eyes. The way she asked felt so close to love that I started to shake. The shooting on Delia's television continued, muffled by the closed bathroom door. The sickly sweet smell from a bowl of potpourri on the back of the toilet saturated the air in the tiny room, making me feel suffocated. I leaned over my knees, sliding my fist along the lines in the linoleum. "Can you promise you won't drink anymore?"

Sirens wailed on the TV. I chewed the inside of my cheek.

"No," she said. "I can't. But I'll do everything I can to stay sober the rest of today. And tomorrow, same thing. And the day after."

I dug my nails into my palm. "That's not enough."

She said, "It's all I have."

I hung up and carefully erased the record of Mom's number from Delia's phone.

At the end of my shift the next day, I asked Pony if he could advance me some money.

"That's no big deal, since I'm paying you in cash," he replied, probably the nicest thing he'd ever said to me. He paid me for the four days I'd worked since the last payday, taking a $140 straight out of the cash register. I vowed to make breakfast at home and take my own lunch to work. I needed the five dollars a day he was docking me for eating his lousy oatmeal and weird casseroles concocted from leftovers.

Delia had already left. I hung up my apron and stood outside on the sidewalk, calculating. I owed Delia a hundred. Once I paid her, I'd have fifty-eight bucks left. Being on my feet day after day, I couldn't continue to ignore that my boots no longer fit. On the way to Delia's, I stopped at a discount shoe store but couldn't find anything comfortable for less than twenty-five dollars. I settled on some sneakers, plus two pairs of desperately needed socks, since I hadn't brought enough with me. The salesclerk took my money way too cheerfully. I still needed tampons, toothpaste, and shampoo, since I'd been using Delia's, plus new underwear. I bought the tampons and toothpaste and a bottle of shampoo that smelled like bubble gum but was only ninety-nine cents in the bargain bin. Not counting my rent money, I was down to about sixteen dollars, with two more days until payday. The underwear would have to wait.

Delia noticed that I was practically broke after I paid her that evening. "I usually earn a lot more," I told her. "Back home, I earned ten or fifteen an hour walking dogs. I'm only working at the restaurant until I find something better."

She gazed at me for a minute. "So am I, Kayla."

It was only nine-thirty when I collapsed onto the foldout couch. I could have gone to see Remy, but I didn't want him to think I needed entertaining every evening. I wondered where Rebel was and whether he had enough to eat. I missed seeing Elvis poke his head out of hiding places. I took out my notebook. If I finished the poem Remy liked, would it change anything between us?

I knew the answer. I stared at the lines of my poem, but the longer I stared, the less sense they made. I tossed the notebook to the floor and turned off the light.

I thought about Mom's half-baked apologies, her lame threat to call the cops. *I love you. Come home.* Sure, she was trying, maybe harder than ever, but it didn't matter, it would never be enough, I would just keep raising the bar. Jump, Mom. Higher. *Higher.* Even though it won't make a bit of difference. You can jump all the way to the moon, Mom, but you can never, ever give me back what I've lost.

But I'll still make you try.

Sadness uncoiled in me and I cried quietly at first, my face pressed into the pillow so Delia wouldn't hear, then louder, because I stopped caring who heard and couldn't have held back the rush of pain and loneliness and regret even if I'd tried. The TV blared in Delia's room, and maybe she was asleep, because she didn't come to investigate even when my cries rose to full pitch.

Or maybe she did hear, but she knew I needed to be alone.

When I could finally open my fists and uncurl my body from around Delia's spare pillow, when I could breathe without shuddering, I kept imagining a man named Desmond, tall and big-boned like me, as he watched my mom walk out the door. Did he try to stop her? Did he call out her name? Did she even give him a chance? Did she leave in the middle of the night or while he was at work, when he couldn't protest?

I turned onto my side, trying to get comfortable, but it wasn't the thin sofabed mattress or the bony springs underneath that made me squirm. If I didn't go back to Mom, I'd be doing exactly what I hated most about her, the thing that hurt me the most.

Leaving.

THIRTY-FOUR

It was a mistake to wait until the end of my shift the next day to tell Pony I was quitting. I hadn't wanted to hear him blast me all day about quitting only eight days after he'd hired me, but my strategy backfired: I didn't notice when he left earlier than usual, so I didn't have a chance to collect my last wages.

I found Remy at his apartment hauling amps and a mike down to his VW for a solo gig that night. "I'm going back to Rio Blanco," I told him, helping him carry one of the amps. His expression changed several times, and I couldn't read any of it. He set his gear on the sidewalk and hooked his finger onto the neck of my T-shirt, tugging me gently toward him. "When?"

The day was warm and airless. Remy smelled of coffee and fresh sweat. "First thing tomorrow."

"Damn," he said. "Just when I'm getting used to having you around."

Was that his way of saying he'd miss me?

"It makes sense, though," he went on. "We've got gigs over in Boulder and Colorado Springs, then down in Phoenix. I'll be gone a lot."

He didn't ask why I was finally going or if I really had to leave. I might as well have said I was going to the grocery store.

"Rem, could you do me a favor?" It surprised me how easily that came.

"I'll try," he said, climbing into the back of the bus to arrange his gear.

"I could use a ride to the truck depot where I'm meeting the guy who drove me here. Fridays, he drives to Albuquerque."

He sat in the open side door of his VW. "I'd rather give you a lift to the bus station. Can't you take the bus this time?"

"Sure, if you've got sixty-four dollars to spare." I folded my arms. "'Cause I don't."

"Right. I guess I know about that." He wiped sweat off his forehead with the back of his hand and went back to organizing his gear. "What do you know about this truck driver, anyway?"

"He's a good guy." I shoved my hands into my pockets. "He spent a bunch of time trying to help me find Rebel."

Remy grunted inside the bus, shifting his stuff. "Maybe I should meet him."

"What for?"

He shut the side door and came close, running his hands up and down my arms, sending sparks of warmth through me. "So I know you're safe."

His concern surprised and pleased me, and I smiled.

"Kayla, I'm serious," he said, frowning. "The last thing I need is for you to get knocked off by some weirdo pretending to be a nice guy."

The last thing *he* needs? For a moment, our eyes locked, and I no longer believed that my safety was tops in his mind, but he pulled me close again, his hands caressing my head and back, and he said softly: "I just want you to be safe."

Neither of us spoke while we held each other, my chin on his shoulder, his unshaved cheek bristly on mine. "It's too bad you can't come hear me tonight," he said, his tone lighter now. "Your last chance for a while," he said. "I'd sneak you in, but . . ."

"No." Stepping back, I shook my head. "I understand. Just meet me here at six-fifteen tomorrow morning so I can make that ride."

He grimaced. "Six-fifteen?"

"Otherwise, I have to walk across the city while it's still dark."

"I guess it won't kill me." He brushed his lips against my hair before jumping into the VW. He started the engine and shifted into gear. I could have gone to him for a kiss—he looked as if he expected me to—but I stayed put, sensing miles between us already.

"See you in the morning." I tried to smile. "Sorry to get you up so early after a gig."

"Maybe I can go back to sleep after."

Watching him drive off, I started feeling sorry for myself. What's wrong with me? Why didn't he beg me to stay? Just before I could get too miserable, I remembered that Remy owed me hundreds of dollars, yet he practically choked over the idea of driving me across town. I could come to Denver, I could leave—it was all the same to him as long as I didn't mess up any of his plans.

Shoving my hands in my pockets, I felt the list of animal shelters. I looked at it one more time, then dropped it in a trash can and headed to Delia's. I didn't have a lot to pack, but I was ready to do it.

It wasn't quite seven A.M. when Remy parked near a huge warehouse lot with semis rumbling in and out. We both hopped out of the bus. I couldn't see Barlow, but I pointed out his black and purple truck to Remy. "Barlow's probably in the cab. If you want to meet him, let's go."

"Wait," Remy said, reaching out to me, brushing his knuckles lightly down my neck. "This is probably it till Halloween, right?" He traced the edge of my ear with his thumb.

I closed my eyes for a moment, trying to still the part of my heart that leaped for joy: See? He wants me!

But it wasn't enough. I wanted more now. And I wanted him to know who I really was.

"Remy, I won't be back for Halloween."

"Why not?"

A guy walked over to Barlow's cab and gestured for him to roll down his window. "I think we want different things."

A muscle twitched at his temple.

"And there's something else."

He reached back and took hold of his ponytail. "What else?"

"I'm only sixteen."

The color left his face. "When do you turn seventeen?"

"Next August."

He looked away.

"Didn't you suspect?"

He smoothed his hair back with both hands. "At times."

"Why didn't you say anything?"

"Why didn't you?"

He looked pained, or nervous. Or maybe both, like me.

"You still want to meet Barlow?"

He kicked a stone at his feet. "Sixteen?"

Somewhere inside my rib cage, relief collided with a sickening ache. "I better go." I put my arms around him. He flinched slightly, but he hugged me back. "Don't worry about me. I'll be fine!" I said. I grabbed my backpack and jogged over to the semi. I looked back once, half hoping, to see if he was following. He was in the VW bus, his head resting on the steering wheel. I couldn't tell if he was watching me or not.

The driver in the black and purple cab wasn't Barlow. He was young, with dark hair and a handlebar mustache. "Where's Barlow?" I asked, frantically scanning the other cabs in the lot.

"Check with the office," he said, rolling up his window.

"Wait! Are you heading to Albuquerque?"

"No passengers," he mouthed through the glass. The huge truck lurched forward. I ran to the depot office and asked the guy behind the desk where Barlow was.

"Got pneumonia," he said. "He'll be down for a week, maybe two."

I felt like arguing with him, telling him Barlow could not be sick, that someone had to give me a ride. The guy shrugged and said, "Sorry."

Outside, Remy was waiting. He lifted his head off the steering wheel and gestured with one hand as if to say, *What's going on?*

I might still have a job if I hurried to work. Delia would probably let me stay on with her, if she hadn't already scooped some other stray girl off the streets. If I was careful, in two, maybe three more paydays I might have enough to buy a bus ticket and get myself home.

I was halfway to the VW. Remy's arm rested on the door, his hand beating a rhythm on the orange metal. He looked at his watch and gestured again, more impatiently this time. "Kayla!" he called to me. "What's up with your ride? I need to get out of here."

I had to shut my eyes for a moment before I could wave him off. "Go ahead!" I yelled, my voice catching. Then I turned and went back to the guy in the office. "Do you have a phone I can use?"

When Mom answered, I asked as matter-of-factly as I could, "Do you still have that credit card?"

THIRTY-FIVE

Mom had the late shift at Circle K and couldn't meet my bus, but that was fine with me. It was Shirley and Sherrie I wanted to see first. I was surprised to see a light on in the store and the two women talking near the cash register.

"Our traveler has returned," Shirley announced, unlocking the front door when she saw me.

Cocoa's bed was now behind the counter. He climbed out of it and came over to greet me. I bent down to scratch him, trying to collect my thoughts. "I took the money," I announced, "but I want to pay it all back. I have a hundred dollars in the bank I can bring you tomorrow."

Sherrie said, "Just tell us: are you okay?"

"I'm fine."

She looked concerned. "Were you in some kind of trouble?"

"I wasn't pregnant, if that's what you mean. I didn't even use most of the money for myself."

"Someone else was in trouble?"

"Kind of. But everything is okay now."

Shirley asked, "Who are you trying to protect, Kayla?"

I shifted my weight from one foot to the other. "No one. The person I gave it to didn't know it wasn't mine."

"Stolen," Shirley said, looking pointedly at me.

"Stolen," I repeated reluctantly. "From you."

Shirley squinted at me. "You sure that person didn't know?"

I felt embarrassed. "Pretty sure."

Sherrie held up her hands. "Wait a minute, wait a minute. Kayla, you turned in your key before the money was stolen, so it couldn't have been you."

My face getting warm, I explained how I'd done it. Shirley went back to the Dog Palace and returned. "That window's unlocked, like she said."

Sherrie sighed, her bifocals on their chain rising and falling on her chest.

Shirley lifted her gaze to the ceiling, then focused again on me. "Is the person you assisted helping you pay us back?"

I looked down at my feet. "Probably not."

Shirley set one hip on a stool by the counter. "So, you want to work it off."

I inhaled deeply. "I do."

"You expect us to trust you with our dog. Or around our store."

My knees felt kind of shaky. "I'm just asking. I'll understand if you say no."

Sherrie had been looking out the window. She turned. "Why did you come back, Kayla?"

"To pay you back."

"Is that all?"

"Well, for my mom, too. To give her another chance."

Shirl turned to Sherrie. "What do you think would be better for her, working it off, or some time in juvie and then working it off?"

My heart jumped. "You're going to report me?"

"Why shouldn't we?" Shirley said. "That was a lot of money. How do you know I wasn't counting on it to pay for something important—medical care for one of us? Rent on this store? What were you thinking when you took it?"

My stomach turned circles. "Did you—did you have any problems like that?"

"No," Sherrie broke in. "Shirley, what's minimum wage now?"

"Five fifteen."

"Roughly a hundred and eighty hours, Kayla," Sherrie said. "A hundred and sixty, if you bring the hundred tomorrow. That's what you owe us."

"Okay."

Shirley said, "You stay out of the Palace—there's no money there anymore, but still—and you don't walk the dog. That's Sherrie's job now, good for both of them."

"Sure."

"You do whatever we ask—scrub the toilet, put a thousand stickers on labels."

"Fine."

"*And* you go to school."

I stiffened. "I was planning to anyway."

Sherrie picked up Cocoa and scratched him behind his floppy ears. She spoke almost cheerfully. "If you mess up again, you'll be dealing with much worse than the likes of us."

I swallowed. "You want me to start tomorrow?"

"There's one more condition," Sherrie said. "Have you seen your mom yet?"

"We've talked."

"Did you apologize to her?"

"Are you kidding?" I sputtered. "For what? I came back. That's all the apology she needs."

"That's our other condition."

I couldn't believe this. "Do you have any idea what she's done to me? She's lucky I was willing to come back."

Sherrie adjusted the pin on her blouse. "She is, but that's not what we're talking about."

"That's between her and me. What's it to you, anyway?"

Sherrie said to Shirley, "You know what I'm talking about?"

"I know," she replied.

"Would you explain it to her?"

"Kayla," Shirley said, "we want our money back. If you've got a big rift at home, you're not going to stick around. We'll lose our money."

"My apologizing won't do anything! I'm here. She's the one who has to change now."

Sherrie said, "I'm not saying she doesn't. Just that every disagreement goes two ways."

"Look, I'll do double the hours I owe you. Whatever you want."

"No deal. We already told you what we want."

"You're butting into someone else's business."

Sherrie smiled. "Sometimes we just can't help ourselves."

"So you want me to apologize, even if I don't mean it?"

Sherrie screwed up her face. "No. Only if it means something to you."

"How are you going to know when I've properly apologized?"

Sherrie folded her arms. "I guess we're just going to have to trust you."

I'd read that a lost dog can travel alone for hundreds of miles to get home, so I checked for Rebel on my way up the dark road to the trailer. The lights were off in Sam's house. Rebel's chain lay on the ground, where tiny dirt drifts threatened to bury it. I picked it up and coiled it neatly near the house before finding the hidden key and letting myself in.

The only sound inside was the refrigerator humming. It had never seemed so loud before. I searched every room with the crazy hope that Rebel would crawl out from under a bed, dusty and sheepish, or burst out of a closet, frantic and delighted to see me. As I locked up the house, I thought that "gone" had to be the longest, most painful word in the English language.

The trailer's front light cast a dim glow over our empty yard. I went

258

around to the back of the trailer and felt inside Elvis's cage. He wasn't hiding in his little house like I'd hoped.

Not wanting to go inside right away, I sat on the front steps hugging my backpack to my stomach, the lights of the valley spread before me.

A car charged up the road and careened into the yard, its headlights momentarily blinding me. Mom jumped out of the Escort and tried to hug me. I stiffened, and she could feel it. She stepped back and ran her hand lightly over the top of my head.

I got up and went inside. The door opened easily and clicked shut just as smoothly behind Mom. Dropping my pack in my room, I noticed the space at the foot of the bed where Elvis's cage used to be. I hadn't thought it would bother me so much if Elvis was gone, but it did. The small room seemed even tinier than before, as if it had shrunk in the time I'd been away.

Mom asked, "Are you hungry?"

"Kind of." Right then, my stomach growled loudly. I crossed my arms over it.

"Sit," she said. "I'll make you something."

Feeling like a visitor, I sat on the sofa and watched her fix me a hamburger. She scooped macaroni salad from a deli container and piled it next to the burger. She added a piece of lettuce and ketchup and set it on the table, sitting down in another chair. I took the plate over to the sofa.

She asked, "What happened in Denver?"

I swallowed. "It didn't work out."

She got up, put the frying pan in the sink, and turned on the tap. The hot pan hissed. With her back to me, she asked, "Is he staying there long?"

I kept my eyes on my food. "He'll be on the road a lot."

She picked up a scrubber and stared out the window over the sink. "And the dog?"

Tears welled up in my eyes. "I don't know," I whispered. "Someone took him."

She glanced at me quickly before turning back to the dirty pan and scrubbing it. When I finished eating, she took my plate and washed it, standing at the sink afterward, both hands on the edge of the counter. Then she sat next to me on the sofa, taking my hand and holding it tightly between hers.

Uncomfortable, I pulled my hand away. "I talked to Sherrie and Shirley about the money."

Her eyes widened. "It was you."

"We have a plan for me to pay it off." I didn't mention that I hadn't accepted all the terms of that plan.

"What did you do with the money?" she asked.

I crossed my legs. "That's between them and me."

The silence between us felt enormous. I stood abruptly and she jumped up, too, but she sat again when I mumbled something about needing sleep and stalked off to my room.

In the morning, I checked Elvis's cage again. The rat was nowhere in sight, but his water bottle was full. Had he run off or died? Or was he still alive and coming back to drink, and Mom had been refilling the bottle? I regretted turning him out. Maybe I'd underestimated Mom. I found some crackers in the trailer and put them in the cage, meanwhile scanning the surrounding rocks and brush for a flash of black and white.

I started up the slope behind the trailer. Shrubs were turning brown or gold, and the prickly pear cacti were covered with purple stumps where earlier they'd had oval-shaped red-purple fruits. I thought getting up high and looking out over the valley and far mesas would be soothing, but when I reached the overhang where Remy had first taken me, I sat down and cried.

Returning to the trailer, I fell asleep on my bed with my sneakers on. When I woke, Mom was there, heating canned soup and toasting bread. I'd skipped lunch, and now, smelling the food, my mouth watered. Uneasily, I sat at the kitchen table.

"I'm going to an AA meeting tonight," Mom said. "You could come with me, if you want. They're pretty interesting. There's another meeting, too, for families."

"That's your business, not mine."

She started to say something but turned away. "What are you going to do, then?"

"I don't know. Maybe call Luz."

"Good idea."

No way was I calling Luz, who I fully expected to pull some holier-than-thou big sister routine on me. I tried watching TV, and then I walked down to the big rock where I'd seen the meteor shower. Thin clouds blocked the stars, and the only sign of the moon was a dull whitish glow. I lay on my back but couldn't relax on the cold, hard stone.

I sat up and remembered how Rebel chased rabbits, like there was nothing else that mattered in the whole universe. Maybe I could do that with school and with paying back Shirley and Sherrie. I could chase those rabbits like crazy. It scared me to think about it, but maybe I'd even ask the school counselor about college. I shivered as more clouds dimmed the soft glow of the hidden moon. The thick blackness around me seemed both frightening and full of possibility, an expansive velvety landscape where I was alone but not stranded. I started home comforted by the fact that I had a plan and pleased that it was all for me.

The following Monday, I went back to school. I'd missed a ton of work over the two weeks I was absent, and I called Sherrie and

Shirley to say I couldn't work for them until I caught up. After I hung up, I admitted to myself that that wasn't the real reason. I could have squeezed in a little time here and there. It was just too hard to face them. Their insistence that I apologize to Mom sent me spinning in circles whenever I thought about it—which I did, every day. Sometimes I even planned what I might say. But I couldn't do it. My mother didn't deserve it. What she'd done in the past and might do again in the future were a million times worse than anything I'd done to her. I appreciated her helping me get home, but it didn't change the fact that she was unreliable.

A few days after I got back, when she was out, I peeked under her bed. No rum bottles, beer cans, or whiskey bottles, just the box of chocolates Shirley had given me when I'd started walking Cocoa. They were nearly gone, the box full of wrappers. Maybe Mom was holding it together now, but that didn't mean I should go soft on her.

When I'd been home for a week, I dropped by Big-Time Bargains to give them the hundred dollars I'd had in the bank. "Thank you," said Shirley. "But you're racking up interest on the rest. Aren't you caught up yet with schoolwork?"

"Hello to you, too." I turned to Sherrie. "My mother is doing okay."

Sherrie asked, "And you?"

"Look, you told me not to fake it."

"You think a deadline will help?"

I scowled at her.

"You look a little like Cocoa with that face. Are you all right?"

"I'm fine." I tapped my foot impatiently. "What if I get a job someplace else, pay you from that?"

"You're still living at home?"

"I guess that's what you'd call it."

"And school?"

"Check for yourself. You'll see how much they love me there."

"I suppose I can't expect miracles. We'll take your money, long as you earn it legally."

As I left, Sherrie asked again, "Are you sure you're okay?" I pretended not to hear.

A week later, when I was nearly resigned to having to work again for Shirley and Sherrie, I got a job at Bailey's Grocery, where I earned slow, steady money stocking shelves. The work was boring but easy. Cans of peas and tubs of yogurt didn't chase rabbits or beg to go on walks, and once I'd set them on the shelf, they stayed put. Walking dogs would have paid more, but so many people knew the two women and Sam, I figured my reputation as a dog walker was probably shot.

When I got my first paycheck, I cashed it and took the money to Shirley and Sherrie. They wanted to chat, but I made an excuse to leave. They were friendly enough, but I got the feeling they were disappointed in me. It wasn't anything they said or did, just the way their eyes bored into mine, as if they sought a glimpse of what was in my heart.

Another week passed. That sense of possibility I'd felt sitting alone at night on the big rock seemed like a dream, hard to hang on to or even remember. I had days when finishing high school, reimbursing Sherrie and Shirley, and not running off like my mother were not enough, when doing everything right felt wrong, but I didn't know what else to do.

Meanwhile, Mom was staying sober. She went to work, to AA meetings, to her support group at New Horizons. She talked to Bell at least once a day, still whining about money and work but just as often laughing over God knows what. She went out a lot with Redbone, or he came over, but mostly they kept their romance out of my face. She never talked about being a whole new woman anymore or starting a whole new chapter, but for once in her life, she really did seem different. One morning about six weeks after I'd returned from Denver, she asked me to have dinner ready when she got home. "I've only got half an hour between work and my meeting," she complained. "I really need your help."

"But I get home from Bailey's only a little before you," I said, "and I have a math test and a history paper due tomorrow."

"Kayla, can't you just . . ." she began in the wheedling, exasperated tone I knew so well, and then she stopped. "I'm sorry," she said. "You're busy, too. I'll grab a sandwich on my way to the meeting."

She was sorry? She'd get her own dinner? Just like that? Startled, I watched her drive off.

Another day, I caught her reading my savings account statement. She didn't know I'd seen her, and she pretended she hadn't touched it. For a week, every time she opened her mouth, I braced myself to say *No, you cannot borrow money from me,* but she never asked.

One evening, Bell stopped by to take Mom to an AA meeting. When Mom went to the bathroom to put on lipstick, Bell tried to get me to go with them. "What do you think of your old mom, celebrating sixty days of sobriety tonight? She's something, huh?"

"She's done it before," I said, slipping away to my room.

Bell stuck her head in. "Not like this, I'll bet."

"I guess," I said, shrugging. I was relieved when they left. It was true, though. Sober and keeping a job. Keeping Redbone. Not a word about moving. Still, I didn't see why I should apologize to her.

On a Friday afternoon a couple of days later, I found Mom's list of amends to Grandma Esther under the kitchen sink, behind the garbage pail. I read the whole thing this time. It was one long, awful list, and I tossed it into the trash, where I thought she'd meant to put it. But when I heard the Escort pull up, I grabbed it out of the garbage and showed it to her as soon as she walked in the door.

"Do you still need to burn this?"

She took it from me and was quiet. "Where do you go on your long walks?" she asked. "Do you have a special place?"

I shrugged. "A few."

"Can we burn it at one of those?"

The temptation to fling *No!* in her face was so strong I barely stopped myself. I suspected a yes would mean a lot to her, though her face showed nothing. I almost said no just to see if she would react.

I could raise the bar, or the hoop. Light it on fire. Build up a higher wall of flames.

Jump, Mom. Jump.

She was waiting.

I bent down, pretending to scratch my knee. "Okay."

The sun hadn't set yet, but it had dropped behind a wide band of high, thin clouds. In the cool October air, Mom followed me up the hill behind our trailer, stopping occasionally to catch her breath. I scrambled onto the huge sandstone slab that jutted toward the valley. She climbed up after me. She stood for a moment looking out over broad streaks of color and shadow and the wide sky that held it all together.

"Do you need to read it out loud?" I asked.

"Nope," she said. "I read it to Bell. That was enough. I'll just look it over once more."

Relieved, I watched a flock of large white birds approaching in V-formation. When they were high overhead, they seemed to get confused, uttering guttural cries and losing their elegant V. They turned first in one direction, then another, making ragged circles in the sky, sunlight reflecting brightly off the undersides of their wings each time they changed direction. Bird after bird attempted to take the lead, but others would break away repeatedly, turning the group around once more. I felt frightened for them, wondering if something was wrong.

Finally, one bird took the lead and the rest gradually fell into place. Flying again in a perfect, noisy V, they headed south.

"Cranes," Mom said, watching them fly off. "They migrate along here. Bell told me."

"I thought they were lost."

"It's what they do." She held her lighter to the paper, and the two of us crouched low, shielding it from the wind with our hands. While the paper burned, I wondered if it would help me to write down what I'd done to Rebel and Elvis, read it to someone, and burn it.

When only scorched bits of paper and ash remained, Mom stood up to go.

"I'll be along," I said. "I want to watch the sunset."

"Mind if I stay with you?"

I shrugged.

A blanket of rippled clouds stretched across the sky, and I expected the sunset to be a good one. We waited in silence, but the brilliant blaze I anticipated never happened. Instead, the clouds turned from white to gray, and only a small, thin layer near the horizon glowed faintly pink before fading. We stood shivering, each of us hugging herself.

Mom watched the darkening horizon, looking as peaceful as I'd ever seen her. My mind filled with questions for her: Did she like it here? Did she think about moving again? If she could be anything, do anything, what would that be? Did she think about Desmond? Wish she hadn't walked away from him? Why hadn't she told him about me?

I crouched down and drew circles in the dirt. "When I was in Denver, how scared were you, really?"

She took a cigarette out of her shirt pocket and flicked her lighter several times, but it wouldn't light, and when the cigarette snapped in half between her fingers, I couldn't tell if she'd done it on purpose or not. "Terrified," she whispered. "Completely terrified."

The whole sky was now uniformly gray, blending with the soft darkness around us. Without a word, Mom started down the hill, her boots crunching on the gravelly dirt.

"I'm sorry," I practiced saying to the deepening sky, and a little while later I went down to the trailer, too.

A few evenings after that, I found a letter from Remy with an L.A. return address. It was on the kitchen table, where Mom must have left it for me, along with a note in her handwriting: *Off work at 7. Meet for enchiladas?* I took the envelope to the sofa and tore it open.

There was a note written on music paper and twenty-five dollars wrapped in a second sheet. He wrote that he might be in Rio Blanco sometime and would like to see me. He wondered if I'd ever finished "What You Want."

Was he trying to buy it? Or was he starting to pay me back the five hundred dollars?

His handwriting was also on the paper he'd wrapped around the money, lyrics to the song he'd written about me and sung the first time I heard Terra Luna play at Billy's. It looked like his first draft, with words and phrases crossed out and rewritten, a little different from I'd heard it that night. Had he sent it on purpose, or had he used this piece of paper by accident? Did he still sing that song? Did he substitute other girls' names for mine?

His timing was perfect. That afternoon, Mrs. Ramirez had told us to write a poem about love for homework. While everyone else in my class had groaned and written the particulars of the assignment, I'd scribbled my half-finished poem from memory. Later, I'd taken my notebook up onto the sandstone ledge. My hands had grown stiff from the cold as the sun disappeared and the rest of the words came to me.

I found a fresh sheet of paper and recopied the poem neatly.

What You Want
by Kayla Hanes

Love isn't always what you want
or where you want it.
It's burnt sienna when you wanted magenta.
A high, dry desert when you longed for a meadow.
A marching brass band when you needed one wooden flute,
one simple melody.
It's definitely not a pot of gold
but a single, tarnished coin
with two distinct sides,
negotiable
only in a foreign country
if you travel those shores and
learn to call them home.

Satisfied, I tucked the new copy into my poetry binder. Tomorrow I'd drop it first thing on Mrs. Ramirez's desk. Maybe I'd ask her if she thought it had potential as lyrics to a song. If so, maybe she'd know where I could send it.

I read Remy's note and the song he had written one more time, dropped them into the trash, and left to meet my mom.